The Salvagers

By John Michael Godier

www.jmgodier.com

Facebook: johnmichael.godier

Twitter: @jmgodier

Cover art by Sabrina Flynn

Facebook: SH.Flynn

Dedicated to all those people daring enough to expect a bright future for our species.

Chapter 1 June 5, 2461

"Men go abroad to wonder at the heights of mountains, at the huge waves of the sea, at the long courses of the rivers, at the vast compass of the ocean, at the circular motions of the stars, and they pass by themselves without wondering." - St. Augustine

There it was, filling the windows of my bridge. The richest and most famous lost shipwreck in the solar system, presenting itself as welcoming and free for the taking. And I knew that it belonged to me. I had found a legend. More accurately, it was *the* legend.

I shouldn't have trusted my senses. I should have held my emotions in check. I should have realized that my mind was bathed in that fog that clouds a person's ability to recognize realities and spot future challenges during the initial moments of a discovery. The more I admired it, the more flawless it seemed—pristinely preserved, shining gloriously new. The polished steel plates of its hull reflected the sunlight like diamond facets as it slowly revolved against the black backdrop of space.

It was pure, dumb, blind luck that we found it. A minor course change in any direction over the previous month, and we'd have missed it entirely. It would have been a passing speck of light to be dismissed as just another chunk of ice or rock like a hundred trillion others dotting the solar system. It must have looked that way to countless other people, for it was well within the main trade routes to the Jupiter colonies, and it was only by chance that no one ever got close enough to see it for what it was.

Our course brought us just barely within the range of our telescope's ability to identify it. I can't say why I even bothered to look through the eyepiece. Maybe it was the regular rhythm of the light rising and falling that suggested it might be manmade. I wanted a look nonetheless, so when I floated away from my command station and trained the telescope on that bright dot and saw that it was a ship, dead in space and of a style that confirmed its identity, I knew that my greatest moment had come.

"All stop!" I yelled to my crew.

Over my 30-year career as a salvager, I'd learned to temper my ideas of what it might be like to find a Holy Grail treasure wreck. In my line of work, unless you keep your expectations in check, you will always meet with disappointment. Like the treasure hunters who plied Earth's old Spanish Main and found that the wood was always rotten and the sunken galleons no longer looked like ships, a wreck in space was almost always a crushed and shattered heap of metal. And that was the most you could expect. Sometimes it was just a widely scattered field of debris or a fresh crater on an asteroid. I'd learned to put little stock in the errant pipe dreams of finding that one perfect ship the other salvagers fantasized about—the one that wasn't utterly destroyed.

I had always tried to restrict my visions to strictly realistic expectations. I imagined the legendary wrecks as torn-open hulls with loose coins dotting zero-G minefields of human remains and jagged steel ready to shred space suits and punch holes in salvage vessels. Relics like that were no longer ships. They were shipwrecks, pitiful victims of violent accidents and failures that could offer only one certainty: they were always ready to take one more life.

I'd never dared to envision this particular wreck intact. Seeing its perfection disarmed me. I gathered enough rationality to ask myself whether I was seeing it through rose-colored glasses because I knew what was on the ship. Then the beauty of it finally overwhelmed me again, forcing me to make peace with the thought that it was real. I wasn't alone. Emotions ran high in every member of my crew. They also knew about the cargo; it was the fabled treasure of the Golden Asteroid, the stuff of legends since its loss 200 years earlier.

We maneuvered closer, watching the ship's name rotate into view. It was emblazoned boldly in matte black letters across the mirror-polished plating of the hull. *Cape Hatteras*. Seeing its name thrilled us and left us with no uncertainty. There would be no need for lengthy research in dusty half-forgotten archives poring over construction invoices to match up half a serial number on a fragment of wreckage. We knew unequivocally what ship we had found.

Our slow rising approach brought its enormous bulk into a better perspective. Over 700 feet long and 100 wide, it dwarfed our tiny *Amaranth Sun*. Its newness was striking and unnatural, looking as though someone had just finished building it and then shut off the lights before promptly forgetting that it had ever existed.

The *Cape Hatteras* was a mining vessel launched in 2258 by the Union of North American Governments (UNAG), the successor state to Canadaska, the Mexican Confederacy, and the United States Mark IV, themselves reboots of countries whose original names most people had forgotten. It had one mission: collect as much gold as possible from the asteroid 974-Bernhard and return it to Earth. The UNAG needed rescue from deep national debt and took a gamble, spending nearly a trillion dollars in the currency of the day on the mission. If all had gone as planned, it would have returned a hundred times that sum.

The UNAG was desperate. If they didn't find a major source of income, they'd have gone bankrupt within a decade and been forced to go the way of the governments they had replaced. It was the same old modus operandi of those times: borrow, spend, go bankrupt, remonetize, and finally come up with some new and unblemished name for the nation. And then, like a tired old scow dressed up with a fresh coat of paint, they would start the cycle over until the next time the polish wore off.

The loss of the *Cape Hatteras* had nearly made that

bankruptcy immediate. If it hadn't been for a last-minute round of weapons sales that balanced the books, the UNAG would have faded into history. They survived but at a shameful cost: the deal fueled the last major war on Earth. A horror that tore apart Eastern Europe and Asia and left 200 million dead after two decades lost, the Eurasian war finally ended in a stalemate with no one winning a damned thing. But it did teach a lesson to the unions: if you're going to have a war, do it in space. Earth itself has been at peace ever since, ruling her empire of colonies, the politics of home always reverberating throughout the solar system.

We circled the *Cape Hatteras* and then moved forward to inspect the bow of the ship. Its bridge windows were as black as holes in space, showing no obvious signs of damage but otherwise revealing nothing. Even the direct light of the sun seemed to disappear without a trace into that dark void. The eeriness of it evoked the uncertainty of what had happened after it finished its mission to 974-Bernhard.

974-Bernhard was also called Walton's Rock after the scientist who had discovered it. Dr. Walton was a preeminent astrogeologist and had spent decades studying the asteroid. It became a singular obsession for him. He was convinced that it held the key, one way or another, to solving all of Earth's troubles. He might have been right in some sense.

Unlike most asteroids it was filled with heavy metals by virtue of having originally been the center of a large protoplanet's core. An unusually slow rate of cooling allowed the heaviest metals to concentrate before finally solidifying. Then it was blown to bits by the impact of an object two-thirds its size, leaving a chunk of metal and rock floating in space and presenting easy access. Most of it was useless iron and nickel, along with uranium, thorium, and other radioactive scrap not worth the trouble to haul back home. But it was also loaded with gold.

Walton attached much more importance to it than the value of its metal. From early on he got out into the media to promote his discovery, but when no one shared his vision he grew despondent. The poor man faced every kind of negativity imaginable. Some said that it was too expensive to mine, others commented that it ought to be preserved as it was, and someone even suggested that it be blown up with a particle laser so everyone would quit fighting about it.

It all proved too much for Dr. Walton. His mental health declined, and he started saying all kinds of crazy things such as that the asteroid was the metaphysical equivalent of the fusion reactor, that it held the key to spiritual happiness, and that it was a transmitter to contact aliens through dreams. His rants became stranger the older he got, and the media were more than willing to let him keep spouting for the entertainment value. He even believed that the UNAG was sending secret missions to 974-Bernhard so they could steal it from him. In the end he was right about the asteroid's resources, and a decade after he died the *Cape Hatteras* project commenced.

We hadn't seen anything that suggested an accident. The hull plating of the ship was intact, and there was no torn or twisted metal that would indicate a violent decompression. We moved on to get a look at the engine nozzles arrayed across the stern. Amazingly, they were sparkling clean, as though someone had recently scrubbed them. Maybe that was a clue, we thought. Perhaps something catastrophic had made the ship's fusion reactors shut down, effectively marooning the crew in outer space. Residues accumulate in engine bells during their use, so to perform a cold restart on a ship's engines you must first spray low-temperature cleaning gel into the nozzles. Then you go through a very involved and tedious process to get everything running again. We speculated that they might have lost power and were trying to get the engines going when they simply ran out of time and oxygen. My crew kept theorizing as we explored further, but my thoughts drifted back to the cargo.

The *Cape Hatteras* had mined the asteroid for nearly a year. The ship was equipped with an automated smelting system; as they mined the asteroid, the system would cast the gold into bricks refined to a perfect .9999 fineness. The crew would then catalog and securely strap each brick onto pallets in the cargo hold until they filled it with a titanic amount of gold. It was enough to increase the supply on Earth by a third. If melted into a single block, it would have been 70 feet long and 20 wide and high. They were about to begin their ten-month journey home when contact was lost. No trace of the ship was ever found.

So many questions haunted the *Cape Hatteras*'s fate that its fame ensured a dedicated following of enthusiasts. Hundreds of books had been written about it, all of them with a different theory about what had happened. In addition to salvaging its cargo, we hoped that that we'd be able to lay all that controversy to rest and solve the mystery once and for all.

The UNAG's earlier conclusions about the accident had only added to the conundrum. An official panel was convened to figure the whole thing out, but their answers fell short of satisfying anyone. They determined that the *Cape Hatteras* had inferior hull plating, claiming that it was too thin to withstand a hit by one of the billions of small boulders that race at high speed around the asteroid belt. One, they proposed, must have struck a weak point in the armor, violently decompressed the ship, and killed its crew of five instantly; however, they had no real proof, just some telemetry readings and a few minutes of footage taken by an orbiting telescope. None of that evidence was released to the public, ostensibly out of concern for the victims' families. But that evasion led to a veritable fire storm of public speculation that only grew worse as the years wore on, shifting the story from a human tragedy to a romanticized legend.

Not seeing anything revealing in a horizontal trajectory, I ordered the *Amaranth Sun* to a vertical position relative to the sun, hoping that our realignment would give us a better chance of spotting something. I wanted no movement at all in order to take advantage of the derelict's own rotation, but the axis of the ship was such that not enough sunlight was reaching where we wanted to see. I ordered our spotlights turned on and set in a diffused pattern that illuminated much of the *Cape Hatteras* in a bluish light. Again we saw nothing but an expanse of perfectly intact hull.

I joked with my crew that the ship might still contain a breathable atmosphere. In truth, that was highly unlikely. In all of my years in space, I'd only heard of one ship that stayed pressurized for over a century, much less two. Even 30 years was often too much to ask. The mothballed Solar Regatta ships at Mercury had all gone to vacuum. But the improbable wasn't absolutely impossible, so I allowed myself some small measure of hope because an oxygenated atmosphere, however compromised, would make for an infinitely easier salvage.

Hope was a good thing, but I had to be careful. It's a tool as much as an emotion, and when misplaced it can lead to disaster. When Earth-bound sailors became spacemen, they kept their old maritime traditions. But hope can eventuate in good luck, so I abandoned the last remnants of my stoic rules and for the first time allowed myself the irrational expectation of an easy salvage. In hindsight, I jinxed it.

I wasn't new to searching for that wreck. In my younger days I'd spent eight years looking for it on and off. She was supposed to be among the asteroids between Earth and Mars, in a sort of parking orbit where Walton's Rock used to be. The asteroid didn't have the gravity to hold the ship indefinitely, so the two separated over time, and 974-Bernhard was now halfway around the sun from where the *Cape Hatteras* was projected to be.

In a search for it I had covered tens of thousands of square miles, sweeping back and forth until the money ran out and the investors lost heart. I wasn't the only one. No fewer than 100 failed attempts litter treasure-hunting history. They all failed because the ship just wasn't where it was supposed to be, so more recent expeditions were forced to widen their search area to an impossibly large swath of space that would have taken centuries to cover. It had become a long shot.

I thought it probably never would be found. I had chalked up the whole thing to the uncertainty of the solar system. Jupiter can deflect an asteroid in a close encounter, and then that asteroid's gravity can alter the course of anything it passes. Even if it's just a tiny deviation, it is still cumulative, and after 200 years something can be a million miles away from where calculations indicate it should be. It doesn't take long to become a needle in a haystack the size of the Sun. But even that consideration didn't explain where we found the *Cape Hatteras*.

We're not talking about relatively small distances such as a million miles. It was *200* million miles away from where it should have been. The *Cape Hatteras* was completely outside the asteroid belt in lockstep with a large trojan asteroid that had settled near Jupiter in a resonant solar orbit. It's really not an asteroid, but rather a burned-out comet full of ice and carbon. In its glory days it would have traveled in and out of proximity to the Sun, the melting ice periodically releasing a gaseous comet's tail. 974-Bernhard had taken too many trips and no longer had enough horsepower to form much more than a fuzzy haze. All we could surmise was that it must have passed through the asteroid belt one last time and picked up the derelict before Jupiter's immense gravity finally captured them both and dragged them to a quiet retirement at a Lagrange point about 20 million miles from the planet.

We were in the area by accident on our way to Earth, after salvaging an old NASA probe from the late 21st century. The Smithsonian was paying us to bring it home, saying something about its being the first probe to carry a true fusion engine. NASA had wanted to study an impending Jovian comet impact close up, but were left with little time to test the new propulsion. In case the fusion engine failed, they equipped the probe with one of the most powerful chemical rockets ever built to ensure the mission's success. It was never needed, and that left us with several full tanks of unstable rocket fuel to contend with.

There was no way to vent it into space, and the

Smithsonian wanted that rocket engine as much as the rest of the probe, so we detached it and stored it in the only safe place we had: strapped to the heavy plating that covered the stern of the *Amaranth Sun*. We'd have been in serious trouble if those had exploded, but no one ever said salvage work was without risk.

To be completely honest, I hated retrieval missions. They were mundane and boring. Treasure hunting is far more fun. But pleasure is one thing, and paying the bills is another. The simple fact is that, if you're willing to spend the time, the solar system is filled with trash and artifacts left over from centuries of human exploration that someone is always willing to pay for.

Unfortunately, I wasn't the only salvager in the solar system. If any of the others found out that I had located the *Cape Hatteras*, I'd have been dealing with ten ships pulling up next to me, all looking for a way in followed by a government vessel full of archeologists wanting to preserve it for posterity and finally a transport of lawyers to sort it all out—no doubt for a modest cut.

I wanted to avoid that scenario at all costs. Captain Camden D. Hunter and lawyers do not mix.

Chapter 2 Day 2

One of the first things I learned decades ago as a novice 24-year-old adventurer is that it's always easier to ask forgiveness than it is to ask permission. If you bog yourself down waiting for permits from Earth, all you do is hand your prize to someone else. Many an unwary salvager forgot that and spent more time and money in court fighting rival claims than the profits they gained from their haul—and that only happened if they *won* their case. To come out on top, you must go ahead without permission and have the job finished before anyone else finds out.

The risk you take with that approach isn't very high. They've still never thrown anyone in jail for salvaging in space. But things can easily bog down in a quagmire of legal action, despite the unions' agreement that the ancient system of maritime law would apply in space. Even so, that finders, keepers system hadn't stopped legal battles in the 18th century, and it still doesn't stop them in 25th. Everyone wants a piece of what you've got, so they'll creatively interpret every law on the books to get you in court. With that in mind, my highest priority was to keep my discovery secret.

It was a daunting task because in order to fund the project, I needed investors. *Quiet* ones. I'd never made enough off my salvages to fund my own expeditions and for something as big as the *Cape Hatteras*, I needed salaries for 30 specialized personnel, a large and fully equipped salvage ship and enough food, fuel, and supplies to last a year or more.

I wasn't worried. Investment money was everywhere on Earth, and if anyone could entice an investor I was the man. I have a good track record. In my career I'd found eleven wrecks, and every one of them turned a tidy profit. But the *Cape Hatteras* was in a league of its own; Nothing I had done so far could compare. It was also the reason I had chosen this career. I had wanted to be a treasure hunter since the age of eight, when I read a book titled *The Lost Ships of the Solar System* by Netea Krahs—a relative of the previous owner of the *Amaranth Sun*. The first chapter was dedicated to the *Cape Hatteras*.

In those days I used to daydream about the odd parallels between my life and the story of the *Cape Hatteras*. I was born 150 years to the day after the ship was declared lost in what was officially called Sononmaz Province in the UNAG, the bureaucrats' name for what everyone else still called Arizona, Sonora, and New Mexico. The first officer's last name was Hunter, though I could never find out whether I was related to him. My mother was born not far from Cape Hatteras, where I'd been many times on family vacations. My young mind drew every kind of minor connection between myself and that ship.

I'm wiser now in my old age, but I was still disappointed that I'd never found the wreck. I think the real blow to the dream came when I found myself fantasizing about going home to Flagstaff and retiring. I thought that maybe I could work for another decade and then hand the reins to my son. I didn't see much time left for the *Cape Hatteras* in those remaining years. But then everything changed.

Before tackling the project, I had to come up with a game plan. I summoned my crew of three to the bridge for a meeting.

"Whatever happened to 974-Bernhard?" Kurt asked.

"It's still out there," I responded.

"Why can't we mine it? If it's still loaded with gold, we wouldn't need investors."

"About fifty years ago some prospectors staked a claim, even though there wasn't much left after the *Cape Hatteras* had stripmined the metallic half of the asteroid. I've been there. The camp is just a collection of prefab units and mining equipment. It's a very radioactive environment, and excavating deeper means drilling through nickel-iron as hard as steel, but they do manage to produce small amounts of gold from deep down. It's a hard life for little return."

"You could probably convince Ed Iron if you turned on the charm," Stacey said.

"I intend to try him first," I replied. "I'm sure he'd keep quiet about it, but he's not dumb. He'll want a full plan and methodology before we speak directly."

"I wouldn't worry," Kurt commented. "This is going to be an easy salvage. You know what violent decompression usually does to a ship."

"Yeah, the jet of escaping air spins it to hundreds of revolutions per minute. This one is barely turning at all. With a few strap-thrusters in the right places, we can stop it. Then we cut our way in," Stacey suggested.

"We don't know whether it's decompressed," I said, worried that I might sound silly.

"What are the chances that thing still has air in it? One in a million?"

"Probably, but we should still find out. Do we have a drill and pressure sensor on hand?"

"I can improvise a drill," Neil said, "but we don't have a pressure sensor. I didn't think we'd need one for the probe salvage, so I never bought one."

"We could try the laser spectrograph," suggested Stacey. "It may be able to tell whether there's air behind those windows."

"I never thought we'd use that thing. I'm glad I didn't have it removed during the last refit," I said.

The *Amaranth Sun* had just been refurbished a year before. The job had cost me dearly, mainly because the ship was never intended to be a salvor but instead an exploration vessel. It still held the record for the second furthest manned expedition into the outer solar system. Its design gave it an important advantage: it had an enormous range, but alternatively it could sit in space for years if properly provisioned. That's a plus if you need to remain alongside a wreck for months at a stretch.

The spectrometer was a relic left over from my ship's exploration days. I considered it useless, but it hadn't been worth removing. It didn't take Stacey long to configure it and get a result. The spectrometer detected no air at all. The salvage would have to be done using lunar-grade environment support systems, also known as moon suits.

With that in mind we drafted our game plan, which we finished in less than a day. There was no way Ed wouldn't want in on it. Still, sending the proposal is always the hardest part when you're asking for money. You always second-guess what you've written. We just had to wait for Ed to receive it, look it over, and initiate direct contact if he were interested or send a polite no if he weren't. It was a tense two days before we heard back from him.

It took about 45 minutes for radio transmission to reach home from where we were. Pleasantries take hours with delays like that, so it's standard procedure to send a message in text detailing what you want to say beforehand, thereby avoiding lengthy conversations. You also learn to speak in paragraphs rather than sentences, and you never get used to seeing people's reactions long after you've finished speaking. Ed's text reply was simple. It read: "I'm in." His image appeared moments later on the communications screen.

"Cam," said Ed, "it's good to see you. I got your report. It's an amazing find. Fantastic, I must say, absolutely fantastic." Although he was usually businesslike and always poker-faced, his excitement showed in the tone of his voice. I could safely predict that I'd snared one of the wealthiest men in the southwestern UNAG. "Imagine it!" he effused. "The *Cape Hatteras* found. I can't fathom what it might be worth today."

That was no small statement for Ed, who knew real wealth. He had made his fortune by manufacturing airtight domes for the colonies. Now he was an old man resting on his laurels, spending his time funding treasure hunts and adventurers, living vicariously through them from his mansion complex in Roswell, New Mexico, and always turning a nice profit.

"Sorry about the delay in getting back to you. It's a tall order for me right now, since I've got something big in the works that I'm not at liberty to discuss. I've had to involve a few others. You know them already: Marty, Babe, Mrs. Li, Renier, and Volkov—the usual suspects. I got your list. You'll have everything you need and then some. We've already found a good salvage ship for you. It's called the *Hyperion*. We'll have her out to you in nine months. Nothing but the best. It's still hard for me to believe that someone finally found that wreck. How I wish I were a younger man; I'd love to be out there with you. Sorry I can't get that ship to you sooner. I understand the need to get this project going, but logistics are what they are."

It's a reality of working in space that you can't do anything fast. Earth was millions of miles away, and we weren't equipped for a major salvage. We'd need the *Hyperion* to do the heavy work. The *Amaranth Sun* is a small vessel with little cargo space. It's just big enough to tie NASA's antique probe to the side and transport it home. It would not bear the immense treasure of the *Cape Hatteras*.

"I see in your report," continued Ed, "that you're going to do a complete survey. Good call. We'll need to know what we're up against and keep the surprises down. Another thing, we'd also like to bring the ship itself back, a tow ship will meet you at the end of the the salvage. B.T. Hall is planning a new resort in lunar orbit. This would be just the thing to boost the draw. You know how big lunar tourism is. Leasing the *Cape Hatteras* could mean a nice secondary income stream for us. Maybe enough to send you out to look for something else. I've got my secret project in the works, and there's also the *INS Elichpur*. It's never been found, you know."

Since I was going to be filthy rich, I wasn't certain I'd ever want to salvage again. But then I thought about the *Elichpur*. It had disappeared while on its way to deliver rare artwork bought by an eccentric billionaire who had lived in isolation on Mars almost a century ago. It was worth a fortune. I'd have to do it, and I was dying to know what his secret project was.

"Sounds great, Ed. I'm ready," I replied. "I've got enough on the *Amaranth Sun* to stay here for a while, but be sure to send supplies and fuel. I also can't stress enough that you guys need to be low-key. Do everything you can to keep this quiet."

I trusted Ed to be discreet, but he was just one of five investors. I knew all of them personally. When you're as rich as they are, bragging rights are more important than making more money, and I could easily imagine word of my discovery getting out at the country club over 100-year-old single-malt scotch.

"Don't worry," Ed reassured me. "I've got it well in hand. I've had my lawyer draft a stiff confidentiality agreement. Anyone who leaks information will lose so much that they'll be broke. I'm also having the whole thing compartmentalized. Only the investors know the big picture. Everyone else won't know enough to put two and two together, and we're having the specialists on the *Hyperion* agree to isolation from the public for the duration of the project."

"Thanks Ed. This is the big one! I'm glad to have you along."

"Glad to be in on it, and thank you for coming to me first. There's one other thing. Do you have the full sensor logs for your ship? All the way back to when Van der Boort owned it? If you do, could you please send me a copy?"

That seemed an odd question. The logs had nothing to do with the *Cape Hatteras* salvage, but I did have them.

"I do, and I'll send them along immediately."

I then sent a few other messages to keep our affairs in order back on Earth. Most important was the matter of the Smithsonian. They sent a nasty reply when they found out that their new exhibit would be delayed by at least a year, but I figured that if I refunded their money and still delivered their probe, they'd get over it. I could afford losses like that with the solar system's greatest treasure in my hands.

Chapter 3 August

Three months had passed since my conversation with Ed Iron. There had been little direct contact other than the reports I was sending every two weeks. I wrote them to sound adventurous, despite its being a simple survey, and his replies consisted of no more than two or three excited words about the mother lode. That hands-off approach was his biggest virtue. As long as he was kept regularly informed, he didn't interfere.

Ed's salvor was still months out, giving us plenty of time for the survey. We wanted to thoroughly *understand* the derelict. We photographed every weld and rivet and pored over each image for hours, thereby gaining confidence that when the time came we could get the job done safely and with a minimum of surprises. That did nothing, however, to relieve our feelings of anticipation. Those only grew worse until they finally gave way to outright impatience.

Our first hands-on experience with the ship came when we tackled the problem of stopping it from spinning. That was something we could try to do before the salvor arrived, so I declared the survey finished on the morning of day 92. When on a long salvage mission, you seize any opportunity you can to break the humdrum routine and celebrate. Kurt and Stacey marked the event with a "feast" consisting of dehydrated turkey and all the trimmings we could approximate . . . and my *last* bottle of whiskey.

The next day Stacey and I were discussing the specifics of just how we'd stop the ship from spinning when Kurt shot in to begin his bridge shift. He was smiling and energetic. He'd obviously had a good sleep after the whiskey the night before, but I think most of his energy was coming from coffee.

"Good morning! Do we have a solution?" he asked.

"We think so," I replied. "We'll have to deploy the pneumatic strap-thrusters first. Neil tells me that he can set them up inside of a week." Neil was the ship's engineer and my son, and also the best spacewalker among us. "We won't have to do any guesswork. The *Amaranth Sun*'s computers will do all the calculating. When Neil says they're ready, Stacey will have the computer touch them off. It'll be as easy as crashing into an asteroid."

"You hope," Stacey said wryly. She had a penchant for being a logical foil to my optimism.

"Always say it's easy. Then it has no chance of failure," I said, causing Stacey to roll her eyes.

"What can go wrong?" Kurt asked, a little disconcerted by Stacey's tone.

"Nothing," I said.

"Everything," she retorted.

She was right, of course. Things have a habit of never going as planned. The first snag we hit was the length of the straps. The *Cape Hatteras* was a huge ship, bigger than most vessels of our day. When Neil unrolled the straps, they didn't reach halfway around. He came up with a workaround by drilling holes in the outer hull plating and riveting the thrusters in place. He then put a spot weld around the edges for added strength, but the whole thing wasn't as sturdy as those braided nanolatch straps would have been. What started as a week's work grew to six, and when the time came to test the rig I was petrified.

I hadn't said anything to anyone, mainly because there weren't any alternatives, but I was skeptical that the plan would work. Neil's workarounds were often ambitious to a fault, and I'd never heard of anyone riveting thrusters in place. I worried they might tear a section of hull plating off and put an end to any easy way of pumping an atmosphere back onboard.

Stacey manned the thruster controls; Neil kept visual watch through a window; and Kurt and I monitored the data from the *Amaranth Sun*'s displays.

"Unless anyone has any objections, I think we're as ready as we can be," I said. No one objected.

"Ready. Four, three, two, . . ." At one Stacey hit the button.

A burst of white mist shot out of seven of the thrusters, but the eighth broke off and spiraled wildly into space.

"Daughter of a Ganymede flagellant!" Stacey exclaimed. "We lost one. Nice workaround Neil."

Neil and Stacey had a bad case of the usual rivalry between pilots and engineers.

"I said it was a workaround! Have you ever tried welding in space? That ship was spinning, taking turns freezing and boiling once an hour. That's hell on a makeshift weld joint," Neil responded defensively.

"Yeah, blah blah. Moon suits are clumsy. Don't forget to add that one too."

"Pilots have no sense of mechanics. You wonder why your ships break down all the time," he said. "Did you tell the computer to give it a little extra?"

That jibe hit home. Stacey had once burned out a reactor on a Roper Model 12 moon flyer during her training days. Those things are nearly impossible to break, and they're widely considered to be foolproof, but she managed to push it too hard and was left stranded on the Sea of Tranquility for a week until a crawler could pick her up. She lost five pounds living on crackers and mustard packets.

"It's still spinning," I said. "Could you two hold the rivalry until *after* we've figured this out?"

"We'll have to use some of the reserve air," said Stacey. "I'd rather we didn't have to because we can't refill the thrusters without bringing them back onboard. We lost that option when someone *welded* them on," she said, firing a parting shot at Neil as he returned to his window. "Still, we've got good reserves, and I don't think we'll use them up completely in a second try. I don't see any other choice."

"Alright, do it," I responded, more than a little disheartened.

Stacey had the computer recalculate the ship's spin rate. It came up with an answer faster than I felt comfortable with.

"That's it?"

"It's your computer. It says it's ready."

That wasn't comforting. The *Amaranth Sun*'s computers were *usually* reliable, but they were first and foremost navigational quantum computers. Using them for something else required the computer to write new software for itself. That usually meant glitches.

"Well, let's try this again."

This time Stacey didn't bother with a countdown. She just hit the button, and the thrusters fired almost too fast for the eye to see. I held my breath and hesitantly looked at my panel. I saw nothing but welcome, wonderful zeros.

"I think it worked," I said.

"Looks as though it's stopped," Neil said as he checked the derelict visually.

"I think we've done it," I said. It took a moment to sink in before we broke into cheers. It was beautiful. The *Cape Hatteras* was sitting motionless with a slight dip to port just off our starboard bow. Stacey moved the *Amaranth Sun* alongside, leaving a space of about 50 meters between the ships.

"Next step," I said as everyone calmed down, "is to set up a scaffold around the center of the ship. We should have enough titanium pipe for it."

We'd never built a scaffold on a wreck before because it wasn't usually necessary. However, a fully intact derelict had to be treated as a ship in space dock rather than as a wreck. Cutting into the hull was an unfortunate necessity since handles can accumulate ice or jam from thermal fluctuation, so there's no way to open a hatch on a spacecraft from the outside.

"Shouldn't be a problem," Neil said. "I doubt it will take a week, and I'd definitely like to get rid of all that pipe. You ordered so much."

"Never know when you'll need it. Of all the things I've learned out here, you can't ever have enough pipe."

"You must have gotten it cheap."

"That too," I responded.

"You know, that ship doesn't look like a violent

decompression at all," Neil said. "When you see it up close, you don't see any bent metal or debris. The windows are perfect, there's no cracks or frost on them."

"Can you see anything inside?" Kurt asked.

"No, just blackness and a few empty seats."

"Glad you looked and not me," I said. "I don't like the idea of seeing frozen bodies floating around. There's five of them over there *somewhere*."

Neil looked a little pale. I don't think he'd considered that certainty.

The pipe project went more smoothly than the thrusters did. Neil got the last bar welded in place six days later and then spent some time taking close-up photos of his work. We studied them as intently as we had with the hull pictures. I wanted everything to go smoothly after the episode with the thrusters, and there was still time to have Ed launch an express unmanned cargo pod with anything we might need, including a little whiskey.

About four months before the *Hyperion* arrived, we could do no more. The wreck was ready for salvage. With the scaffolding it looked as though it belonged to someone, and it was so thoroughly mapped that we knew the exact count of rivets the ship had—3,221,801. With nothing left to do, we were considering a trip to the Trojan asteroid. It was about five hours away by hyperboard and was likely loaded with interesting gemstones, perhaps even diamonds. Most comet diamonds were ugly and industrial-grade—Earth has plenty of those—but sometimes very large flawless ones can be found that dwarf anything back home. It was worth a look around, and I figured the crew could use some time off playing in the wide-open.

I'd walked on several trojans, so I volunteered to stay and mind the ships. I thought my crew would be in for a treat: dead comets are among the most alien-looking landscapes around. I promised that they would see amazing natural ice sculptures covered in coal-black carbon dust and large caverns through the porous surface, all surrounded by a halo of ice and gas that reminded me of a light fog on Earth.

We planned to get some sleep in shifts before they'd leave in the morning. I was looking forward to some time alone; I wanted to admire my prize without anyone's bothering me. But then came the next disaster. It started when I awoke to Kurt's yelling. He was floating in the air outside my door, his round face the only part of him poking inside.

"Cam! Someone's here! There's a ship!"

I acted instinctively, but my body was moving faster than my brain was. I pushed out of the bunk-bag violently, bounced off the far wall and hung in midair.

"What the hell are you talking about?"

"There's some kind of ship about 35 kilometers out. They're not responding to communications. They've got to be jumping the claim," he said with urgency.

"Move us in close to the *Cape Hatteras*!" I ordered, grabbing a jumpsuit and slipping into it fast and forcefully. "I want them to know we own it."

I had been foolish in thinking that I could keep my find secret.

Chapter 4   Staking the Claim

You learn a different sense of urgency in space. A distance of 35 kilometers really means ten hours of difficult maneuvering before you can stop at just the place you want. I remember a really tricky project years ago as a hand on Will McInerny's legendary *MS City of Paris III* salvage. It had been making a delivery run to the newly founded Miranda colony at Uranus carrying a fortune in gold foil that was intended to be used as radiation shielding. They were making a gravity-assisted course change through the Jupiter system, and an unorthodox low pass of Ganymede, when its tenuous atmosphere proved enough to tear off a hull panel and expose a master fuel line. As soon as the sunlight hit it, the line superheated and the fuel tanks exploded in a chain reaction, one right after another, pulverizing the ship.

The crew escaped. Luckily the bridge was designed to serve as an escape pod and was jettisoned the moment the first tank blew, but the ship was a total loss otherwise. The foil had shredded into any number of inch-sized pieces that circled all the way around Ganymede, making it look like a miniature Saturn. The ship had exploded at such low altitude that we had to make constant course corrections to get it just right, besides dealing with the cumulative effects of the same friction that had wrecked the ship. Finally, we deployed a mesh net and collected the foil, but it took us five months just to get started. We considered that to be lightning-fast as far as working in space goes, though Will is still out there retrieving tiny bits of gold foil that we missed the first time.

We watched helplessly as the other ship made its slow approach. If there had been an information leak, they couldn't have gotten out there that fast on their own without our knowing. Ships are registered at every port they stop at, and Ed had people monitoring them all. No, these people had been lurking already, probably sitting somewhere nearby. Maybe they knew something about the *Cape Hatteras* that we didn't, or, worse, they had found it before us and were getting supplies. That scenario would make *us* the claim-jumpers.

The *Amaranth Sun*'s bridge was in disarray. Stacey worked at her station faster than an ice miner on Oberon to learn whatever she could about the mystery ship. Her closed-top coffee cup was floating above her, leaking little globules that formed a tiny solar system around her head. Kurt meanwhile was nearly hysterical, looking as though the approaching ship was full of pirates ready to fire a broadside. He scrolled through a listing of every active ship's radio identification number, but I don't think he could have found it at the speed he was going.

"What do you have, Stacey?" I asked.

"I think it's a salvor. I can't tell which one. It has a beacon, but we haven't found it in the listings yet. No idea what size it is. We can only see it head-on, but from the diameter I'd say it's at least a 300-foot ship."

"Could be armed. You know what happened at Europa," Kurt chimed in.

Talk like that sent an icy chill down everyone's spine. That robbery had irreversibly changed the equation for anyone working in space. Jupiter's moon Europa was one of Earth's many official colonies, but it was the odd one. A group had gone out there a few decades ago to create a utopia, drilling beneath the surface to reach the abundant heat and water below. But they were dreamers and didn't take the slightest precaution to defend their colony. They grew their own food but also *other,* more illicit plants, which they shipped back to Earth in little capsules that fell somewhere different every time. They were always one step ahead of the authorities and were masters at skirting the issue diplomatically.

About a year ago a ship with no beacon fired a shot, cracking the ice near the settlement and sending a column of water spraying into space until it froze solid before crashing back to the surface, dropping boulders of ice just feet from their colony's domes. The pirates admittedly had style. They sent a message that read: "Arrrgh! Ye know what we want." They then appropriated the year's crop, which was packaged and awaiting transport later that week.

No one knows who the pirates were, and the unions had little reason to patrol for them. They were too busy keeping up their old rivalries and worrying about what rock belonged to which union, though none of them wanted lawless Neptune or the outer reaches of the solar system. It was the first time anyone had ever armed a ship in space with an old-fashioned projectile cannon—a really big one. I was surprised that we hadn't seen piracy in space before then. It seemed natural, since there's so little law enforcement and so many places to hide.

"It's not the pirates, Kurt. They never struck again. They're probably retired on a private island somewhere on Earth, permanently high and giggling about the size of their bank accounts. Besides, the *Amaranth Sun* is fast. We can get away from just about anyone once we get moving," I said.

He seemed to calm down a bit, and Stacey finally got around to gathering up her coffee blobs.

"Still," I added, "we should be prepared for anything. What can we do to keep them from taking the *Cape Hatteras*?"

"Easy," said Stacey. "Spin it."

"Honey, how are we going to do that?" asked Kurt before I had a chance to pose the same question. Kurt and Stacey were long-time partners in love and work.

"Fire the thrusters using the last of the reserves. I think we can spin that thing to at least five revolutions a minute, maybe more. Once our salvor gets here, we can attach lead-tipped inertia weights to slow it back down. The claim-jumpers haven't got that kind of time. Soon we'll have them outnumbered two to one, and I doubt they'd outnumber our crew," Stacey said. We expected to have 30 more personnel when the *Hyperion* arrived.

"And we hold a wildcard. Since they know, it won't make much difference if the whole solar system knows too. I can radio a press release announcing the find of the *Cape Hatteras* and have all eyes on us in minutes," I said.

I didn't want to do any of that, however, unless I had no other choice. It could take weeks to stop the *Cape Hatteras* from spinning again, and that's assuming we'd be able to get the inertia weights to work. Those things are notoriously tricky. They consist of a powerful magnet that sticks to the hull after being fired from a compressed-air gun. Attached to the top is a reel and a heavy lead weight that rolls out fifty feet or so. The effect is to slow down the rotation like a spinning ice-skater extending her arms, but they need to be in precisely the right places, and they must land mechanism up. That's not always how it works out.

Still, it was a solid option. Since we had found the *Cape Hatteras* already rotating, I had requested an ample supply of inertia weights. Most wrecks don't require them. The weights are heavy and expensive, so it was unlikely that the claim-jumpers had any with them.

The only question I had was whether the thrusters lacked enough reserve air to spin the wreck fast enough. If the thrusters failed, and we were going to have to fight for it, we'd need to grapple the *Cape Hatteras* and hit the engines hard. We didn't have the power to tow it, so we would have to send it twirling at high speed into deep space. The encroachers would never be able to get a man on it to fix strap-thrusters, but that approach also meant that the wreck might end up spinning on more than one axis. The derelict would then be nearly unsalvageable.

When I entered the engine room, Neil had a panel off the ceiling and was floating motionlessly while peering into it.

"Neil, how are my engines?" He hadn't heard me glide in. Zero-G makes for quiet movement.

"You scared the hell out of me," he said.

"Sorry."

"Your engines are fine, but your electrical power isn't. Remember that burning smell from a while back?"

"Yes," I said hesitantly, growing concerned. When we were working on securing the NASA probe to the *Amaranth Sun*'s side, the whole ship suddenly smelled like melting plastic. In a closed oxygen-rich atmosphere, that's dangerous. Fires are almost always deadly on ships in space.

"Well, you know, it was just a short. Not a serious problem, or at least it hasn't become one. We don't carry much extra wire onboard because it's not usually something that fails. So I rigged it, using what I had. But the gauge is too small, and I've been keeping an eye on it ever since. If you have to accelerate beyond normal parameters, it might fail. You'll still have your engines, but you won't be able to steer."

"We'll just have to hope it holds together," I said. I trusted my son's judgement. He was a natural engineer, as far as running a ship was concerned. He had just turned 25 and could rig his way out of anything. But when he was worried, I was worried. It meant that he couldn't think of a contingency plan.

"Cam, we've got a radio message up here," Stacey yelled.

I shot back to the bridge. The first thing I did was to peer out at the approaching ship through a porthole. It was closing much faster than it should have been. Worse, even though it was still 20 kilometers away, you could already discern lighted bridge windows in the telescope. That detail confirmed that it was a big ship and that, if it were a salvor, it could easily handle the *Cape Hatteras*. There could have been a crew of twenty or thirty on a ship that size.

Just then the radio console flashed. The strong signal strength made it clear that it originated from the other ship.

"Cam Hunter, looks like you've found a fish bigger than you can reel in," a voice said.

I recognized it immediately. It was Finley Pace, a salvager like me but also a notorious claim-jumper. He had the most gravelly voice I've ever heard.

"Well, at least you admit it's mine. That's more than you do for most people," I said.

"Oh, I'll go that far, but there's no way you'll salvage it with that mouse of a ship you have."

"I've got another one on the way from Earth. It will be here in just a few days."

"You're going to be waiting a lot longer than that," replied

Pace. "Earth is ten months away for a salvor, and I know you haven't been here that long. I've been tailing you since you picked up that old NASA probe. So what ship do you think it is?"

"Just an old cargo vessel. Can't find any records on it." I was grasping at straws. At any moment he could train a telescope on the derelict and see what we had.

"We could always cut a deal, split it 50/50, and have it done before the government gets involved," Pace said, trailing into a cough. He once had a successful business working on salvaged spacecraft and returning them to service but destroyed his lungs in a decompression accident.

"I appreciate that, but my investors won't go for it. I've already got the funding and percentages worked out and inked."

"That's a shame. I'd have loved to do the *Cape Hatteras* all nice and legal," he said, revealing that he had known all along the find's identity. "But you don't have a way to secure that ship, and you can't stop me from taking it in tow."

"I'll rope it and spin it so fast that it will just be a blur, Finley. You won't see the inside of it for a year or more, and by that time my salvor will be here and you'll be outnumbered."

Finley dropped communication without a response. I glanced out the window again. All I could see was his ship surrounded by a bright white halo. He'd hit his main engines hard and was coming our way. He meant to ram us.

Chapter 5 Spin

I'd never heard of an intentional ramming in space, but if Pace believed his bow could take it, there wasn't much I could do to stop him. The close positions of my two ships made it impossible to tell which one he was aiming for. My gut feeling told me he was after the prize. If you embed your bow into a derelict ship, that's as good a way as any to make it yours. Alternatively, the whole thing might have been a game of chicken to drive us away from the *Cape Hatteras*. We had no way to know until it was impossible to escape.

What we did know was that the margin for error was zero. If he was aiming for the *Amaranth Sun,* a light bump would do fatal damage. Our hull would breach, and we'd end up just like the *Cape Hatteras* and her crew. I didn't think Pace would do it, but if he were after us, we could either abandon the derelict and punch the engines or die. Either way Finley would retire rich in the lawless outer solar system.

We had to act fast.

"Stacey, spin the *Hatteras*!" I yelled. Without hesitation she fired the pneumatic thrusters. We saw the white sprays shoot from them, but the ship was still motionless. If they had worked at all, they spun it so little that we couldn't see the rotation.

"What the hell happened?" I asked frantically.

"They fired, but it looks like they all went off at once."

"At once?"

"They're in stabilization mode. The computer didn't understand why we would want to spin it again, so it corrected the order, believing it was getting faulty information. Damned artificial intelligence. Cam, we've got no reserves left."

"Nice work, Stacey! We've got to grapple," Neil exclaimed. "Dad, bring us around, and I'll go out and attach the lines to the stern of the *Cape Hatteras.*"

That was a very dangerous idea, and I wasn't certain we had time for it. If Neil was out there when Pace's ship closed in, we could lose him in several different ways, not the least of which was vaporization by Finley's engine wash.

"Do it," I ordered half-heartedly.

I followed him to the airlock, despite knowing that he didn't want me involved. He was always independent, wanting to save the day by himself and take the credit for it.

"Sure you want to do this?" I asked, placing my hand on his shoulder and hoping fruitlessly that he would reconsider. "I'd rather have a son than a treasure ship."

"I can do it. I've suited up and worked in space a thousand times. You said yourself that I've got more experience than you had at my age. And you *know* I'm fast," Neil said. His confidence was well founded but did little to ease my worries.

Neil suited up and climbed into the airlock. I watched as the atmosphere drained off and the outer door rotated open. He pushed himself out, spun around, and took up the ends of two steel mooring cables. I can't say I liked the idea of losing them. It's a pain to dock a ship without lines to draw it in. The astronauts of old always seemed to manage it, but it's much safer to use a winch.

Neil fired his suit thrusters and headed for the *Cape Hatteras*. I shot to the bridge, which was the only place that had a starboard porthole where I could see him. I probably shouldn't have watched at all. Nothing up to that point had been so intense on my nerves.

He started by covering the distance between the two ships much faster than I thought he should have. One of the lines he was carrying flailed about, for a moment appearing as though it might foul and whiplash him off into space. He was lucky it didn't. He fired his suit's thrusters just in time to make soft contact near the stern of the derelict.

I've never seen anyone move that fast in a moon suit with its massive thruster array attached. Space may be a weightless environment, but everything still has inertia and bulk, and that makes movement far from effortless. And you get weak in space. Despite the periodic injections of nanotechnological microrobots that maintained us on the cellular level, time in the gravity centrifuges was still required. Even with all of that, and regular exercise, you *will* get weaker working in space no matter what you do. As the old saying went, "The strongest man in space was nothing in a bar fight on Earth." Somehow Neil wasn't showing it. He got the first line connected in record time and then scrambled to the side of the *Cape Hatteras* to connect the second.

Once the job was finished, the idea was to punch the engines hard, tightening the shorter cable on the stern and pulling the derelict along, giving it some speed. Then we would sever it, in turn tightening the second line and imparting a fast spin. We hadn't had time to work out the physics of it all, so we left it to providence that we wouldn't cause the derelict to tumble on multiple axes. If the whole process went well, both the prize and the *Amaranth Sun* would be well off in two slightly different directions, moving faster than Finley Pace's big unwieldy ship could follow. If it worked, the first thing I planned to do was to hang a portrait of Sir Isaac Newton on the bulkhead and sacrifice an apple to it. Then we'd rendezvous with the *Cape Hatteras* and radio a course correction to our salvor.

"Got it!" Neil exclaimed. "Coming back over." He hit his thrusters so hard that he brushed past the airlock door, smacking squarely into the exposed mechanisms on the far wall and tearing a hole in his suit.

"Close it! Close it! I've got a leak!" he yelled. I slammed the button to start the compression cycle, and it became a helpless waiting game. There was no way to know how fast or slow the leak was. It takes less than 30 seconds for the pressure to come up to one atmosphere, but that's an eternity when your suit is losing air. It's a terrible way to go, and it doesn't work as you might think it does. You exhale forcefully, but at the same time you feel your lungs stretching like balloons as the air you do have expands. You panic as your brain senses your inability to take in enough oxygen. The feeling hits you in the chest, a fear unlike anything else. Losing air also means losing heat and moisture, leaving you feeling incredibly cold and terrified, your skin drying painfully fast, and you're struck with stinging pain as the blood vessels in your eyes burst and your lungs are destroyed by barotrauma. Then you pass out.

Twenty-five seconds. I could see Neil struggling. I looked for anything I could do to speed up the process. Finding a wrench stowed on the wall next to the door, I grabbed it and banged on the glass of the window. It was unbreakable.

Fifteen seconds left. "Jesus, he's passing out," I yelled, but the others couldn't leave the bridge. I banged harder with as much strength as I could muster. I saw his face pressed against the glass of his helmet. Ten seconds. He was turning blue. Ice was forming in his eyebrows as his body was robbed of moisture. Five seconds. He had stopped moving. Then came the green light. I spun the door open as fast as I could while yelling to Stacey to begin the maneuver.

I felt the ship burst forward and then stop a moment later as the first cable went taut. I opened the inner airlock door and pulled off Neil's helmet. He was breathing. I felt relieved, but that didn't mean he was uninjured. His color began to return. It hadn't been too late. He regained consciousness, coughing hard and opening his eyes and blinking frenetically to wet them.

"Are we moving?" he asked, wheezing.

"Yes!" I exclaimed as I pushed myself through the door frame, pulled a 90-degree spin, and shot to the the bridge. The *Amaranth Sun* was barely moving.

"Half a kilometer per hour," Stacey said as I careened through the doorway.

"Full thrust?"

"As much as it can give," she said with some disappointment. I guess she expected the *Amaranth Sun* to save the day, but the laws of physics are immutable. But it *was* moving, if only slightly. I looked down the hall to check on my son. I could see him, still wearing half his moon suit, working in the engine room. I remembered the jury-rigged wire.

"Neil! Is it holding?" I asked.

"For now, but if it fails, we'll be dead in the water," he said, not sounding well at all after what he'd just been through.

"Three kilometers per hour and increasing exponentially," Stacey reported.

Most captains get sentimental over their ships. They anthropomorphize them, pet them. Old Will McInerny used to brew an extra cup of coffee each morning and pour it into the recycler just to give his ship that extra kick. That's not me.

"Come on, you bastard!" was the most endearing thing I could come up with as I kicked a bulkhead.

"Ten kilometers per hour," Stacey said.

"I smell burning back here!" Neil relayed. I hoped he was making it up for effect.

"Twenty."

"Fifty." We had less than two minutes left before Pace would be on us..

"A hundred"........"Two hundred"......... "Five hundred"...... "A thousand."

"Sling it!" I yelled.

Stacey cut the first line. We felt a jolt as the second line went taut, then a major lurch as the *Amaranth Sun* spun on its own, the final line being cut by the computer at just the right moment. The maneuver had worked. I saw the *Cape Hatteras* rotating wildly as we spun around. Stacey fired the hydrazine thrusters, righting the *Amaranth Sun* just in time for us to see Finley's salvor pass between our ships. We were receding from each other at thousands of kilometers per hour. It would take him days to stop and calculate our new trajectories. We'd be long gone by the time he did any of that, and catching up would cost him a lot of fuel. Given that he'd been out there for a while already, I figured he was probably running low. And, even if he did overtake us, he'd never stop the *Cape Hatteras* from spinning. We had won.

I watched Pace through the telescope for several days thereafter. He seemed to give up and content himself by heading onward to Jupiter. I never did find out which ship he was aiming for.

We updated Ed Iron and the *Hyperion* about what had happened. Four days later we caught up with the *Cape Hatteras*, but there was little else we could do. It was tumbling so fast that its details were a blur. Stacey had no sooner completed the braking maneuvers to bring us alongside than we lost power. Everything went black.

Chapter 6 Dead in Space

Four and a half months in space with nothing to do. We had main engines but no navigation computer, no lighting other than the glow of a few critical instrument panels, and just enough power shunted around the short to support basic systems like air recycling. It was the deep-space equivalent of camping out.

When too much current passed through the wire, the copper vaporized. The whole line was gone, and we had nothing left to replace it. We even tried to raid the NASA probe but found it to be full of useless fiber-optic cable and inaccessible traces on circuit boards.

The *Cape Hatteras* sat spinning about a kilometer off our port bow. It had shed our steel scaffolding and the pneumatic thrusters. Its center was wrapped like a mummy in our cut mooring lines, but otherwise it seemed intact. I tried to radio the *Hyperion* again without success. Our limited power, we surmised, wasn't producing enough of a signal.

We simply had to wait for reinforcements. The real salvage would begin when the *Hyperion* arrived. It was a 300-foot vessel constructed just two years earlier and it was the most advanced and capable salvor yet built. I was delighted to have that ship. It certainly cost enough to rent, from what I understood.

Ed Iron wanted us to have the best, but he also wanted regular communications. I knew I would get an earful when we regained contact, but I couldn't have controlled what had happened. In a certain way the lack of communications gave me an advantage: when I did eventually establish contact, my account of the claim jump would make for one hell of a surprise read for him. I started writing it on a quantum pad for lack of anything else to do.

I don't like using quantum pads. There's something very invasive about setting a sensor by your head and letting it scan your thoughts. Everyone uses them, and it's an old technology, but the idea of thinking a picture and having it appear on a machine seems disturbing and voyeuristic. It's also inaccurate. The human brain doesn't remember sufficient detail to make a decent digital image. However, I didn't have a working computer for dictation, and the quantum pads had inexhaustible batteries.

Unfortunately the endeavor didn't take up *enough* time. There were days when we had nothing else to do except chat. The *Amaranth Sun* is a tiny ship with a small crew who are around each other all hours of the day. That's not so bad when you have work to do, but when you don't the nerves fray easily.

Neil spent weeks recovering from his decompression injuries, mostly resting in his cabin or doing reduced duty in engineering. But once he felt okay, he and Stacey were at each other's throats. I tried to diffuse things by ordering exercise regimens because the centrifuge pods were offline, but I also hoped the physical activity would blow off steam.

It wasn't enough. By the end of those months we weren't getting along, and I had taken to spending most of my time in my cabin. I even cleaned it, in total darkness, just to see how well I could do, although I wouldn't know until the lights came back on. Neil kept to himself in engineering as much as he could. Stacey and Kurt stayed on the bridge and squabbled, which sometimes made for entertaining listening.

When not on a mission, they lived together on the east coast of Florida. Treasure-hunting was the glue that bound them together. When at home, they'd go beach-combing and look for coins that washed up from the old Spanish wrecks that lay offshore. A few months before finding the derelict they had asked me to marry them the next time we were on Earth. I am a ship's captain, after all, and I was looking forward to performing the ceremony, but at times they argued so vehemently that I figured their marriage would go as badly as mine had.

When the *Hyperion* and its crew finally arrived, we didn't see them. There's a small window in engineering that lets you look out from the ship's stern, but no one was regularly checking it. The radio receiver was turned off to conserve power, so when they appeared it was a complete surprise and a very scary sight. The salvor was a huge cylinder that looked just like Finley Pace's ship. We stopped breathing until we saw the bright flashing of Morse greetings.

Our first order of business was to dock the ships together and repair the *Amaranth Sun.* Within hours they had an airtight corridor running between us. I opened the hatch to see an old friend of sorts. The scowling face before me was that of my ex-wife.

"Where's my son?" she asked.

I hadn't been told that she would be part of the mission. I didn't dislike her—in fact, we were on amicable enough terms—but it was still a shock to see her. Kurt and Stacey had always wondered why my marriage failed. I told them that the answer was simple: I was one of those self-absorbed people who just could not sustain a relationship, even with the perfect woman—which Janet was not.

"He's in engineering, and he's fine. Did you come out here because you were worried?" I asked

"No, I came out here because I'm eminently qualified and the pay is unbeatable."

"I know you better than that."

"No, you don't! Ed Iron figured that since we knew each other I'd be trustworthy, even if there was personal friction. There won't be. Now point me to my son."

Clearly she wasn't in the mood for talking, so I directed Janet to Neil. I didn't believe her story. She was never concerned with making large amounts of money. While there's no question that she's a fine engineer, having graduated top of her class at the University of Copernicus Crater, I knew that her presence had more to do with Neil than it did with my salvage project.

I followed her back to engineering. Neil had the look on his face of someone who wasn't quite sure whether to be happy or very scared. He could get away with his youthful shenanigans with me, but he wouldn't get far with her.

"Give your mother a kiss," Janet said, "and a hug. How are you, baby? Is everything okay?"

"I'm fine, Mom. Don't worry about me," Neil said.

"You haven't been doing anything dangerous?" she asked him, darting a look at me with virtual lasers shooting from her pupils.

"No. Safety first is the golden rule!"

He sounded like a ten-year-old. I used to say the same kinds of things to placate her.

"Well," she said, turning in my direction. "I guess we need

to fix this *ship* of yours. Where did you buy this bucket, a used-vehicle dealership on Mercury?"

She opened a panel against the back wall. I didn't think it had anything to do with the failed wire.

"There's nothing in here but substandard trash. No wonder you're floating around dead in space. Oh come on," she said, "look at this quanzistor," yanking it out with uncomfortable force. "Don't you ever do maintenance on this ship?"

"Yes, I'll have you know it went through a complete refit just. . . ."

"Refit or not, this shouldn't be in here. These things have dates on them, and this one expired two years ago. I can just imagine what the food in your galley is like."

"It's up to date, I swear!"

"Feeding my son dried kelp from fifteen years ago. You're the cheapest person I know."

"I am not cheap!"

"You don't think you are, but I'll bet your supplier is altering dates. You're single-minded. It's always salvage, salvage, salvage. Just cursory thoughts about anything else."

"I'm not that bad!"

"Well, we did find those old steaks," Neil said.

"Thanks, Neil! Stop sucking up to your mother!"

"I am not sucking up. Those steaks were a year past their date! They were awful. They had to have been from a milk cow or something."

I didn't want to admit anything in front of Janet. Yes, I had bought them on Mercury. And, yes, I had gotten a great deal on them. And, yes, I had bought forty cases of them at a bulk price. And, yes, they probably were from dairy cows. But Neil could have given me a little slack.

"I should tell her about your two feuding female friends on Mars," I said.

"Father, you know I don't like girls yet."

I rolled my eyes.

"And it was three," Neil added.

"Of course he doesn't like girls! Both of you, stop it!" Janet commanded. "Cam, you're wrong, and my little angel is right. Now let's get to fixing this bucket."

"I've missed you," I mumbled sarcastically.

She wasted no time in summoning the engineering team from the *Hyperion*. They had my ship up and running in two hours. Their efficiency was incredible, and it was great to see the lights on again. There were even spacewalkers installing new mooring lines to replace the ones we lost. I went to explore the *Hyperion* while they finished.

It was a gorgeous ship, full of enormous interior spaces. When you're stuck on a tiny craft the size of a three-bedroom house, you get used to small spaces. The *Hyperion* was like a palace, its spaciousness seeming almost too much. It had two rotating sections with gravity and a gymnasium instead of a kitchen/gym/dining-room combo like what we had on my ship, along with a large cargo hold and even a recreational room with gravity. The people onboard could sit around on couches, have snacks and watch the latest holovies sent from Earth. On the

Amaranth Sun we had to hover on the bridge and watch 400-year-old classics on a two-inch instrument display.

"Jealous?" Captain David Keating asked.

"Yeah, you've got more than one bathroom," I said.

"Three, and each bedroom has a unisex urination facility," he replied.

"Lovely. A suction cup at 4:00 a.m. Isn't technology wonderful." He chuckled.

I didn't know David personally, but we seemed to be starting on a good footing, or so I thought.

"Captain Hunter, on a more serious note, it's both a pleasure to meet you and a joy to be a part of this salvage. I don't have to say that the *Cape Hatteras* is legendary."

"I know. It's difficult to grasp the magnitude of this discovery. I think of nothing else, and yet it still hasn't entirely sunk in. It's historic."

"It may be more historic than you think," Keating said.

"Oh?" I responded, not certain what he meant.

"Yes, we didn't want to radio any of this, and you apparently couldn't have received it anyway, but the investors hired a researcher to look into the *Cape Hatteras* story in depth. Two centuries out, the classified status of the investigation was a bit easier to break into with Ed's influence, but it still had unusually strong covers. You wouldn't believe how secret this whole thing was. It had the highest level of classified status. What we found out was that the whole story hadn't been told to the public."

"That's no surprise. Did you discover anything specific?"

"Yes, we did. First, there was no telescope footage. You're aware of the public fervor; everyone wanted to see it. It was a sensation when they refused to release it. The UNAG government at the time said that it was very graphic and that everyone should respect the feelings of the crew's families. But the evidence never existed as far as we can tell. It's mentioned in the official report but not in any of the classified documents, and we've got most of them, we think."

"Most of them? Some documents are still missing?"

"Yes, there is a reference in several of them to another file or group of files. The archivists said they should have been released too, but they simply didn't have them. Probably erased decades ago by mistake, or so they claimed."

"Or the UNAG government still doesn't want it revealed that they lied about the footage."

"That would make sense. They wanted an open-and-shut case with no questions asked. Something straightforward such as that the ship was hit by a meteor and violently decompressed. If other factors were involved, a bad component installed by a lobbyist's contractor or something of that nature, then it might have been worth covering up and keeping it that way."

"Or they just wanted to get past the fact that a huge investment had just disappeared with no return. I would have wanted to bury it and move on too. Did the researcher discover anything new about the actual cause?"

"No, she didn't, but the investors saw your photographs of the *Cape Hatteras* and concluded that something wasn't quite right. They hired naval historians, archeologists, and engineers, all of whom are here now, and they all agree on one thing: the ship did not suffer a violent decompression."

"So what do they think happened?" I asked. Our suspicions were confirmed, but the academic side of it was news to me.

"No consensus yet. We'll find out when we go in," he said.

Chapter 7 Day 178

Captain Keating asked me to stay for dinner aboard the *Hyperion*. I considered declining because I wanted to get back to the *Amaranth Sun*, but I sensed that the invitation was a veiled order from Ed Iron. The occasion was to be an official question-and-answer session that would make its way home as an independent report.

The dinner started out very ceremonially. I have problems with formality, always feeling out of place. Keating dined with his officers and the academicians from Earth at a long table in one of the gravity sections separated from the general crew. The *Hyperion* was a nice ship, but it was still designed to be a utilitarian salvor—except in the officers' mess. It was large and lavishly decorated. Oak paneling lined the walls, and the ceiling had a fixed crystal chandelier ingeniously designed to look as though it were floating freely, all lending the room the feel of an expensive restaurant. Most remarkable was the transparent floor that revealed the rotating star fields, giving the impression of traveling in a glass-bottomed boat in space. I'd never seen anything quite like it. The room was darkened enough that you could discern the individual colors of the stars glowing like white, red, and blue gems from a shipwreck at the bottom of a coal-black ocean. The view was distracting. I had to make a conscious effort to maintain eye contact with the people sitting around the table.

Full maritime protocol was observed. Keating sat at one end of the table and I at the other as the captains present. I looked past the two rows of faces that led to Keating, who gave the impression of a lawyer preparing for a cross-examination with an almost regretful look on his face, as though he weren't relishing the idea of grilling me in front of the others.

The scene reminded me of the old 18th-century Royal Navy ships. I was in the position of the captain who had lost his ship to mutineers and was being dragged back to the admirals amid an air of absurd civility. Keating was a Yorkshire native and an old Eurorussian naval man—they were known to cling to tradition—and that led me to expect his questioning to be tough. I had little reason to be concerned, but words can be misinterpreted with disastrous results, so I tried to prepare myself as best I could in the short time it took for everyone to settle in.

"Captain Hunter, if I may ask, how is it that your ship has ended up dead in space while the *Cape Hatteras* is spinning?" Keating asked, finally breaking the awkward silence.

The question was blunt, as I expected, but I was somewhat relieved. I was ready for that one after having written my report to Ed Iron. All I had to do was to paraphrase it. I wouldn't have been prepared for a question about why my communications receiver was turned off. I'm not sure that power conservation to keep the toilets flushing would have been an acceptable answer, and I was worried that my first impression on the scientists would be a jumble of excuses.

"We were attacked by a claim-jumper," I said, spinning my story before Keating had time to respond. I told them about a succession of close scrapes, which weren't all that close, embellishing freely. Everyone was staring at me absolutely captivated. Thankfully none of my crew, especially Stacey, was there to dispute any details of my narrative.

"His ship missed us by inches," I elaborated, "but it was too much for my poor jury-rigged *Amaranth Sun*. We lost *everything*. I had to suit up and spend a week working inside the exhaust bells just to get the engines back."

Our engines had never gone offline, but a cold start of a ship's engines made for a harrowing story.

"I was never sure whether the reactors would accidentally come back online and incinerate me. But here I am! And we're all in for a treat, my friends. Answers to one of the greatest historical mysteries *and* the derelict's vast treasure lie right outside. More gold than any human eyes have seen in two centuries, and it's ours," I said, sweeping my arm with a flourish as a fine view of the *Cape Hatteras* presented itself through the floor, as if on cue.

My audience gasped and applauded. I knew that at least half of them had enough engineering knowledge that they must have known I was dramatizing, but a good story is a good story nonetheless, and making yourself popular during a first encounter is essential. My ploy worked: Keating never asked about the receiver.

We spent the rest of dinner in deep discussion about the adventure to come, and by the end of it Keating was just as engaged and excited as everyone else. I think he was relieved that his boss would be satisfied with everything I'd said. I left the *Hyperion* with a feeling of success in endearing myself to everyone, helped in the end by copious quantities of French brandy.

I got back onboard the *Amaranth Sun* at about midnight. I hadn't had a drink since our whiskey celebration of months before, so I hadn't been inclined to moderate my intake at dinner. I made my way to my cabin hoping that I wouldn't run into anyone. I was so drunk that my hands were slipping off the handholds, and at one point I had to close one eye to see where I was going. I made it to my quarters and zipped myself into the bunk-bag, even though I wasn't all that sleepy.

I was in that state of intoxication where your mind is churning, not yet at the stage of passing out. Maybe I should have had one more drink. I kept going over what Keating had said when I first boarded the *Hyperion*. The *Cape Hatteras* did not look like a wreck that had violently decompressed. It looked like a mothballed ship waiting to be brought back into service.

Eventually I fell asleep. I don't think anyone could have woken me without extreme difficulty. My dreams were nothing short of strange. I remember one in which I saw myself and my crew dead and frozen on the *Amaranth Sun*. I felt that somehow we had died from a disease that we had contracted on the derelict. That wasn't possible, the low temperatures the derelict had sustained for centuries would have sterilized it, but it was still disconcerting.

The next morning the *Hyperion's* crew got to work immediately on the *Cape Hatteras*. Their first step was to deploy the magnetic inertia weights. It took them over a week in 24-hour rotating shifts. They took great care, planning every step and going over any potential snags to ensure they were ready. It paid off: they attached them with no mishaps.

It was beautiful to watch them operate. The velocity of the spin reduced as they let out the line, leaving the *Cape Hatteras* in a rhythm of slow rotations, much as we'd initially found her. Then they installed sophisticated hydrazine rockets, much better than pneumatic thrusters, to bring it to a complete stop.

Our situation was much improved. The rockets had plenty of fuel, and someone had the foresight to look up the diameter of the *Cape Hatteras* and send straps long enough to encircle the ship. More importantly, they were 360-degrees directional so that we could maneuver the derelict remotely from the

Hyperion and have some evasive-action capability if Finley Pace showed back up.

In addition, we set a slow, meandering course to throw off any calculations Pace might perform to locate us, changing the heading of our group periodically, with only Keating and I knowing when and where the salvage operation would occur. If you take precautions like that, it is impossible to be located based on your previous positions. Finley would have to search by using telescopes and time-lapse photographs, which could take years. I was satisfied that Pace was no longer a concern, even if he did leak word about the discovery. Still, I intended to soil his name from Earth to Pluto for what he had tried to pull.

We rebuilt the scaffolding around the *Cape Hatteras*, work I found frustrating because I don't like to do the same thing twice. On December 24, 2409, we were ready to cut into the hull. We celebrated Christmas Eve onboard the *Hyperion*. One of the crew played guitar quite well, banging out tunes all night while we sang along. He mentioned that he wanted to eventually play professionally. I wondered if he realized that he would soon be so wealthy that he could do whatever he wanted.

On Christmas Day, back on the *Amaranth Sun*, I set up a "tree" consisting of a bunch of dried rosemary twigs from the galley. I crowned the bundle with a flashing stick-on emergency beacon without thinking. The light blinking through the galley's porthole prompted the *Hyperion* to call and ask whether we needed assistance. Everyone went to bed early that night, for the next morning we planned to start cutting into the hull of the *Cape Hatteras*. Excitement made sleep difficult. I couldn't have gotten more than four hours before Kurt popped in to wake me.

By the time I had finished my obligatory two cups of coffee and suited up, there was already a large crowd maneuvering through the scaffolding.

"You're finally here. We're ready to begin," my ex-wife said.

"It's 6:00 a.m. I'm not late. I'm on schedule."

"You always were a slow mover in the mornings. Early bird gets the worm, spacebrain," she said, flashing me a dirty look through the glass of her helmet.

Janet then gave a thumbs-up to two men on either side of the target area. They pulled down their gold-plated visors, and a moment later their plasma cutters fired blindingly. It was so intense as to be hard to watch, but I couldn't help myself. Janet saw me struggling to shade my eyes and pulled down my visor, taking a swipe at me for not remembering that I had one.

At nearly the halfway mark we hit something, a bulkhead that wasn't on the ship's blueprints, behind the hull plating. That's not unusual. When you build a ship, sometimes things don't end up as the plans might suggest. Certain areas might be shored up with an extra rib, or a dividing wall might be installed afterwards. The torches we were using weren't going to be able to penetrate it.

It cost us several hours to bring a heavy-duty torch over from the *Hyperion*. They tested it before applying it to the hull. The torch shot out a stream of fire easily 60 feet long, making it look like a flamethrower, but when they applied it to the hull, all you could see was an intense pinpoint of light. I worried that it might damage the interior of the ship when it burned through.

At 2235 hours the cut section floated free, and they signaled for me as the cutting crew withdrew. I motioned for everyone to tune to the global comm frequency so that whatever

I said would be audible to all. I had planned to make a speech, but when the moment came it didn't seem appropriate. Everyone had been waiting all day. I simply said, "Here goes!" and peered into the blackness.

"I can't see anything," I reported.

The problem was that none of the lights on the scaffolding were pointing directly into the ship. I turned on my head lamp. Still nothing. Then I remembered the visor. I figured that I might as well get some laughs out of my gaffe, so I turned around and lifted it. After the laughter stopped, I said, "Alright. Let's try this again."

I had read a book years ago about Howard Carter and the moment he broke through to King Tutankhamun's tomb in Egypt. He could see statues and riches, but all I could see was part of the far wall of the corridor. I poked my head in a little further and saw a black passageway leading away in either direction. It led to unimaginable treasures and mystery, so when someone asked on the comm what I could see, all I could do was to parrot Carter. "Wonderful things," I said.

Chapter 8 Day 205. 2300 Hours.

After that long day I should have left things at poking my head inside. If I had been an archeologist instead of a salvager, I'd have followed strict protocol and waited until morning to go in. That was the smart thing to do—start fresh and rested, ready to be methodical and careful. But I was a treasure hunter, and although I intended be sensitive to anything I found, I needed to live the moment and go deeper inside.

I called for Neil to accompany me, due to his close experience with the ship. An archeologist had arrived on the *Hyperion*, so I asked for him as well to temper our enthusiasm with a dose of professionalism. He jumped at the chance with as much excitement as Neil did.

I liked Dr. Maheshtra, or Sanjay as he preferred to be called. After shaking hands with all the academicians during the dinner party on the *Hyperion*, it was clear that professional enthusiasm abounded. But Sanjay stood out as the only one who seemed willing to admit the absolute importance of the gold. I could work with a man like that, so I decided that he would be the first of the scholars to see the derelict up close.

I went first by lightly pushing myself into the interior of the *Cape Hatteras*. I found myself in a passageway running the length of the ship that was similar in function to the central corridor on the *Amaranth Sun.* The ship had two, one on either side, that formed a kind of enclosed promenade extending from the bridge to the engineering compartment. We had chosen an entry point near the center of that passageway, or as close to it as we could get without having to slice through a main rib.

It was pitch black in there. I had a miner's light on the top of my helmet, so I flipped it on, producing a disappointing six-inch patch of illumination. I wasn't going to see much with it, and I hadn't thought to grab a flashlight from the *Amaranth Sun*. I had the others turn their headlamps on.

"First thing in the morning, we'll need to bring in some decent lighting," I said.

Sanjay and Neil followed closely. Everyone else remained outside, both to minimize the impact we would have on the pristine ship but also to rescue us if need be. While the *Cape Hatteras*'s exterior looked great, the inside could easily be a mess of dangerous debris. Our communications with the outside world would be blocked by the ship's thick steel hull, so I left instructions that if we weren't back in two hours, someone should come to look for us.

"Right or left?" I asked.

"Left, to the bridge," Sanjay said.

"Right, to the treasure," Neil retorted.

I had to break the tie. "Left. The gold isn't going anywhere."

Ever since Keating had filled my head with burning questions, I was eager to find out what had really happened to the *Cape Hatteras*. The bridge was the most likely place to find some answers. We edged our way down the corridor. I'd like to say I was being safety-conscious, and that did play a part, but there were also five bodies somewhere on that ship. I didn't want to lunge head first into one.

The ship's interior was as cold as deep space. I noticed a thin coat of frost on the walls. That required condensation—not something you see in shipwrecks very often. Frost can form only in a pressurized atmosphere. In a violent decompression things happen so fast that any moisture goes right out the hole. The *Cape Hatteras* must have lost its air very slowly, allowing its moisture to freeze out. That was a clue.

All of the compartment doors were wide open, which was odd. The first thing you do during a decompression is to close doors. On larger ships like the *Cape Hatteras*, they're built airtight so you can seal off the area where the leak is. If the derelict decompressed slowly, there should have been plenty of time to shut them and save the ship. For some unknown reason its crew didn't do that. We stopped at each open door, shining our tiny miner's lights into the darkness beyond.

The first room was a galley, spotlessly clean except for a coating of frost. Food packets and prepared meals were stacked in containers mounted to the walls, with a metal table and a cooking unit in the center of the room.

"They're probably still good," I told the others. "There really isn't much that can happen to food in open space. It's just a few degrees above absolute zero in here, with no light or air to damage the provisions. I once heard of a crew doing a run between Saturn and Earth that ate 90-year-old food on the mothballed ISS XII station when an accident thawed their own supplies. They claimed that the meal was delicious."

"Is that where the milk cow steaks came from?" Neil asked. I ignored him.

We floated forward, not lingering too long in the galley. A long row of assay facilities, control rooms for mining equipment, and computer labs followed, but no sign of the crew. Just aft of the bridge we found the communications center. That was where we most expected to find a body, since in the event of a disaster you always want someone sending maydays. In the vast distances of space the chances for rescue are slight, but at least you could consult with engineers back home, talk to your loved ones, or simply make sure everyone knew what had happened.

The instrument settings revealed that a crew member had been in contact with home. The dials were set to the standard emergency channel—a direct line to the Admiralty Administration in Montreal—with both the record and transmit tabs depressed, meaning that someone had been making logs and transmitting them at the same time. But whoever it was, he or she hadn't died in that room.

Things were much the same on the bridge: there was no sign of anyone. The computers weren't working, as expected. Then we noticed something odd: the ship's wheel was stowed. That seemed unlikely during an emergency and a cold restart. With no engines you wouldn't have the ship automatically navigating and maintaining its heading. I wondered whether it were possible that the crew of the *Cape Hatteras* may have intentionally set a course to Jupiter and allowed the ship to run out of fuel. The ship was last reported to be in the orbit of 974-Bernhard and had only enough helium to return home. It shouldn't have been underway anywhere as far as anyone knew, and if it was then it *should* have been in the direction of Earth. Two centuries ago there were no colonies at the gas giants for refueling, meaning that going out there was a one-way trip.

"We've got to get a look at the ship's logs," I said. "This wreck just gets stranger by the minute."

"I'll make it my top priority when we restore electrical power," Sanjay replied.

"Can we go and see the gold yet?" Neil asked.

"We should make a full circuit down the other corridor. It will take us to the hold," I said. I had the schematics of the *Cape Hatteras* memorized, having had a poster of them in my room when I was a kid.

We passed down the twin corridor on the other side. It was a mirror image of the other, with no sign of anyone. The only difference was that the doors to the crew's quarters were closed. That's standard, since no one leaves the door to their private space open. We left them unexplored as they were possible locations of the bodies.

"Once we get to the hold, we should be able to pass through the engineering compartment and come out the other side through a second door. We'll be in the same corridor we started in," I said.

We passed a transverse corridor that led to the other side of the ship. Its floor was cocked at an odd angle, the entry stoop sitting two feet above the level of the corridor, frozen where it had been when it lost power.

"What's down there?" Neil asked.

"Crew amenities. We're in a rotating gravity section. There's a gymn, recreation area, and dining hall."

"Do you think the crew could be in there?"

"Maybe, but I doubt it. You don't watch a movie when your ship is losing air."

"Unless you don't know it's leaking out," Sanjay said.

"We'll see several of these crossings. The next one leads to the secondary reactor rooms."

"Shouldn't we explore those areas?" Sanjay asked.

"I'll leave that up to you and your colleagues. You can be the first to explore them." I responded. Those rooms were of little importance to my goals that night. It was late, and we needed to move on and see the gold. We reached the door to the hold a short time later. Unlike doors elsewhere on the ship, this one was closed tight.

"We'll have to crank it open by hand. Stand back," I warned. It was well worth playing it safe. If the hold was still pressurized, the escaping air would be powerful and might carry debris, possibly even gold bars that could shatter a space helmet. It wouldn't be the first time that happened. A salvage crew was sent to retrieve a capsule left by the fifteenth manned mission to Mars, abandoned nearly four centuries ago. Everyone assumed its pressurization wouldn't have held up that long, but when they popped the hatch it blew plastic shards from a broken computer screen straight into a man's space suit, killing him. I wasn't going to take that chance, even if it was one in a million.

I stood to the side of the door and cranked the manual release. There was no rushing air, and the compartment door slid open easily. Then came that sudden flush of excitement you feel in your chest when something truly wonderful is about to happen. We must have moved faster than at any other time in our exploration that day to get ourselves inside that hold and shine our tiny lights on the cargo. We were not disappointed.

"It's still here!" I said, as both of my companions were struck speechless.

Row after row of gold bars flashed brilliantly in our miner's lights. It was more than a bank vault, it was a royal treasury. I'd never seen anything like it, even in old pictures of Fort Knox.

The bars were stacked neatly, strapped to metal pallets across the forward quarter of the hold.

"We're so . . . rich," Neil said.

"And I thought my grandchildren would still be paying off the loan for my degree," Sanjay remarked.

I did some quick math in my head. Even after dividing it into shares, I was now one of the wealthiest men in the UNAG. We stayed for half an hour marvelling at the magnitude of the haul. We were looking at the fabled treasure of the *Cape Hatteras*. Fairytales were told to children about it. I'd bet every salvager in the solar system started their career specifically to look for it, and I was the one who had bagged it.

"It's late," I said. "We need to move on. Everyone's waiting for us, and we need to get back to the salvor and come up with a plan for tommorrow."

It was hard to stop staring, but when we finally moved on we ran into a problem: the doors to the engine room were welded shut from the inside. To go through them, we'd have had to cut our way in, and we weren't prepared for that. The path across the hold was blocked by a large mass of stowed mining gear, so we were left to return the way we had come until we found one of the transverse corridors.

"It's not unusual to weld a door shut if you don't need it. They had two and may have decided to install additional equipment and needed the extra wall space," I said.

"Is it possible the crew welded themselves into the engineering compartment to save themselves? Would there be any advantage to doing that?" Sanjay asked with a slight hint of India in his speech that I hadn't detected before. I suspected he was nervous.

"Well, the walls on ships are usually built thicker in the engine room in case something explodes, but it's probably no more airtight than the rest of the doors. It's just armored," Neil said.

I didn't think the crew would be in engineering either. It didn't seem like the place you'd go to spend your last moments. When you're losing your air, you don't need propulsion; you need rescue. You'd put on a moon suit to buy a few more hours and head for the communications room.

I paused for a moment, thinking that I should bring something out to excite the crowd. I unstrapped a bar of gold and pulled it along behind me. It would weigh over 200 lbs on Earth, but in zero-G it weighed nothing yet still required significant force to get it moving. Mass is mass.

"I'm sure everyone's still out there. I don't want to come out empty-handed," I said to my companions.

We made our way through the first transverse corridor and on to the entry cut. I followed close behind my companions. Our communications returned, and we could hear everyone talking. They were waiting for some confirmation of success. I didn't say anything but just pulled the bar around and let it float freely in front of me. Everyone erupted into cheers. For the rest of that night we were very happy people, spending what was left of the evening drinking champagne on the *Hyperion* and talking about how wealthy we were.

Even the most stoic academicians seemed to join in and contemplate how much money their percentage worked out to be. We had a rough idea, but everyone wanted to know *exactly* how rich they were. I'd counted one of the facing stacks in the hold and made an estimate. It was beyond anyone's expectation. We believed that the ship was carrying *more* gold than had been assumed. We weren't just wealthy; we were filthy rich. Every one of us, or so I thought.

Amid the excitement I wish that someone had stopped for a moment to look around before we went merrily rocketing back to the *Hyperion*. No one had bothered. But if they had, they might have noticed that a new star had appeared. It would have been bright enough for anyone who navigates in space to have noticed. It marked the full-throttle engines of a ship, distant and weeks away, heading straight for us.

Chapter 9 Day 206

We spent the next morning coming up with a method of unloading the gold over coffee. The ideas ranged from floating it across freely to ferrying the bars between the ships using transport pods. The engineers had the best suggestion: a bucket brigade and a conveyor line. It seemed be the fastest way and involved little risk.

The plan was to use a pair of pulleys, one attached near the hole in the *Cape Hatteras* and the other outside the cargo hatch of the *Hyperion*. We would number and catalog each bar before sending it across in a bag attached to the line. The people on the other side would wheel it around, unload it, record it in the ship's manifest, and strap it down securely in the salvor's hold. Then they would return the empty bag on the other side as a new bar arrived. With any luck we hoped to move as many as 50 bars a day.

Cataloging would be the most important part. I couldn't just toss the bars in the hold and be on my way. It wasn't my personal gold; it belonged to the investors and employees too. We would get our fair share when the time came, but we had to be meticulous to avoid disagreements. Once the treasure was cataloged, the hold would be sealed and guarded, with only myself and Keating having access. When we reached Earth, we would unload the cargo at an old orbital dock colloquially known as "Waterloo." We chose it because that's where the *Cape Hatteras* had launched its mission. It seemed appropriate for our expedition to return home to Waterloo Dock 4b.

When we arrived at Waterloo, we would check each bar against the records again, accumulate a good-looking pile, and then call the press in for photographs and holograms. We would need serious security, so Ed Iron had contracted a private firm in Kathmandu that specialized in guarding transports to the outer solar system. It was made up of Gurkhas, still the toughest and most capable warriors in the solar system.

We studied the gold bar I had brought over the night before. It was interesting how meticulous the *Cape Hatteras* project had been. The bar was neatly assayed and stamped with its exact weight recorded on top. Impressive work for something done in space.

I couldn't help but think what might have happened if the UNAG had recovered the gold. History might have been different. At the time Earth was still using fiat currency, trading paper instead of something valuable. It was hard to imagine that from my perspective. The world had operated on a gold standard before paper currency, and then it had returned to gold afterward.

By afternoon we had finished installing the pulleys and lines. It was time for me to get back inside the *Cape Hatteras*. I chose Sanjay and Neil to accompany me again. They knew the terrain already, and we weren't yet ready to fill the derelict with sightseeing historians.

Before going over, Neil and Dr. Maheshtra had to prepare for moving a fusion generator to the *Cape Hatteras* for running the portable lights. Once we did that, we could send engineers to work on restoring power. If the ship was out of fuel, we'd need to fill the helium tanks. As it turned out, they were completely dry.

We then had to figure out some way of transferring helium from the *Hyperion* to the derelict. I left that to the engineers, but even I knew that connectors from 200 years ago were much different than those of today. The engineers would also have to build a smaller tank inside one of the five monsters on the *Cape Hatteras* rather than filling the whole thing. We didn't need the engines, just electrical power.

"I'm going over ahead of you," I said to Neil and Sanjay. "I'll get the lights in position and run the power lines. I'd also like to look around a bit more, unless you need help moving the generator."

"We've got it, I think, but be careful," Neil said.

I took three sets of lights with me. They were originally designed for the deep ocean but worked just as well in space. Their frames had magnetic feet, so I could set them up anywhere on the ship. I intended to put one in the hold, one at the entrance looking down the corridor, and one on the ceiling of the bridge.

I slipped through the cut, set up the first light near the opposite wall, and plugged in the line that would supply the bridge lighting. I was delighted to find that each individual light swiveled—the older models did not—so I could illuminate the corridor from two different directions and cover everything.

I had brought a tube of low-temperature rubber and applied a coating on the edge of the entry cut. Sharp edges and burrs are dangerous things in space; one accidental swipe could easily cut a hole in a moon suit. That was such a worry that nearly all ships designed over the last few centuries had no sharp edges anywhere. While I was slathering the entry cut, I examined the derelict's construction.

It was very old-fashioned. Instead of a microcomb hull behind the outer plating, a lightweight design that allowed comm signals to penetrate, it was built of solid steel. That was the first thing I'd seen that betrayed the age of the otherwise spanking-new appearance of the *Cape Hatteras*. I figured that it must weigh five times what a comparable ship of its size would today, but that didn't mean it was weak. On the contrary, old does not necessarily mean bad, and if Finley Pace had rammed it, I think it would have pushed back.

When I was satisfied that I had applied a good coating of rubber, I made my way slowly toward the bridge, feeding out electrical line as I went. Moving backwards was a little disconcerting. If a body floated up and bumped me, I'd turn to see a 200-year-old face sporting milky frozen eyes.

I wondered how a micrometeorite could have done any damage to the *Cape Hatteras*. The hull was *thick*. At most a collision would have made a little crater that probably wouldn't have left a corresponding dent on the inside, much less cause an air leak. What I saw stood in direct contradiction to the assertions of the official investigation.

Once on the bridge I pushed myself to the ceiling and positioned the next light. I took a moment to look around. No theory I'd heard fit what I was seeing. Unless the leak was on the bridge itself, there should have been some sign of activity. The swivel chairs all pointed forward, there were no closed-top coffee cups, papers, or computer pads lying around. It looked as though someone had cleaned the bridge before leaving, as though the ship had been mothballed for storage.

I stopped to look at the panel in front of the captain's station. When we restored power, I hoped that would tell us everything. His logs would have been stored on its computer, and there was no good reason why a ship that well preserved wouldn't have all the data intact. I thought of the commanding officer of the *Cape Hatteras*, Captain John Andrew Nelson.

He was an interesting man, one of the last people to command both ocean and space vessels. His first command was one of the final warships to sail Earth's seas. His last assignment was the *Cape Hatteras*, and if he had survived he might have led some of the great missions of the following years before a quiet retirement after making fleet admiral. Instead, his end came mysteriously in the cold of deep space.

I made my way back down the corridor to the hold. I was in new territory and found the door open on that side. If this section was consistent with how we'd found the rest of the ship, when the lights came on we should see an open engineering door. I shone my light toward it but couldn't make anything out. I didn't want to go any closer and find a body on my own.

I set the light up near the entrance, feeling silly for being scared. I was like a schoolboy in an abandoned house, reinforcing his own fears by thinking about them. I stayed with the most comforting thing on the ship—the gold. I trained my light on it, hoping to switch mental gears and get back to planning. I intended to keep that six-inch spotlight right there until Sanjay and Neil got on board.

I felt my foot touch the floor's plating. I must have been moving slightly on residual momentum. When I directed the miner's light to my feet, I instantly felt nauseated and weak. I knew that feeling: I once had fainted from drinking cold water on a scorching hot day, and that's what it felt like before going black. I tried to think of a cause, but my mind began flitting in and out of consciousness.

I shook my head and sobered briefly, enough to focus. It had to be low oxygen. I panicked and tried to assess the condition of my suit. I tried to check my air gauges, but before I could the feeling passed. I was abruptly fine again and looking at my feet, though I didn't recall moving my head back in that direction.

I glanced back up at the gold. There is a difference between true fight-or-flight scared and helplessly frozen terrified. I felt the latter kind. I was like an animal in headlights, locked on what I was seeing but not quite capable of comprehending the imminent danger.

On the edge of a gold bar in front of me was scrawled the words, "You're not supposed to be out here yet." I thought someone had written it there to frighten me, but I realized it wasn't possible. I had been looking at that same brick just moments before. The writing transmogrified into the color of blood and liquefied, boiling and subliming away in a puff of red steam.

I turned to flee only to be confronted by a dead man. He was wearing no moon suit. His flesh was dried and reduced, his paper-thin lips contracted into an unnaturally wide grin. Instinctively I glanced upward, expecting desiccated and sunken eyes, but they were still brown and bore life in them. He was looking at me. I could hear his labored breathing in the dead of space—impossible without air and through a thick helmet. My suit filled with the smell of simultaneous life and rot.

As I jolted back in stunned shock, my miner's light falling on his jumpsuit revealed the name Nelson embroidered on its breast. It was the captain of the *Cape Hatteras*. Like a thought placed in my head by someone else, it became powerfully clear that I had to get out, abandon the wreck, and never return. Otherwise I would become like him.

The cargo bay suddenly was illuminated in flashes of unearthly blue light. I could see more bodies of the dead coming toward me. The scene went black. I closed my eyes in terror and held them tightly shut. They would take me in the darkness. The light returned, rising stronger and whiter, painfully bright through my eyelids.

Then I felt the moment of waking. I opened my eyes; I had somehow fallen asleep. I knew the comfort you feel when you awake from a terrible dream and experience the epiphany that it wasn't real. The light in my eyes was the superlight, Neil and Sanjay were onboard plugging them in. I moved to look past it. The dead were gone, leaving only a lighted cargo hold filled with treasure and mining equipment, but the dream's vividness left me trembling.

I shot down the corridor until I bumped squarely into Sanjay, banging my helmet against his.

"What's wrong?" yelled Neil on the comms.

"I just. . . . I'm sorry, Sanjay," distancing myself so that he couldn't feel my shaking. I didn't tell them about what had happened. I figured that it was better to look foolish for going too fast rather than look crazy for seeing a ghost in a dream and being terrified of it.

"You're too used to your own ship and getting impatient in your old age," Neil said as he helped Sanjay get his bearings again.

"Treasure hunters, you're all just big kids! I'll be on the bridge playing with my toys," Sanjay said with a good-natured grin.

I had no idea what had happened. Maybe a moment of low blood pressure or worse. I made a pact with myself to have the medic onboard the *Hyperion* take a discreet look at me. I never followed up on that resolution.

Chapter 10 Day 207

The next morning I appraised the wreck as I coasted across the gap for the third time. The *Cape Hatteras* looked profoundly different. With our lights shining through some of the portholes dotting the side of the ship, it seemed alive again, a place where living people worked instead of the dead and sterile place it had been the day before.

Neil and Sanjay had positioned more lights and there were now four engineers working onboard. The interior looked something like it might have 200 years ago. I could see various instrument panels every few feet down the corridor. They were still lifeless, but it wouldn't be long before they had power again. Seeing them gave me confidence that we would soon gain control of the prize.

I was struck by how much more technology the derelict had than a modern ship. The wreck had layer upon layer of automation. People were barely needed at all; they were almost a token presence in case something went wrong. The *Cape Hatteras* was three times the length of the *Hyperion*, yet it had a crew the size of the *Amaranth Sun*'s. Only five people were needed to mine that asteroid. But that same complexity led to accidents and malfunctions, and within fifty years after the loss of the *Cape Hatteras* designers began emphasizing simplicity.

I wanted to see the treasure in the new lighting, but I was hesitant to return to the hold. After my strange experience the ship itself didn't bother me, but the hold did. I felt as though someone were watching me whenever I was in there. I hadn't told anyone about the incident, nor did I plan to, but my feelings of dread when on that ship contrasted sharply with the enthusiasm of the others.

I planted my feet on the derelict's floor plating near the spot where I had dreamt my ghosts. I felt a sustained groan in the ship vibrating through the frame that made it seem as though the *Cape Hatteras* were a whale and I was in its belly. The vibration, I thought, was probably that of the engineers working inside the fuel tanks. Earlier they had informed of a welcome way to save time. They had devised a flexible fuel bladder, eliminating the need for constructing a metal tank. With a little luck it would be less than a day before we had partial electrical power.

"We need to access the engine room, Cam," my ex-wife said as she lumbered into the hold in her moon suit, complete with magnetic boots—she preferred not to float unless she had to. "We know you want to limit access to the hold. God knows why. It's not exactly easy to stuff a bar of gold down the pants of your moon suit. But your overactive imagination needs to get out of the damned way so that we can get this ship up and running."

"You know the bodies are probably in there, darling."

"Well, *darling*, get them out so we can go in."

"I can't. I have to supervise preparations for the gold transfer," I said. "You'll have to do it yourselves. Be reverent toward any dead crew members you find, we don't want any bad publicity over that. You'll need to access from the port side. The starboard door is welded shut."

"You always were squeamish," Janet replied.

"I'm too busy to be squeamish."

Truth be told, I was squeamish. I hadn't been looking forward to dealing with the dead crew. When they were located, we were to arrange a service and proper burial in space. I knew that I'd have to officiate, but I didn't mind that. What bothered me was the prospect of having to view the corpses before we put them into the coffins. I couldn't dodge that. It was customary for a commander to identify the bodies for legal purposes.

I knew they'd probably be mummified and very much dead, unlike the case in my dream. That bothered me even more. It was always possible that the same thing that killed them might one day get me. I was probably being superstitious again, but you have to be that way when you're dealing with something bigger and more powerful than you are, whether it's an ocean or the vast expanses of space.

Part of the engineering team filed past me. I knew that theft was unlikely, but even so I watched their every move as they passed the mountain of gold. I couldn't help myself. If I screwed things up, I'd have been finished. My investors were rich and powerful people, and if I didn't deliver, I'd spend the rest of my life hauling containers full of space station sewage with the *Amaranth Sun*.

I could see them preparing to work near the far bulkhead. No one had been back to that part of the ship, so I was also naturally curious . . . from a distance. Then came yet another surprise.

"Cam, this door is welded shut," one of the engineers said on the comm, "but from the outside."

"What? Why would they block access to their own engine room?" I asked.

"Hell if I know, but we're going to have to cut our way in."

It took six hours to cut the door loose. When they pulled it open, the greatest surprise and disappointment of the expedition to date smacked us squarely in the nose. In front of us was a wall of ice. For some incomprehensible reason the engine room had been flooded with water, ending any immediate hope for electricity. Worse, the ice was glowing bright blue, much like the flashes I had seen in my dream. One of the engineers called it Cherenkov radiation and said it had no business being there.

It took two weeks for the engineers to come up with a workaround. Ultimately, they cut the power mains running down the backbone of the ship and connected them to a small reactor located in one of the transverse corridors. It was designed to run mining equipment, but they said it would do what we needed. When they finally hit the switch, the lights and instrument panels in the corridor burst to life, along with a whole lot of flashing warning lights. If there had been an atmosphere on that ship, the alarms would have been deafening.

I went immediately to the bridge. Its computers were up and running, and they all had red decompression alerts scrolling across their screens.

Sanjay approached me and said, "Hi Cam. May I have a look at the computers now that they're working?"

"Be my guest. See if you can turn off all the flashing lights," I replied, returning to the hold.

I'm not certain what happened next. Sanjay never spoke about it after that day, but I'm guessing that he was scrolling through screens when he screamed. I heard it on the comm and shot to the bridge to find Sanjay struggling to get away from the computer station.

"Are you alright? What's wrong?" I yelled, fearing that he

had cut his suit.

"Sorry, Cam. I . . . ," he said, looking panicked. "Turn off the open comms, Cam. I need to talk to you directly."

I set my frequency to that of his suit.

"Cam, this thing just spoke to me,"

"What?" I wasn't certain what he meant.

"The computer terminal. I was trying to view the engineering reports, and I got a message that access was restricted. I was wondering why when ten seconds later I felt ill, as though I were going to be sick. Then I heard someone speaking."

"Was it the others? Did you have open comms on?"

"No, this wasn't coming from a speaker. It was a real voice."

"That's not possible, Sanjay. There's no atmosphere in here, no sound."

"It was inside my helmet, Cam. Right next to my ear," he said.

"What did it say?"

"It said we weren't supposed to be out here yet."

"Was it male or female? What can you tell me about it?" I asked. I wondered whether Sanjay would ever want to set foot on the derelict again.

"It was strange, Cam. It spoke very calmly but haltingly. It was deep, like a man's voice, but the cadence wasn't quite right," he said. "It was as though it were *trying* to sound unnatural."

"Or didn't know what human speech sounds like?" I asked. "You know, just because we've never found alien life doesn't mean it's not out here hiding."

I quickly regretted blurting that out. Sanjay went silent for a moment to fathom my unfortunate bombshell. Everyone knew the legends from the earliest exploration of space about astronauts seeing unexplained phenomena: lights and discs following them to the moon, strange radio signals from deep space that never repeated, and even disembodied voices like what Sanjay had heard. Some people said that those stories indicated an alien presence of some kind. Others said that they were just stories. But with more people venturing out into the solar system, such reports had declined.

"Cam, I hold a Ph.D. I'm a rational man; I've been trained to be objective. It wasn't aliens, and ghosts don't exist. There must be another explanation," he said.

"Is it possible that you fell asleep and were dreaming?"

"Why do you ask?"

"Just eliminating possibilities," I said.

"I don't think so. I mean, I might have been. I don't know," he responded.

"Sanjay, keep all of this quiet. We don't need to spread fear among the crew. It's not just you. When we were bringing over the lights, I could have sworn that I saw something in the hold. There was writing on the gold telling me to leave, and then it sort of melted away. I think I had fallen asleep and was dreaming."

I didn't want to tell him that it was blood-red, and I definitely didn't want to mention the corpses.

"Fell asleep? I'm not narcoleptic, Cam."

"Neither am I. I don't know what's going on here. Maybe something's not right with space in this area, or, God forbid, a claim-jumper is messing with our heads to scare us off, maybe with electromagnetic waves. I've heard they can affect your thinking. Let's try to figure it out on our own. Keep it between us."

"Yeah, that's best. You're right," Sanjay said, still breathing heavily.

"Tell you what. I'm going to order a buddy system. Nobody spends time alone on this ship from now on. I'll also restrict access to the engineers and essential personnel. You can work the bucket brigade with me and continue your work. It will take time, and I know the other scholars won't like it, but I can't see any other way until we figure this thing out. I'll have Keating announce it on the *Hyperion* tonight and say it's for safety reasons."

He nodded in agreement.

"Did you have any luck with the computer?" I asked, changing the subject.

"No, it's locked on the decompression warnings."

Just at that moment my ex-wife and a few of the other engineers entered.

"Is something wrong? We heard a scream on the comm, and then you two went silent," she said.

"It was nothing. Sanjay's suit is malfunctioning. It was giving the wrong oxygen reading. He was just on his way back to the *Hyperion* to have it checked out."

Sanjay and the other engineers left the bridge, leaving me and Janet alone.

"The computers are running," I said. "Sanjay found the engineering display, but he can't access anything."

"He's an archeologist. Let me deal with the engineering programs. It's probably just some common security protocol. Easy to get past if you know what you're doing."

I stayed with her for several hours while she tried to find a back door into the program. Apparently it wasn't as easy as she expected, but I didn't want to rub it in. I also didn't want her to be alone. Whatever was affecting us seemed only to do so when people were alone, and the last thing I needed was for her to get spooked too—if that were even possible. She was the type of person who would try pick an argument with the disembodied voice and convince it that it didn't exist . . . and then tell the entire crew about the incident.

Eventually she found a way past the lockout. There was an emergency feature hidden in the programming that allowed the captain to input a code and go anywhere he needed. The code was ultra secret at the time, known only by the commanding officer of the ship and the admirals on Earth. It was still redacted when Ed Iron's people looked into it, but with some difficulty they were able to convince the archivists to release it, probably with a monetary incentive.

Janet put in the code and then spent fifteen minutes studying the numbers on the screen. Finally she turned to me and said, "Cam, this ship was decompressed on purpose."

Chapter 11 Day 208

"Intentionally? That's absurd!"

So exclaimed the eminent naval historian Dr. Lawrence Webb aboard the *Hyperion*, team leader of the academic contingent. He was already reeling from my order to restrict academic access before anyone other than Sanjay had been aboard. The idea of an engineer revealing a major discovery rather than a scholar sent Webb over the edge.

"First, we have the commission records. Second, we have the telescope footage. With all due respect, Janet, you're an engineer, not a historian."

"I know how to interpret technical data. Your views are at odds with everything we've seen on that ship," she responded.

"Your whole argument hinges on the commission's work," I interrupted. "We already know that the telescope footage didn't exist, and the commission had far less information than we do right now. She's right, that ship was set to decompress!"

"You're indulging in conspiracy theory," Webb said dismissively.

"I don't think a computer record that's been in cold storage for two centuries is going to lie. It's as authoritative as things get," my ex-wife interjected. The rest of the salvage personnel listened to her intently. She obviously had cultivated respect among them on the journey from Earth. "It's right there, irrefutable engineering data proving that the ship was ordered to vent its air. We've got everything except a picture of a finger pressing the button."

"Data can be corrupted," Dr. Webb retorted.

"Or falsified," I said.

"By whom? The crew? You haven't found them yet. You don't know what they were doing at the time of the disaster."

"They were UNAG military," I said.

"That doesn't mean anything. Not *everyone* was dishonest in the government of two hundred years ago, though I'll admit that many of them were."

"Yet you're willing to trust the findings of a UNAG commission," Janet added.

"We're going in circles," I said, hoping to steer the conversation away from the speculative. "We don't have enough information. We need to find those crew members and get a look at Nelson's logs. Has there been any progress in thawing out engineering?"

"It's going to take another week, probably longer," Janet replied. "Remember, the temperature over there is still near absolute zero. Water behaves like solid rock in that kind of cold. Melting it requires powerful directional radiant heaters, and we have only two."

"Is it possible to restore heat and atmosphere to the ship? Would that speed things up?" I asked, hoping to finally get an atmosphere on the derelict.

"Definitely, but I'd have to divert everyone away from the effort in engineering."

"Seems like a good gamble. If we can do that, the ice would melt on its own. We then could adjust the bucket brigade to work through the airlock. That way we could seal up the entry hole," I said.

"No issues maybe, but still a pain in the ass and a delay," Neil added. "Especially if they're just going to haul the ship back to Earth. Why not study it there? Why do we need to get into engineering to finish the salvage?"

He had a good point, and he liked working in moon suits.

"It's pristine. We need to document it as it was," answered Sanjay. "Modifications, people working, and movements from towing will destroy information. It's best to be methodical. Besides, the bosses at home want this thing to turn a profit in more ways than one. They want a sensation ready for reporters and the public. They won't want to wait for us to finish a study."

He was right too. Ed Iron's response to my report had been little more than a flurry of excited musings about how we were going to unveil the find and squeeze every drop of profit we could from it.

"That's true. There's also the fact that we need to find the crew," I said. "It's not in the best taste to haul them back to Earth in a salvaged-for-profit venture. They need to be buried at space, with Ed's public-relations people pumping up how reverently we treated them. They're heroes. He sent coffins and flags for that very reason."

The engineers worked for two weeks modifying another small fusion reactor to increase available power. After Neil welded the entry cut closed, we ran a hose from the *Hyperion* to the *Cape Hatteras*, pressurizing the derelict quickly. We sealed off the crew quarters and other rooms that didn't need oxygen, using helium to equalize the pressure. It was safe enough to breathe if any leaked.

The derelict still had abundant liquid oxygen and nitrogen reserves. Using a spare air recycler from the *Hyperion*, eventually we intended to open each of the doors and allow the helium to be scrubbed out and new air added. Within a few months we'd have a complete atmosphere on the derelict, with the recycler producing its own oxygen.

We would also finally lay the decompression question to rest. If it had been decompressed intentionally, the ship should be airtight, provided that Neil's welds were okay. If it had been an accident, on the other hand, the air escaping through the hole would be immediately apparent. I ordered everyone on the *Cape Hatteras* to remain suited until we knew for certain. It would be up to me to test the air.

"Geezer, I'm reading a breathable atmosphere with no loss of pressure," Neil said, as we floated near the sealed entry cut. We had been monitoring for several hours.

"I'm not a geezer. I'm getting younger. I think I noticed gray in your stubble yesterday."

"No, you didn't, and if there was it's Stacey's fault," he responded.

"Don't mind her. You know she marches to a different drummer. All pilots do."

"So do engineers, but at least our drummer has rhythm."

"You're just flustered because there aren't any unattached girls on the *Hyperion*," I said.

"You might be right about that," he said with a chuckle. "All that wisdom you've got comes from being older than the solar system."

"Yes, I was salvaging when Earth was a baby."

I loved my son. I just wished that he didn't think he was immortal.

"Well, here goes," I said, as I flipped the three latches on my helmet and lifted it off. I stood there for a moment breathing while Neil watched my lips for blueness. Even with the warm air from the *Hyperion*, it was cold enough to see my breath. "Looks good," I said. "I think you can remove your helmet."

"It smells like the inside of a refrigerator," Neil said, as he lifted it off.

"And metal. It's all this frost and space-smell," I said. Something that's been exposed to space acquires a very peculiar metallic odor.

It took a few days for the ship to warm up. When we began to move gold, Sanjay and I served as the bucket brigade, with Neil in his moon suit manning the airlock. The job went slower than I had hoped. The airlock was designed for automatic operation, and using the handcrank was inefficient. Nevertheless, it was nice to work in a short-sleeve shirt. The only drawback was the inability to escape easily. I hadn't forgotten my dream, and the engine compartment door had been left open to release the water, allowing that eerie blue light to flicker out.

The water floated out in globules. There was nothing sensitive in the hold, so we just let it accumulate. It would either coalesce on the walls, or sometimes a blob the size of a basketball would jellyfish past to be captured by an engineer named Roberts. He'd net them in bags and leave them in the airlock to be disposed of when we were conveying gold. He must have done that a thousand times before the engine compartment finally stopped leaking.

When it did, Roberts volunteered to go in first. I don't know whether he had more guts than the others or whether they felt he deserved it for being the waterboy. Whatever it was, what happened next has bothered me ever since.

"He's ready to go in," Janet said as we gathered near the steel door leading to the engineering compartment.

The Cherenkov light was a warning. There might be more dangerous forms of radiation inside, so Roberts donned a moon suit to take advantage of its shielding. He pulled the heavy door open. The interior had the eerie look of a fish aquarium in a room with no other lights on. I grabbed a moon helmet and switched on its comms, hoping we could receive him through the thick bulkhead.

"It's laid out as in the ship's blueprints," he said. "I'm in a room with three doorways. The left leads to the exhaust nozzle feeds, the center to the engine access panels, and the right to the main engineering control compartment. The Cherenkov light is coming from there. I'm going through the door. Reading no dangerous radioactivity. There is. . . ."

And that was it. The blue light went out, and he fell silent. Worried that he might have been injured, Neil and I suited up and charged in. We found nothing. He had disappeared without a trace.

We presumed him dead three days later and held a service. I never really knew anything about him other than the idle conversations you have while working on a ship with someone. We had nothing to commit to space, so we took the only thing from his quarters that seemed to have meaning to Roberts: a well-worn copy of *Ulysses* by James Joyce, with copious notes written in the margins. I suspected that there was more to Roberts than anyone knew.

In the weeks that followed we carefully explored the engineering compartment. Whatever took Roberts wasn't there anymore. There was also no trace of the crew. We had seen every part of the ship, at least at a glance, and one thing was clear: there were no crew members on that ship when it decompressed. However, if Roberts could disappear mysteriously, they might have too.

We were out of our league. People do not simply vanish into thin air. Janet suggested that a malfunctioning reactor could vaporize a person, but there was no evidence of that, and none of the reactors in that room had power. No one liked suggestions of a new phenomenon in nature, and all we had left that might provide an answer was Nelson's logs.

Unfortunately, we couldn't find them. Like everything else in the databanks, they were hidden in some obscure folder, probably in the middle of a program file. Rather than spending months combing through the computer's files, we hoped there would be something in the government records on Earth that might help.

I contacted Ed Iron, who sent his researcher to the archives and got back to us after a few days. As it turned out, hiding files was standard military procedure at the time of the ship's loss. They sent us a key, but it wasn't necessary. They hadn't told anyone that they possessed the logs themselves from the beginning to the end of the mission. They sent a copy to the *Hyperion*.

That stood in direct contradiction to the commission report, which claimed that the logs were never transmitted home. It confirmed that there was indeed a cover-up, and it also explained why the communications equipment on the derelict was set to transmit.

With the scholars busy poring over the logs, I was able to enjoy a reprieve from their insistent requests to be allowed on the derelict. I didn't have time to read the logs. I needed to focus on removing the gold, though I was astonished that the UNAG had given them to us. I guess they figured that we'd eventually ferret them out of the computer anyway.

We had removed most of the gold by the beginning of the month. Only a relatively small amount remained onboard the derelict, so I left the job of transferring it to Sanjay and Janet while Neil and I returned to the *Amaranth Sun*. There had been no further manifestation of the blue light or other strange occurrences. It would only be a few more days before I had little choice except to unleash the academic specialists for the study phase of the mission. Webb would have Ed Iron countermand my orders if I didn't. I didn't mind, though. My part of the mission was nearly over, and I could relax while academicians completed their study under Webb's leadership. It would be his baby after the gold was unloaded.

I was preparing for a meeting to update the *Amaranth Sun*'s crew when a message came through. "Hunter, nice trick, spinning the *Cape Hatteras* like that!" Finley Pace said as he broke radio silence and made his presence known. Apparently he had maneuvered in behind us after I had transferred to my ship. For a second time we hadn't been on the lookout and were caught off-guard. I had left the job of detecting approaching ships to the *Hyperion*'s superior equipment. That proved to be my biggest mistake of the entire salvage operation.

"Not much you can do now. It's mine. We've got two ships to your one, and I've got directional thrusters on the *Cape Hatteras*," I said. "You won't win this one."

Keating's voice then came over the radio. "I'm sorry, Cam. Ed signed a bad contract. Most of my cut would have gone to the owners of my ship. My core crew would have received little more than peanuts from those greedy bastards. I can't let that happen."

Keating had defected. I probably should have suspected when the day before he had asked to dismantle the corridor between our ships. I had assumed that he simply wanted better maneuverability. The tiny *Amaranth Sun* could do nothing against two salvors. Even worse, the scholars had made it less than halfway through Nelson's logs, and I had never bothered to transfer a copy to my ship. With the *Hyperion* gone, I had no access to them.

Chapter 12 Day 217

"December 8, 2259. Log of Captain John Andrew Nelson, Commanding Officer, UNAG Mining Vessel* Cape Hatteras. *In synchronous orbit with the asteroid 974-Bernhard. Seventeen days from completing operations. The mission is a success. We have already begun preparations for the voyage home."

Keating spent most of the day transferring the remaining academicians and much of his crew to the *Cape Hatteras* using his pressurized corridor. I could hear his announcements on the radio. He convinced them to go freely by declaring that I had opened the ship, and he suggested a tour for all personnel to be led by Dr. Webb. Webb fell for it. He was always ready for an opportunity to pontificate.

I couldn't contact anyone.The *Cape Hatteras* lacked working communications, and Finley had our transmissions jammed. I tried in vain to send a Morse message with the *Amaranth Sun*'s spotlights, but no one was watching. All I could do was observe as the traitor marooned most of the expedition's unsuspecting personnel. When he was finished, Keating was left with a few loyal crew members and most of the gold.

I wasn't worried about the safety of the people aboard the *Cape Hatteras*, other than the possibility of someone else disappearing. They would be fine until Ed Iron's tow ship arrived. I don't think Keating wanted them dead: I saw his crew transferring supplies to the derelict.

The whole thing was a set-up from the moment Ed rented that ship. Pace knew most of the captains in the business, including David Keating. He also knew that the *Hyperion* was the most likely ship for Ed Iron to rent, being the newest and the best. All Pace had to do was to contact Keating and cut a deal over a secured channel.

But there was still one problem remaining: me. I was on the bridge of the *Amaranth Sun* with Stacey, Kurt, and Neil trying to figure out what to do when another message came through.

"Alright, Cam, you've got a choice. I know you haven't been able to contact Earth, and by the time that tow ship gets here, we'll be rich and retired in the outer solar system. You can let us board your ship so we can disable your engines, or I can ram you. Either way, no one will ever know where this gold went. I'd prefer option two, but I'll give you the chance to save your crew," Pace said.

"You'll just have to kill us, Finley, and dent up that pretty ship of yours."

He didn't respond but just rolled his ship in our direction. I had to act fast. He was much closer than in our previous encounter.

"Stacey, engines, full thrust, any direction!"

"I have a reinforced bow for ramming," announced Pace, "and I've tossed out every bit of extra weight. I'm a fast accelerator now, and your little exploration scow isn't. This is your last chance."

"Not going to happen, Finley" I said. "When I get done trashing your name, they wouldn't commission you to haul iron from the moon."

"I won't need it. I'm as good as retired," he responded.

"We'll see about that."

You're supposed to accelerate a ship like the *Amaranth Sun* incrementally, but you've got more power if you need it for towing and other heavy jobs. We'd already exceeded its design guidelines the first time we escaped Finley Pace, and I knew its frame wouldn't tolerate too many more fast punches of speed. We were no longer pulling anything, so when Stacey slammed the throttle to 110%, it sent us all against the back walls of the ship. *Hard.*

I smacked my head squarely against a light fixture. Shaking it off, I realized that Pace had missed us. If we didn't slow down, he couldn't catch us once we were at full speed. Next came something terribly painful to watch: the NASA probe had broken loose from that jolt of acceleration and was floating freely. It looked helpless, like a small animal about to get run over by a bus. A small jet of hydrazine fired from Finley's ship, signalling that he had altered course to make sure he hit it. The probe pancaked across his bow and slid off.

I had no idea what I'd tell the Smithsonian. The weren't going to be happy, and I prayed that they'd be satisfied with the probe's chemical rocket assembly still strapped to the *Amaranth Sun*'s stern.

The immediate question was where we should go. If we went back to Earth, Pace would have the *Hyperion* in the safety of the outer planets before we could intercept him with a military patrol. We couldn't go back to the derelict. There wasn't much we could have do there except dodge Finley's salvor until he eventually got lucky and smashed us. Worse, he might threaten to ram the *Cape Hatteras* and kill everyone onboard. No amount of gold was worth taking that risk, so I knew I had to stay away—at least for the time being.

The only thing I could think to do was to stay ahead of him. I knew the *Hyperion* had enough fuel to return to Earth with that load, but Pace didn't have enough to make it much further. If he were going to reach one of the rogue colonies, he would have to refuel. There were only two places he could do that, Jupiter and Saturn, and by pure chance they were lined up with each other in their orbits.

Our best chance was to catch him at Jupiter. If we went there and hired thugs, we could get him when he made his stop. If he slipped past us, we might have another try at Saturn if I could find ships fast enough to overtake him. I wanted to be wherever he stepped off his ship, backed by 50 guys with crowbars at the ready.

Jupiter has two major colonies: Europa and Callisto. Io was never colonized, and Ganymede's settlement consisted of an isolationist religious cult. Because Callisto was a major UNAG outpost, I knew that Pace wouldn't go there. They'd want to do an inspection, and the gold was bound to raise interest. That left Europa.

The Europans would never search him on principle. They were pariah drug dealers who had their own problems with their ships being searched. They would sell him fuel without any questions asked, so I had Stacey set a course for Europa. I didn't think there would be a problem finding ships. Most cargo vessels are faster than an empty salvor, and I might even be able to find an armed one, since many of the Europan ships had been carrying laser weaponry ever since the mysterious pirates robbed them. Pace's ship might have become lighter and faster, but the *Hyperion* was weighed down with the gold. Pace wouldn't let that ship out of his sight, so that effectively slowed both of his ships down.

Pace had jammed our signal by using some kind of high-energy beam to haze over the optical coatings on our transmitter, cutting our outgoing signal strength to almost nothing. Europa would have a paycomm location, and their people could fix the transmitter, but it still took three weeks to get there, and I knew that Ed would be very anxious after losing contact. The first message he would get from me would be terrible news. I wasn't looking forward to dealing with that, but then again it was Ed, not I, who had hired Keating.

When we arrived at Europa, I figured we had a two-week window to prepare. I contacted the surface. They barely received our transmission, leading to a long exchange of garbled statements and requests for repeats. They said they'd have a robotic repair drone out to fix the transmitter within a few days. It took them hours to send a tender to pick us up, and when it did arrive the pilot appeared intoxicated.

"I'm Randy, boys, and I'll be your pilot," he said with a slur.

"I'm a girl," Stacey said.

"I hadn't noticed," he said before launching into a boisterous laugh. He had long, gray hair in a loose ponytail, an unkempt beard, and thick glasses. I'd never seen anyone wear glasses other than in photographs from centuries ago.

We boarded the tender, leaving Kurt to mind the *Amaranth Sun*. I looked forward to visiting the colony. They had recently renamed it New San Francisco, and despite its reputation it was one of the more interesting places in the solar system.

"Care for a little toot?" Randy asked, hitting a button on his console that dropped masks from the ceiling which emitted smoke instead of emergency oxygen. I didn't have to guess what it was.

"No thanks!" I said.

"Well, more for us," Randy said as he hit the button again, stowing the other masks. From the well-used one in front of his face he took a hit, pushed it out of the way, pulled a flask from his front shirt pocket, and handed it to me. "How about a little heart of the tarpotch?"

I took a sip out of politeness. It was potently alcoholic.

"Well, here I go again. Hold on," Randy said, with a hint of anxiety in his voice. He hit the gas and started moving away from the *Amaranth Sun*. "I get this right most of the time," he muttered.

"Now hold on," I said, trying to sound good-humored while still posing a serious question. "What happens when you don't get it right?"

"Oh hell, nothing. I'm not dead at the bottom of a crater yet. I just don't want to tear off a part of your ship," he said as he looked backwards past us, frantically changing views to see the *Amaranth Sun* through the portholes of his tender.

"Parallel parking was not my strong point," he added.

He flicked a switch that pushed us back into our seats. Europa doesn't have much of an atmosphere, so we careened toward it with nothing to slow us down. We could see the colony approaching fast. Just when it appeared certain that we would crash, Randy let out another boisterous laugh and braked so hard that anyone not smart enough to wear a seatbelt might have ended up with a permanent imprint of a control panel on their face.

We settled into a hangar situated to the side of a small structure in front of the largest dome.

"Well, there we be," Randy said, holding his hand out for the fare. I gave him 30 UNAG dollars in gold foil. He put it in his pocket and held out his hand again for a tip. He grunted approvingly when I gave him 20 percent.

"Enjoy! Be sure to drink the water!" he said, following it with another obnoxious laugh as we stepped into the corridor leading to the dome.

Chapter 13 Day 238

"December 18, 2259. Log of Captain John Andrew Nelson, Commanding Officer, UNAG Mining Vessel* Cape Hatteras. *Excavating the asteroid has proven easier than projected, and we have reached the ship's cargo limit seven days early. We will use the extra week to explore the rocky portion of the asteroid and collect samples for the scientists back home."

Europa is an unusual moon. On the surface it looks like an ice-skating rink floating in space. You wouldn't think it was one of the most vibrant worlds in the solar system. The surface is just a shell that covers a warm saltwater ocean full of volcanoes and aquatic life.

An enormous hulk of a man with salt-and-pepper hair, a reddish complexion, and a smile the size of Jupiter met us in the reception dome. "Welcome to New San Francisco!" he boomed. "I am the *Very* Reverend Mirador T. Stunt, Mayor of the sovereign colony of Europa and member of the Council of Colonial Governors—*in absentia.* Would you like some hot water?"

We nodded, and he started filling closed-top mugs and handing them out. The Europans had the odd habit of drinking plain hot water. They claim it's full of minerals that give it a flavor all its own. They also admit it's an acquired taste. I sipped. It tasted like water with garden soil in it.

"Can you add tea to it?" Stacey asked, seemingly as unimpressed as I was.

"If you want to ruin it! But if you must, we do have a nice blend grown here on Europa," he said as he bounced behind a desk in the tiny reception module. Europa is just a bit smaller than Earth's moon, so you don't walk but bounce. That requires the ceilings there to be rather high.

Mayor Stunt grabbed a few packets of tea, opened our hot-water containers, and popped them in. "If you want sweetener, just use these controls," he said, pointing out a set of buttons on the mug marked Sweet, Sweeter, Sweetest, and Desweeten.

None of us bothered to consider what else might be in the tea. You just assume that tea is tea, but that wasn't necessarily true on Europa.

"What brings you to our great colony?" Stunt asked.

"Commercial business."

"What sort of commercial business?"

"Waste hauling," I said hesitantly while inventing a cover story. I didn't want to come out and say I was there to hire thugs.

"We don't have waste," boasted the Mayor. "We recycle everything."

"That's not entirely true. Your reactors produce waste gases. Are you venting them into space?

"Well, I suppose something gets vented. Mainly heat, but. . . ."

"Environmentally unfriendly!" I proclaimed. "That gas could easily disarticulate and recombine into something that might end up sealed forever in Europa's ocean. The damage could be catastrophic! And Mayor, it won't ever stop harming your world," I remarked, making it all up as I went.

"Well, I hadn't thought of that, but. . . ."

"I need to speak to your engineers. An arrangement could be made that won't cost you a gram of gold."

"Won't cost, eh?"

"Not a cent."

"Well, I can arrange for you to speak to someone. But. . . ."

"And there are also the home fusion reactors. Anyone with one of those will need us too. But I can't get started without checking the prices for lithium waste on Earth. I'll need access to a communications array," I said.

"That won't be a problem. There is a paycomm in the main dome. But as I was saying, we're hydrothermal. We don't have any reactors at all."

"None?" My hype deflated. I was proud of my charade up until then.

"Not a one, but don't you worry, Mr., umm, Hunter," he said as he glanced at the *Amaranth Sun*'s registration papers. "As long as you're not here to steal our crop and are not with any of the unions, we won't bother you. But that means too that you don't bother us."

"We have no intention of creating any kind of problems for you."

"The main dome is entirely public," the Mayor explained, "and you're welcome to everything in there. We just ask that you avoid the private habitation modules and the growing domes. After the pirate attack we've had to be more security-conscious. Before I was elected, they used to give tours of our agricultural projects. I'd love to give you one now because we're very proud of them, but I hope you understand that we can't any longer."

"That will be fine. We respect what you do here, but our business is the reason for our visit. We have a schedule, and once we're finished we'll be leaving immediately."

"Fair enough, and welcome again! If you need *anything* do come to my office and speak to me or my lovely secretary, Sister Mary Joanna." The aforesaid smiled from behind him and waved sheepishly with a high-pitched giggle. I'd never seen a nun in a bikini before.

We bounced past the greeting desk and through a very high doorway. Beyond it was the central dome. It had a main street aptly named Ashbury running the length of the structure. New San Francisco was arranged much like any other city in a standard grid pattern, so we made our way down Ashbury Street admiring the shops. We stopped to peruse a clothing store that sold entirely domestic plant-fiber products. Most of them had the feel of burlap.

I was struck by how the merchants lived above their shops. In a way the place had an anachronistic feel, something like a cross between a modern space station and an old European city, but with obvious differences. On Europa you could bounce more than ten feet in the air, making stairways unnecessary. The nicer buildings had barber poles that you could climb up or down, but some of the simpler ones had openings with stout netting to grab onto and pull yourself into the rooms above.

At the intersection of Haight and Ashbury was a square with a large fountain. An inscription said that the water was piped directly from the ocean below the ice floor. The fountain was at least 60 feet in diameter. It had to be in order to catch all the globules of water falling back down in the slow motion of low gravity. The whole thing was quite beautiful, but then the scene begin to shimmer.

"Cam," Stacey remarked, "I think there was something in that tea."

"I think you're right," I replied.

"I gotta sit down," Neil said.

We plunked ourselves down on the edge of the fountain and didn't move for three hours. My mind is usually churning, but for that period of time I was drawing a blank. It took effort to think about anything, so I found myself perfectly happy to just sit and stare, occasionally giggling at the open-mouthed looks on my companion's faces.

Neil was the first to stand up and say something: "I feel as though my brain is made out of rocks."

"Mine is. . . ." I said, stopping to clear my throat. "Mine is starting to work again." I put my hand on my forehead and rubbed it.

"Strong stuff," commented Stacey.

"We'd better get moving," I replied.

We ventured sluggishly down a side street. They really did have everything, much more than you'd think for such a low-population settlement. A trading post sold most kinds of things, though apparently their biggest seller was rolling papers. There were organic vegetable stands and several street vendors selling fried tarpotch.

The tarpotch is the only complex animal in the solar system that didn't evolve on Earth, though no one knew what lay in the unexplored subterranean oceans of Saturn's moon Enceladus. The tarpotch is something like a jellyfish, black and formless with no eyes and an almost gelatinous feel. Breaded and fried it was delicious, particularly if you'd been drinking Europan tea.

At one of the stands we bought some tarpotch and bounced along one of the busier streets until we spotted the paycomm building. Stacey and Neil stayed outside, still a little orbital from the tea, while I spent a few hours inside. I wasn't over it either, but I had work to do and thought I could still write a decent letter to Ed. He told me later that it was so full of misspellings and grammatical errors that he had a linguist look at it to make sure I wasn't writing in code. I collected my companions and started looking for somewhere to spend the night.

The only hotel was called the Jupiter Rising, but it was run more like a bed-and-breakfast. The proprietor was a 60-something robust lady named Reeda, who had a naturally warm personality. I'd recommend that hotel to anyone. It was spotlessly clean, and they didn't bleed your bank account for every little amenity as they do on Earth. The best part was the free breakfast.

Reeda rose at 4:00 a.m. sharp, a schedule she kept regardless of whether there were any guests or not, and set out the greatest breakfast spread you've ever seen. Europa is far from Earth, and traditional items like bacon and eggs are prohibitively expensive. A typical breakfast there consists of fried squash, homemade kelp-bread, and a spicy tarpotch sausage ground by a man who could only be happy on Europa. He popped in halfway through our meal. Everyone called him "Sausage." He ground tarpotch, made moonshine in a still, and grew gigantic watermelons and peppers.

"I've been here for years. I'm the last of the real hillbillies," he said as he handed a package of fresh meat to Reeda. "Tennessee has lost its way. It's too modern. Buildings and corporate parks everywhere; even the country isn't the country anymore. I say to Hades with that. Give me the good old days. Here on Europa I've got my own habitat dome. I call it *100 Miles from Memphis*, and I pretend I'm in the old days, listening to radio recordings and watching monochrome movies. I love it here. You can be who you are, do whatever you want, and there's never any pressure."

"Did you have a still in Tennessee?" I asked.

"Heavens no," Sausage said with a broad smile. He seemed to turn into a completely different person. "I was the CEO of a corporation. Three decades of 16-hour days, occasional heart attacks, and not a single vacation the whole time. The last coronary got me thinking, so I retired. Haven't had an event since. Tarpotch has the highest cholesterol content in the solar system, they say. It's a bunch of hooey. Stress is what gets us."

"Sausage grows the most amazing peppers," Reeda interjected. "They'll burn your mouth out. You'll see. I added them to the country gravy."

It was the hottest gravy I've ever had.

Chapter 14 Day 239

"December 20, 2259. Log of Captain John Andrew Nelson, Commanding Officer, UNAG Mining Vessel* Cape Hatteras. *We have altered our orbit in order to focus on the stony side of the asteroid. I have dispatched crewmen Marquez and Galon to the surface to collect science data and samples."

The tone of Ed Iron's reply was angry, but it was more of a vent than anything else. He understood that there wasn't much I could have done. But without the gold exhibiting the *Cape Hatteras* and cashing in the few bricks left on it wouldn't come close to covering the cost of the expedition. He stood to lose a great deal of money if I didn't retrieve most of the gold, and I was already certain that the Smithsonian would sue when I delivered a pancaked hull instead of an intact probe.

Wandering around New San Francisco made me realize that my plan wasn't as clear-cut as I had envisioned. I had expected a population of law-skirting hooligans, but really they were just independent people looking to live apart from Earth and its trappings. If we were going to find the kind of people we needed, our last chance was Europa's only tavern. It was called the Naughty Venus.

Going in there involved stepping through a shifting barrier of smoke. It was so thick you could have cut it with a mining laser. But it wasn't just smoke from Europa's more famous crop. It was also tobacco. The health issues surrounding tobacco had long been solved, but it had never recovered the prominence it once had on Earth. On Europa they smoked it proudly. My throat was burning, so I ordered one of the local beers, taking care to read the ingredients.

I looked around the Naughty Venus. The view wasn't encouraging. A group of 20-somethings hovered around the bar to avoid any interruption in the flow of booze. Some older men sat at one of the tables, their beards and ponytails bobbing in the low gravity as they opined about the recent pirate raid for lack of any weather to complain about. I overheard one say that if they lost another crop the colony would be finished, and the UNAG would have to assume direct rule.

I figured that springing for a round might break the ice.

"Hey, human," said one. "Thanks for the bubbles."

Europans referred to anyone from anywhere else as "humans," as though we were a separate species.

"You're welcome. We're here from Earth on business," I responded.

"Never been there! I'm the first true Europan, born here in 2441," he said.

For someone about age 20 he looked scrawny from the low-gravity upbringing. He probably couldn't have visited Earth without breaking bones.

"Cool," I said, hoping to sound hip by using a 500-year-old colloquialism.

"Heh, yeah, frozen," he said with a chuckle.

I glanced at Neil to take over, and he launched into the slang of the day. It was incomprehensible to anyone over 30. From what I understand, body movements are just as important as the nonsense words.

"Far, Europan, you know the plantation," Neil said, holding his right arm high above his head.

"Yar, human, mang. Tonto and Grandpa do tha' mix," replied the Europan.

I had no idea what they were saying, and neither did Stacey. I assumed that I was "Grandpa."

"Oldie. Melon-good, but mang, Tonto udewatch, sour t'itch," Neil said. The Europan chuckled, and then they fluttered their hands at each other.

"Hey!" Stacey caught on. "What's this "sour" you're talking about?"

"Melon?" I asked.

"What?" said Neil. "I told him you were nice. It's, like, opposite meanings."

They ignored me and continued stringing words and gesticulations together that made them look like drunken dancers. In the end they simply appeared to be whistling at each other and on the brink of kissing when Neil turned to me as the Europan abruptly bounced away.

"Did you offend him?" I asked.

"No. Mission accomplished!" Neil said.

"What do you mean mission accomplished? What the hell just happened?"

"He said he's got the man we need. He'll be back in a few minutes."

Not long afterwards the Europan returned with the Mayor

and Sister Mary Joanna in tow. She waved with a giggle.

"Why didn't you tell me you needed someone stomped?" he asked, as though that were a perfectly normal thing to say.

"We don't need anyone stomped, Reverend. We need to get our property back," I said, mindful that he was still a government official of sorts.

"What kind of property? You aren't smuggling plant products are you? We'd have a problem if you are. We can barely survive pirates, much less competitors."

"No, nothing like that. Just salvage from a wrecked cargo ship."

"Ahhhh, salvagers. Little better than pirates, your lot are."

"Not us. We're doing it legally. It's some of the other salvagers who create a problem and give us all a bad name."

The Mayor sighed and looked at me suspiciously. "I suppose we know a lot about acquiring bad names here on Europa. Tell me what happened. No lies, no deflections, just spill it all if you want real help, instead of that. . . ," he said, as he pointed out a window framing crazy Randy, who was bending over and poking at some gooey stain on the street and chuckling at it.

"We wrapped up work on a ship. . . ."

"Which ship?"

"A cargo ship lost 50 years ago called the . . . *Cape Canaveral.* A salvager by the name of Finley Pace made off with our haul. The skipper of our salvor was in on it." I wasn't lying. I simply made an error in geography.

"I see, I see. And what sort of haul was it?"

"Scrap metal," I said. I was still not lying: gold *is* a metal and can be *called* scrap.

"Scrap metal, you say. It wasn't, by chance, *gold* scrap metal was it?"

"We wish! Just aluminum and advanced alloys," I said. Now I was lying.

He looked at me in silence for a moment, rubbing his beard. "I see. Well, that Finley character passed through here some months ago. He claimed he was looking for the *Cape Hatteras*. I've heard that one before. I told him the damned thing probably either didn't exist or has drifted halfway to Alpha Centauri by now. I guess he failed and made the best of it by robbing you."

"Must be, but my investor wants the goods back. The advanced alloys were of substantial value to him. He builds habitat domes and is always short on raw materials. I need people and ships to intercept the thieves when they pass through this system. It will be sometime within the next two weeks."

"I can help," said the Mayor. "My ship is in direct orbit of Jupiter watching for pirates. It's fast, and I've armed it to the teeth. It'll be more than a match for a couple of salvors. Of course, that's assuming you're willing to pay well for the service."

I didn't tell him about Finley's ram.

"Would $100,000 UNAG dollars be sufficient?"

"I'd need $200,000. I've got a large crew to pay, and I need a confidentiality agreement in writing. I don't want it broadcast that the Mayor of New San Francisco moonlights as a mercenary."

"Done."

We made our way through town to his office. Sister Mary Joanna wrote up a contract in triplicate, handing it to us with a squeal.

"Meet me in two days at Io. I'll be in a polar orbit at an altitude of 4000 kilometers," the Mayor said, signing the contract.

"Does anyone else here have a fast ship? I'd like to have some backup."

"It's just me at the moment. Most people don't need them. Our transports are old and slow but very reliable. Especially when Randy pilots them," he said facetiously.

Having only one ship worried me, but the Mayor was confident that his vessel had the speed and overwhelming force needed to defeat Finley. We were left with extra time to see the rest of the city. Neil and Stacey had heard about a low-G swimming pool across town and wanted to try it.

The Mayor offered to have someone show me the agriculture domes, an offer I readily accepted since I didn't want to admit to Neil and Stacey that their salty old captain couldn't swim. I was met at the fountain an hour later by a young man named Bobby. He looked like something from 20th-century Earth, complete with dreadlocks and beads. He ushered me into the tiered gardens rising hundreds of feet in the air and nurtured by an artificial sun. Vegetables and the cash crop were intermingled. The strong scent of the plants overwhelmed my nostrils, which were too accustomed to the sterile smell of technology and freeze-dried rations.

Europa might have had a reputation for skirting the law, but seeing it in person made it seem like a paradise.

Chapter 15 Cloak and Dagger

"December 21, 2259. 0700 hours. Log of Captain John Andrew Nelson, Commanding Officer, UNAG Mining Vessel **Cape Hatteras.** ***Marquez and Galon have reached the surface. They report an alien landscape of porous spires of rock reaching a hundred feet skyward. A chain of small mountains lies a short distance away. I have instructed the men to explore them."***

Later that afternoon I went to find Stacey and Neil. The swimming was apparently more than they could stomach, and the water was so salty that their clothes had dried stiff. They were desperate for a mist shower, so we cut our exploration short and made our way back to the hotel. A half-hearted hello to Reeda was all any of us could muster.

I collapsed in slow motion onto the bed. I had been walking most of the day, or rather bouncing, and the prospect of a nap was sublime. No sooner had I hit the pillow than I heard a knock and the sound of paper sliding beneath the door. I had a look outside, but no one was there. I retrieved the note.

"Beware the captain of the *Neptune's Revenge*," it said in a sexy female voice.

"What's that supposed to mean?" I asked the digipaper.

"Beware the captain of the *Neptune's Revenge*," it repeated, before flashing a grainy human memory-based picture of the Mayor.

I was more excited about getting a secret spy note than I

was by what it contained. I already knew that I couldn't trust the Mayor. I folded the note away and took a long mist shower, thinking the whole time about my first real brush with cloak-and-dagger stuff. I hadn't a clue about who had sent the warning.

I had little chance of getting any rest, so after fortifying myself with three closed-top cups of coffee I collected Neil and Stacey with the intention of making our way back to the *Amaranth Sun*. They might have been better rested than I was, but neither of them looked well. That must have been one hell of a bad swim.

"Where are you all off to in such a hurry?" Reeda asked as we entered the lobby with our baggage.

"I hate to check out," I said. "I really hate it, sweetheart. I could stay here for eternity and enjoy your cooking."

"You're always welcome back," Reeda replied. "Next time I'll even give you a discount. I'd give you one now, but I have something worth more: advice. My grandson told me that you were looking for unsavory types in that terrible bar earlier. He brought you the worst one he could think of: Mayor Stunt. He showed up here just after the pirate attack and got himself elected by promising to drive them away if they ever came back. He's no good otherwise. He feeds on everyone's fears, and now he's trying to get us into some kind of weird religion he's cooked up. I can see it coming: next he'll want donations. Crooked as an ice crack on Ganymede, that man. If you're going to have dealings with him, watch him closely."

"Did you send the note?" I asked.

"What note?"

"Someone slipped a note under my door. It said as much."

"There was no one here, sweet tarpotch. I've been in the lobby all day. Your friends must be playing tricks on you."

"Must be. Don't you worry. We'll watch our backs," I said as we bounced out the door.

An awful lot of negativity surrounded the Mayor. I passed the note around to the others, who puzzled over who could have sent it. Stacey thought it had to be the grandson, but I was skeptical. Even though he did seem a little odd, why would he use a sexy female voice?

I was starting to think I might have made a mistake. We had no idea of how trustworthy Reverend Stunt was. I wasn't even certain what kind of ship he owned. I regretted not having asked more questions. On the other hand, the contract stipulated that payment was due upon completion of the mission. So what could go wrong?

We wended our way back to the reception dome in order to arrange a tender back to the *Amaranth Sun*. We'd have made it in under ten minutes if we had gone straight there, but we didn't. Instead, we stopped at the trading post to grab a few extra provisions and a supply of tarpotch steaks. Somewhere between the trading post and the reception dome everything went black.

I woke up face down on steel plating with a tremendous headache. Neil and Stacey were still out cold, sprawled across the floor in the center of a poorly lit, windowless room. It was circular with a sliding door that had no handles. It was like a prison cell. Half an hour later my companions started to rouse, and just then the door opened.

"Come with me, Mr. Hunter," a man said as he stepped into

the room. He was UNAG military, with the uniform and insignia of a lieutenant.

"Which one?" Neil asked.

"The old one. The rest of you stay here."

I didn't say a word. I knew that something was very wrong. I was certain that the Mayor had turned us in for planning to attack Finley's ship. I followed the officer down a corridor to await formal charges.

"Captain Masterson wishes to see you," he said.

"Are we under arrest?"

"Not yet."

"What does that mean?"

"It means not yet."

"Can we leave?"

"Theoretically, but it isn't practical."

I kept quiet as we negotiated our way through wherever I was. I could have been out for days. It occurred to me that we might not even be on Europa anymore. The UNAG colony on Callisto had a reputation for tough law enforcement, but Callisto was bigger than Europa, and I should have felt slightly heavier. Then I noticed something else that seemed strange: the floor was moving. I felt unsure of my step. I guessed that the sensation might have been from the drugs they had knocked me out with, but even the construction didn't look right for a colony. It was cramped and compact like a ship. My hand brushed against a wall. It felt warm, whereas space imparts cold on the walls of a ship. Another pair of doors opened onto a bridge. A man I assumed to be Captain Masterson was standing in the center.

"Welcome, Mr. Hunter. It's a pleasure to meet you. Imagine meeting the man who found the legendary *Cape Hatteras*. I'm Captain Laurens Masterson, and you are aboard the UNAG submarine *Lancaster*," he said, bouncing over and shaking my hand with a firm and confident grip.

"Submarine?"

"Yes, under the ice of Europa."

"Under the ice? What the hell are you doing here?" I asked.

"Monitoring the drug dealers above, of course. Did you think Earth wouldn't have a presence here? This is *our* colony."

"How did you get this thing down here?"

"We melted a hole on the far side of Europa and dropped it in from space. We're not the only ones. The Asian-African Union also has a submarine here. We shadow each other and play our little games. We even cooperate occasionally."

"How long have you been here?"

"Approximately five years. Of course, seeing this obligates you to secrecy. I'm afraid you can't tell your companions."

"My lips are sealed," I said, not wanting to push the issue. "Are my people alright and safe? What did you use to sedate us?"

"It's perfectly safe. Just a sleep agent. They've already been sedated again."

"How the hell did you know about the *Cape Hatteras*?"

"We knew you'd find it before you did, Captain Hunter. We *are* the UNAG."

"You were tracking me?"

"We track everyone."

"Forgive me, Captain, but I'm thoroughly confused. Why am I here?"

"Quite simply, Mr. Hunter, we want to help you get your treasure back."

"For what price?" I asked instinctively.

"No price at all. Well, other than the taxes you already intended to pay, I'm sure. And one other thing."

"And that would be?"

"Private access to the *Cape Hatteras* for two days."

"What for?"

"It's classified, " he said.

"Before we go any further, how did you know we found the *Cape Hatteras*? Did you know where it was?"

"I wasn't lying. We knew that you were going to find that ship."

"What do you mean?" Spying was their business, but they'd have to have been psychic to see that one. I wasn't looking for it when we blundered across it.

"The UNAG has always known where the *Cape Hatteras* was. We saw you getting close to it. You gave our tracking staff in Montreal quite a laugh when you nearly passed by it. Imagine missing the biggest treasure in the solar system," he said with a chuckle.

"Why didn't you salvage it yourselves?"

"It's classified."

I instantly worried that Masterson might tell me that I wasn't the legal owner of the derelict.

"You knew all that gold was there, and you didn't bother to get it?"

"That's correct. I can't say why. I may not even know why. But I can tell you that the last thing the UNAG wants is for that much wealth to go to the outer solar system, untaxed, possibly to be used against us. All of the unions agree on that issue."

At least that made some sense. If they didn't want the gold, and they didn't want the ship, then I didn't see a problem with their plan. It seemed potentially well worth it if they were going to offer help. Even so, I wondered what they could possibly want aboard a 200-year-old ship that they could have visited whenever they wanted.

"What do you propose?" I asked.

"We know that you are about to rendezvous with the Mayor of Europa Colony."

"New San Francisco," I corrected him.

"Europa Colony. We'd like to capture him. We have an operative on his ship who has been monitoring his drug-trafficking activities."

"Did that operative send me a note warning about Stunt?"

"Yes, that was from us. If we couldn't kidnap you, we felt obligated at least to warn you."

That was the nicest thing a UNAG official had ever said to me. Their usual idea of being friendly was a tax audit. I then started to wonder whether the paranormal phenomenon that Sanjay and I had experienced on the derelict had something to do with the UNAG. Maybe they had invented hallucination beams, and were trying to drive us away.

"We want you to make your rendezvous with Stunt as planned. Afterwards he will be out in the open where we can capture him after you're safely off his ship. Our operative will let us know if you need our assistance. Should you fail, we will set up a perimeter at Saturn to capture your gold. We have two ships in the vicinity to aid you, plus another that can act as a last resort and destroy them if they get past Saturn."

"Destroy them?"

"Last resort, Mr. Hunter. You could always salvage the gold again from a truly wrecked ship."

"I suppose, but. . . ."

He cut me off with a wave of his hand. "You are to make your rendezvous and go with the Mayor. Then send your small ship to secure the *Cape Hatteras* and await our arrival. Two war cruisers will meet you. We will contact you after your treasure is secure."

Chapter 16 Day 240

"December 21, 2259. 0700 hours. Log of Captain John Andrew Nelson, Commanding Officer, UNAG Mining Vessel **Cape Hatteras.** ***Crewmen Galon and Fitz have reached the mountain chain and report the discovery of a cavern. It will reveal much of the geological timeline of this very ancient asteroid and give us clues about the early history of the solar system. I have authorized the men to perform a full exploration and report back hourly."***

Only a government official could come up with a convoluted and heavy-handed plan like that, but I did feel better knowing they had a ready supply of warships backing me.

"If you'll follow my aide," said Captain Masterson, "we'll surface and get you back to your ship *quietly*."

There was no time to ask another question. I was knocked out again. I remember nothing before waking up on the *Amaranth Sun* with my companions.

"Jesus, how did we get here?" Stacey asked in bewilderment.

"I feel like that crushed NASA probe," Neil said.

"My head feels as though it's been bashed in," Kurt added. They must have knocked him out too when they dropped us off.

"Don't worry, guys," I said. "I know what happened. I can't talk about it, but our chances of success are much greater now."

"What do you mean you know? You weren't knocked

out?"

"I was, but not for as long as you were. I'll tell you all about it when I can, but for now we need to find out what day it is."

"We've been out for 22 hours!" Stacey exclaimed after glancing at the bridge panel.

"Set a course for the Reverend's coordinates at Io. We've barely got enough time to get there."

It was just over a day before we caught sight of Stunt's ship. Its cylindrical shape suggested that it may originally have been a salvor or fuel ship, but it had numerous modifications that none of us could recognize. Strange spheres were attached to all points of the hull, and it appeared to have twice as many engines as a normal vessel of its size.

We established contact with Stunt, and he sent an automated shuttle. I always prefer real pilots over computers, at least until I met Randy, but the shuttle seemed to navigate safely. Automation on that scale was unusual and had to have been very expensive.

I had ordered my crew to take the *Amaranth Sun* and rendezvous with the *Cape Hatteras*. It was an uneasy feeling watching my ship shrinking into the distance, but it was an integral part of Masterson's plan.

The shuttle carrying me slid within the Mayor's ship. He had something that I hadn't seen other than on the outside of a space station: a docking bay. I felt a jolt as the shuttle touched bottom and made a seal. A moment later a hole opened in the floor that revealed a ladder. I climbed down to find the Mayor floating in front of me with his arms folded.

"Welcome to the *Neptune's Revenge*!" He seemed relieved

that I'd shown up.

"Thank you, Reverend Mayor. I'm sorry that I was delayed, but I've never navigated to Io before. Have you had any luck locating our target?"

"Not yet, but don't worry. We've got some of the most advanced tracking equipment in the solar system. We can see four or five times further, and at a much greater resolution, than a ship like yours can."

"That must have cost you dearly," I replied.

"I came into money some time ago. We've got the latest laser communications, sensors, engines—fastest ship in the solar system—and weapons. The engines were designed on Titan and built in Mars orbit. They're state-of-the-art."

Titanian engine design and Martian construction—that's usually reserved for space regatta racers and Union warships. What I really wanted to know about was his weapons.

"Yes, you mentioned you were armed to the teeth. May I ask what sort of weaponry?"

"Lasers, missiles, machine guns, and a little surprise you'll see if we need it."

"Not nuclear, I hope!"

"Heavens no! I'm not a savage, Mr. Hunter. Would you care for a drink?"

"Tell me it's not more hot water."

"No, not that vile water. To tell you the truth, I've never acquired a taste for it, but to be Mayor of New San Francisco you've got to play the part. On my ship we drink coffee. Strong coffee. Or you may also have some of Sister Mary Joanna's cola, if you prefer."

"Coffee, please."

It was delicious. I drank little else for five days. In that entire time I didn't see a single crew member other than the Mayor and Sister Mary Joanna. I heard sounds, the usual knocks and bangs that a running crew produces, but my meals were set out for me, and my movements were restricted to just one floor of the ship. I assumed that the Mayor's cabin was the gateway to the rest of the ship. It was the only area of our compartment that I hadn't seen.

I saw little of the Mayor during that time. When he finally invited me to dinner, I jumped at the chance.

"Sister Mary Joanna sends her apologies," he said. "She's indisposed this evening for prayer."

"Quite alright. She must have a busy schedule. Er . . . what does she do?"

"She's my secretary, of course, among other things."

"May I ask you a few questions about your ship?"

"What would you like to know?"

"What is your crew complement?"

"Forty," he said.

"I haven't seen anyone at all."

"They're down below. They never have reason to come up to the bridge. I prefer compartmentalization, if you get my drift."

I wondered how the UNAG operative on board was going to monitor my status when he couldn't see me.

"Compartmentalization?" I asked, playing dumb.

"Yes. You can't very well be a mercenary and a mayor at the same time without some measure of secrecy. My men never see me. They never set foot on Europa, and the Europans never set foot here. If I need to send a message to the crew, it's done through Sister Mary Joanna."

"She's their commanding officer?" I hadn't even heard her speak, much less act assertively.

"In a way, yes. But enough about my ship. I need to know everything you can tell me about the enemies we'll be up against."

I gave him a detailed report on the *Hyperion*, and I finally broke the news to him about Pace's ramming technique. Stunt wasn't pleased that I hadn't mentioned it before, but it didn't kill the deal. He was confident that he could avoid it. I retired early hoping to get some solid sleep. It was a good thing I did. Just before 4:00 a.m. they detected Finley's ship and, more importantly, the *Hyperion*.

When Stunt awoke me on the intercom, I shot immediately to the bridge. He was already moving to intercept. He might even have been able to go up against a UNAG cruiser with that kind of maneuverability. Within an hour we were bearing down. I decided it was time for a radio message.

"Alright, Finley, we're faster, and you're outgunned. If you want to keep this nice, you'll need to load the traitors onto your ship, hand *Hyperion* over to me along with every bar of gold that was there when I left, and be on your way."

There was no response.

"Perhaps we should fire a shot across his bow?" Stunt asked.

I agreed. For all his nonchalance in the way he suggested it, the result was shocking. The ship shuddered deeply as a stream of 300 rounds fired in a matter of seconds. It got Pace's attention.

"Your ship really is armed. I didn't think you had violence in you, Hunter," he said as he broke radio silence.

"Well, after you tried to kill me, I find it easy. Now hand over my property."

"I don't think so, Cam."

With that he broke formation with his ship while the *Hyperion* made a run for it. Finley's salvor rotated and set a course straight for us. Sister Mary Joanna burst into the room with a wide smile and settled in at the weapons station, while Stunt took the helm. He tried a number of evasive maneuvers, but somehow Finley ended up in front of us each time and was closing fast.

"He's got us, Hunter. We don't have enough distance to shake him. We've got no choice. We'll have to use lethal force," the Mayor said. I nodded, and he pointed at Sister Mary Joanna, gesturing as though he were firing a gun. She squealed and punched a few buttons on her panel. The computer targeted Finley's ship.

"Give up, Finley," I said in a last appeal. He didn't respond.

The Mayor's forward guns roared in a blitz of lasers and lead. They appeared to have no effect.

"Still here, Cammy boy," Pace taunted. "The modifications that let me ram ships can also stop bullets and lasers!"

Stunt grasped his chin as he seemed always to do when he wasn't quite certain if someone was telling him the truth or not. "Deploy the surprise, Sister," he ordered. "Mr. Hunter, if you'll join me in prayer."

"Prayer?"

"Yes, prayer."

Sister Mary Joanna bowed her head.

"Oh great and infinite universe, we ask forgiveness for what we are about to do, and let us be thankful for. . . ."

"He's getting close, Mayor," I interrupted.

"Fire!"

Neptune's Revenge recoiled as though it had hit an asteroid. Finley's ship disintegrated into a cloud of torn metal, bits of which I heard hit our hull.

"What the hell was that?" I asked in astonishment.

"A cannon," the Mayor replied quietly.

"A cannon? But there's only been one instance where someone mounted a. . . . My God, Mayor Stunt. You and Sister Mary Joanna are the pirates?"

She squealed and said, "Arrrgh!"

"Oh, I wish you hadn't said that," Stunt said to her. "Bad Sister Mary Joanna!"

She sipped her cola, staring at him indifferently.

"I was just about to lie and say no. Yes, I am the pirate. Those rubes on Europa are the gift that keeps on giving, and now I'm going to grift them as their spiritual leader. But since you know, I'll have to kill you."

"There's no reason to resort to that," I said.

"I'd hoped I wouldn't have to. I wasn't even going to rob you of your scrap metal. I don't see how it would have been worth more than what you were paying me, unless you found the *Cape Hatteras* or something. But now I have to take it, seeing as how you can't imprint your thumb on a hypercheck when you're dead."

He pulled a particle pistol from his overcoat and pointed it at me. "I'll let you live long enough to watch us kill your traitors. It's the least I can do. I'm sorry, I really am. I hate unpleasantness. After the other ship, Sister."

We were on Keating faster than he could begin evasive maneuvers. A brief laser barrage cut the power lines to his engines and reduced his thrust to a weak sputter. As we moved alongside, the Mayor pressed an intercom button, ordering his crew to board the ship.

But they weren't men. It was a swarm of armed drones that cut through the *Hyperion*'s hull in only a few minutes. I was impressed. It had taken us a full day to cut through the *Cape Hatteras*, yet these hovering robots were through Keating's hull in no time, with an airtight corridor ring mounted. Fifteen minutes later they radioed that the crew had given up without a shot and were jailed in a bathroom with the door welded shut. They'd never seen the face of the pirate who was robbing them.

"Alright, Mr. Hunter, now to deal with you," Stunt said with his gun still drawn. "I really am sorr. . . ."

I heard a zap and cringed, thinking it was all over for me. I opened my eyes to see Stunt's body floating in front of me. He had been shot by none other than Sister Mary Joanna.

"I've ordered the drones to stand down. The ship is ours, Mr. Hunter."

I had no idea what to say.

"Mary Joanna Johnson, UNAG Intelligence," she said.

It was the first time I'd heard her speak, but I recognized the voice instantly. It was the sexy one from the spy note.

Chapter 17 Day 248

"December 21, 2259. 1100 hours. Log of Captain John Andrew Nelson, Commanding Officer, UNAG Mining Vessel* Cape Hatteras. *Crewman Galon and Fitz have been collecting samples as they descend into the cavern system. They report a host of carbon-based minerals containing amino acids, the building blocks of life."

"You're the agent who was watching out for me?" I asked.

"That's me!" She let out a little giggle, but now it rang hollow.

"It's so hard to believe. If I had to make a guess regarding you and the Mayor, I'd have said he was the agent. You always seemed to be, well, just there."

"That's why I'm such a good spy," she said.

"How long have you been watching him?"

"I joined him shortly after his raid on the Europa colony. Play the bimbo, slay the crook."

"So the UNAG knew that he was the pirate?"

"Yes, but it wasn't our place to interfere with Europa's internal business unless they wanted help. They never asked for it. And losing that crop was in Earth's interest."

"In Earth's interest? How? Stopping the drug trade?"

"Yes. The Europan traders are very good at distributing

their garbage on Earth. We haven't had much luck with catching them in the act. The Mayor was bolder, and it paid off for him, but his distributors were sloppy amateurs. He watched them all go down one after another. He'd taken some precautions. None of them knew precisely who he was, but it made him paranoid, and he automated this ship."

"Automated?"

"Yes, Mr. Hunter. There is no crew at all. It was just the Mayor and I plus the robots. If you go down below, all you'll see is computers and drones. When he raided Europa, this was just a fueling hulk with a crew of three and a big cannon mounted on it. Now it's a warship as good as anything we've got in the UNAG fleet. One of the reasons we helped you was to take it out of commission. I needed a way back on board, and you provided that."

"What happened to the original crew?"

She drew her finger across her neck.

"He killed them?"

"We think he ejected them into space. I wasn't with him when he did it, but he talks in his sleep."

"Why didn't you just arrest the Mayor early on?"

"We'd have gotten him if he hadn't tricked the Europans into electing him. The UNAG considered that a bonus. Europa under a bad administration meant only bad things for Europa's economy, so we didn't interfere. But the new crop is set to be distributed in a few weeks, and we intend to stop them. Picking up the Mayor was the first step. The moment he left that moon, he was in *our* territory."

"You mean space."

"Yes, colonies may do as they please internally, but space is *ours*."

"What about the other unions?"

"We all agree on one thing, Mr. Hunter: space is *ours*."

"Call me Cam. No reason to be formal. You just saved my ass."

"Alright, Cam, and you're welcome."

"Well, where to next? Will we be going back to the *Cape Hatteras* as planned?"

"Yep! Don't worry. We'll tow that salvor with us. Your gold is safe. The *Neptune's Revenge* is a powerful vessel. We could pull two or three ships."

"Why didn't Stunt tell me the ship was automated?"

"I'm sure he would have told you that there were 40 people on board so he could charge you wages for them. But it's just us now, and I have full control of the drones."

"How did you gain the Mayor's confidence so easily?"

"By playing dumb, loyal, and sexy."

I didn't want to pursue that conversation to its natural end. I was content just to be in a better position than I had been a few days before. One thing still worried me, however. I couldn't guarantee that the UNAG would relinquish my gold when the time came. It *was* originally theirs. Moreover, they could prove that they had never actually abandoned it. That undermined my claim. But if they did pursue it in court, it would be a very public affair. I doubted that they wanted the publicity.

I contacted Ed Iron from the *Neptune's Revenge*. He assured me that the UNAG was in his pocket, but there was still the matter of just what they *did* want with the *Cape Hatteras*. Two days of access is one thing, but I could see that turning into a week and then finally a confiscation. I pressed Mary Joanna on the issue. She said that it was classified information. She didn't have the whole answer, and if she did she couldn't tell me about it, but she did say that the person who knew the most was on one of the warships with which we were set to rendezvous at the location of the *Cape Hatteras*. I couldn't wait to meet him.

I went over to the *Hyperion* to talk to Keating. He and his loyal thieves were not in nice quarters. The drones had imprisoned four men in a single bathroom and welded the door shut.

"Captain Hunter, you've got to improve our conditions," said Keating.

"Why would I do that?" I responded, speaking through a small hole cut in the door.

"It's what they're feeding us. They're taking perfectly good food and converting it into a more efficient form. When we get it, it's just a paste."

"I'm sure it's perfectly nutritious. It's probably had all the fat removed and vitamins added, and I'm sure you're getting plenty of fiber."

"It's tasteless. We'll go insane cooped up in here."

"Well, I do have some candy treats."

"What do you want for them?" he said, seemingly willing

to do anything I might ask.

"Well, you know, you deserve what you've got. You did maroon most of my personnel on a derelict, but I will trade you for some information. Whom else did Pace tell about the *Cape Hatteras*?"

I was worried that Pace might have reinforcements on the way and that the task of keeping the *Cape Hatteras* secret was spiraling toward futility by the day.

"He didn't tell anyone," declared Keating. "We were to keep strict radio silence. Pace wanted it kept a secret as much as you did. He didn't want the Europa pirates or the UNAG government to know. I don't think he expected you to cut a deal with the pirates. Who was it?"

"How do you know I wasn't the pirate all along?" I said, giving him the candy and returning to the *Neptune's Revenge* and ignoring his pleas for better accommodations.

I spent most of the rest of journey exploring *Neptune's Revenge* and chatting with Mary Joanna.

"Care for some of Europa's best?" I asked her.

"Best what? Not that hideous weed they're all dependent on."

"No, this is better. Sausage's famous moonshine."

I had brought two bottles with me. I thought they might come in handy, and UNAG was good enough not to confiscate them when they moved my luggage to the *Amaranth Sun.*

"That I can handle. I'm so tired of hot water and cola."

I poured a couple of shots. I had a motive in trying to get

Mary Joanna drunk: I wanted more information. I didn't really care if it pertained to my salvage or not. I just wanted any classified stuff I could get out of a spy.

"I know things that certain people would kill to know," she said with a slur as I broached the question of secrets after the fifth serving.

"Tell me one."

"I can't."

"Why not? I won't tell anyone."

"I trust you, Cam," Mary Joanna said, "but I can't tell you. I have an implant that will knock me out cold the moment I say anything that it doesn't like."

"Does that mean you can't lie either?"

"Oh, I can. I'm trained to lie my way past any detector. That's easy, but it's a lot harder to train someone to hold her heart rate down when she reveals a secret. UNAG Intelligence only accepts agents who *can't* do it."

"Was that a secret?"

"What?"

"The initiation rituals of UNAG Intelligence?"

"I don't know. Now that you mention it, it might be."

She promptly passed out. The UNAG's implant worked, but not quite the way they intended. She was out for at least eight hours. I had no idea what part of that sleep was the alcohol and what part was the effects of the implant, but she didn't move once the entire time. Mary Joanna just floated around the bridge like a helium balloon. I finally had to secure her to a wall with a strap when she drifted in my direction and planted her boot against my neck. When she came to, she had only a vague memory of the last few minutes of our conversation.

"Your implant made you pass out!" I said.

"Hard to get information from someone that passes out the moment you start torturing them," she said.

"I wasn't torturing!"

"I meant hypothetically."

"Well, if I ever need to know if there's a spy in the room, all I have to do is ask everyone if they're UNAG agents. Whether they lie or not, the one that goes down . . . "

"It doesn't work quite that way, Cam”

"I'll bet it does," I said, intending to try it some day.

We were faster than the *Amaranth Sun*, so we caught up with them a few hours before both ships arrived at the *Cape Hatteras*. The scientists were happy to be liberated. They had been marooned for only a week, but judging by their reactions it might have been years.

"Cam, we're so glad to see you," Janet exclaimed.

"You can thank me later, darling. It's all part of a day's work for a hero."

"Hero? We've been cursing you for running away when we needed help," said my ex-wife.

"He was going to ram and kill us!"

"Don't make excuses for cowardice, where's that adventurous spirit and go get 'em attitude?"

"No wonder I divorced you."

"You didn't divorce me. It was the other way around. And we never finalized it. We need to do that as soon as we get back to Earth."

She hugged me. I hadn't expected that.

"Just glad to have you back," Janet said. "We've got to talk privately."

"Alright, let's go to the bridge and. . . ."

"Not on this ship, Cam. On that thing you arrived in. I've never seen a ship like that before."

"It's the pirate ship with the big cannon that robbed Europa."

"What? You hired pirates? That kind of idiocy coming from you isn't surprising. But how did . . . ? Tell me later. You've got to order the evacuation of this ship immediately."

"Why? What's wrong?"

"Just get these people off the *Cape Hatteras*."

I ordered the third officer of the *Hyperion*, the most senior officer who hadn't been aware of the plot, to start the process. I also ordered a drone to remove the remaining bars of gold from the derelict. It did in minutes what had taken us days. Janet and I then suited up for the journey to *Neptune's Revenge*.

"Let me get this straight," she said. "You captured the pirate ship, yet you couldn't defeat a pair of unarmed salvors."

"There's a big difference between shooting a pirate captain aboard his own ship and trying to escape a salvor that's trying to ram you."

"Wait, you shot the pirate captain?"

"Well, I didn't. Sister Mary Joanna did."

"A nun shot the pirate captain?"

"She's definitely not a nun. She's a UNAG spy."

I thought I deserved to pass out when I outed her. After exchanging waves and giggles, Mary Joanna left us alone on the bridge, though I'm virtually certain she had it bugged.

"Cam, the Cherenkov radiation returned while you were gone. It took two more people."

Chapter 18 Day 251

"December 21, 2259. 1400 hours. Log of Captain John Andrew Nelson, Commanding Officer, UNAG Mining Vessel* Cape Hatteras. *The first sled of samples has arrived. They are full of a kind of crystal, uniquely formed in the low gravity of the asteroid. My mineralogist on the surface believes they are completely new to astrogeology. I expect several more sleds as the men descend deeper into the cavern."

A week later a pair of ominous-looking UNAG warships positioned themselves near our fleet. These weren't the usual patrol ships; they were Poseidon-class cruisers, the biggest guns of the fleet. Normally having one those off your starboard bow would be one the most frightening sights imaginable. In my circumstances it meant safety and security accompanied by a huge element of uncertainty.

I had transferred back to the *Amaranth Sun*, from which I could see several guns on those warships trained on both the *Neptune's Revenge* and the *Hyperion*. That was a natural precaution because they were recently enemy ships, but I also noticed a smaller gun dedicated to my ship and the bulk of their weaponry targeted on the *Cape Hatteras*. That was the clearest sign yet that they feared something on that ship so much that it warranted the presence of two armed cruisers. I had to find out what it was.

I had been judicious about the information I was giving the UNAG up to that point. I felt it best to save news of the missing people until I spoke directly with whomever was in charge.

"Camden Hunter," came a radioed message. "Please dock your vessel with the UNAG battlecruiser *Portsmouth*. Clearance is issued on our mark. Mark. We will expect you within the hour."

It sounded more like a summons than an invitation. Intimidating, to say the least. Docking rings were extended from both warships, so I had Stacey make extra certain that she got the right one. A mistake might have gotten us fired upon.

Clearly the enormous ship was not designed for any commercial or recreational purpose but instead for a battle in space that would probably never come. Most of the room onboard was dedicated to the weapons systems. I doubt that even Finley's ramming bow could have knocked it out of commission.

"Our companion battleship will be docking with the *Cape Hatteras* immediately. It's a good thing you evacuated ahead of time," the ship's captain said as he greeted me near the airlock.

"Just holding up my end of the bargain. I said that I'd allow two days' access. It's all yours, but I do need to give a warning before your people go aboard. I'm not certain whether I should tell you or a specialist. I think you'll want to discuss it in a more private setting."

"Come with me."

I followed the captain into a small room that looked like a laboratory. A balding man in his sixties turned from behind a workstation.

"Mr. Hunter, this is Dr. Westmoreland, Director of Research at Titan. He's the de facto head of this operation."

"Pleasure to meet you, Captain Hunter," he said. Finally

someone was getting my title correct.

"A pleasure, Dr. Westmoreland. I've heard that your people have done great things at Titan, especially the work on methane as a fusion catalyst. That promises to do great things for our engines."

"Thank you. I'm certainly glad that the captains of the solar system are paying attention to us. If the funding I get from Earth is any clue, you're probably the only people who are."

"Do you have any theories on how to fix the fusion interflow problem?"

"Yes." He seemed a bit hesitant. "I'd love to tell you about it, but time is rather short."

"Mr. Hunter said he had a warning for us. I felt it best for you to hear it as well," the captain interjected, rescuing Westmoreland.

"I do, but I'm curious about your fusion work and what it has to do with what's on the *Cape Hatteras*. Its fusion reactors are two centuries out of date."

Westmoreland sighed. "I can see you're very perceptive. Fusion engine research isn't the only thing we do on Titan."

"Oh? What else do you do? Since I am the legal owner of the derelict, I should be aware of what's going to happen while you're onboard."

"Alright, Captain Hunter. You win. Of course, this falls under your obligation of secrecy as a citizen of the UNAG."

"I understand."

"The engine research is real and successful, but it's a front.

I have nothing to do with it. I specialize in black projects and secret research."

"Black projects? As in secret weapons and new orbital interceptors?"

"Something like that. Titan is a natural place for that kind of work. It's isolated and difficult to get to. In this case, it's research on dark matter. What's happening on your ship involves that. I can't say more."

"Dark matter?" I was shocked. "It's supposed to be entirely non-interactive with our matter."

"It interacts only through gravity."

"I was under the impression that it was useless."

"It is."

"But you said we're dealing with that."

"We are. Now if you'll get to your warning, please."

"We've had people disappear on the *Cape Hatteras* and in our fleet. Three to date, gone without a trace. The only thing we know is that whatever happened was preceded by a flash of blue light."

"We expected that, Captain Hunter."

"You expected?"

"Yes. I also suspect that your people have been dreaming and hallucinating."

"Something like that," I said curtly.

"I apologize for not being at liberty to say more, but what I can tell you is that you were in grave danger every moment you spent on that ship. Danger that we'd hoped would stay bottled up in space for at least a few more centuries until we could figure out a way to deal with it. Your discovery of the derelict has changed that."

"So whatever it is, the UNAG felt it was better off left alone. Was it some kind of experiment?"

"You could say that. Don't worry, Captain Hunter. We have some working theories that they didn't have 200 years ago. We think we can deal with it. And it won't affect your derelict once we've finished our work. You'll have your ship."

I didn't believe him. They'd have salvaged it themselves if they thought it could be made safe.

"I don't suppose you could tell me what happened to the crew? I mean, I don't want to know specifics, but is the blue radiation why there aren't any bodies on that ship?"

"Yes and no. The crew froze to death on 974-Bernhard. The UNAG secretly recovered their remains about a decade after the disaster. Captain Nelson died on the *Cape Hatteras*. We think that he disappeared like your men."

"How do you know what we're dealing with? Have UNAG personnel been aboard the derelict? The ship looks mothballed, as though someone cleaned it up."

"We did send an exploratory mission, the same one that visited 974-Bernhard, but you were the first person to set foot on that ship in centuries."

"Why didn't the UNAG recover the ship?"

"Because there were two other disappearances."

"Two others?"

"Yes, part of the recovery mission. After leaving the asteroid, they were sent to the position of the wreck. They boarded the *Cape Hatteras* in hopes of returning it to Earth. They spent several days preparing for a cold restart of the engines, and then two members disappeared. We ordered the ship abandoned after that."

"That's why the *Cape Hatteras* was spotlessly clean. You were preparing it for a new crew. And the engineering section was full of water and frozen solid. Was that related?"

"Call it a last-ditch effort to make the ship safe to sit out here forever. But I've said enough already. Just two days, that's all we will need, and then the relic is yours with our blessing. Are you going to display it?"

"It's classified," I said.

He chuckled at that. It diffused the tense background of the discussion.

"Yes, it's slated to be a museum ship."

"We would appreciate it if you stayed here with us for the duration. We'll probably need more information from you."

"Of course."

I wouldn't have missed that for the world. I wanted to glean whatever bits of information I could. The *Cape Hatteras* tale was already a great story, but it was getting better—and more valuable—by the minute, and I was the first member of the public to hear these new parts of the saga. I was given quarters that consisted of a desk and a sleeping bag on the wall. I spent most of the first day in my room twiddling my thumbs and doing backflips in zero-G. Sometime late in the afternoon an excited ensign poked his head through the door.

"Captain Hunter, you're needed on the bridge."

I shot to the bridge as best I could without banging my head on an armored bulkhead. I found Dr. Westmoreland and the bridge officers floating around a map table and talking feverishly. On the table was a large diagram of the *Cape Hatteras*.

"What's wrong?" I asked.

"We've lost our crew," Westmoreland answered.

"Your boarding party?"

"No, Captain Hunter. The entire crew of that warship has gone silent," he said as he pointed out the window.

I glanced out but had to take a second look. The other warship was listing and tearing away from the derelict, the pressurized corridor between them fluttering as its air released into space. I hoped to Pluto that didn't include the *Cape Hatteras*'s atmosphere.

"Disappeared like the others?"

"We're not certain. Someone will have to go over and see. It could have been a simple accident that killed or incapacitated the crew. We don't have any information yet. May we ask you some questions?"

"Certainly."

"When your first crewman disappeared, what happened?"

"Well, he just disappeared. One moment he was there; the

next he wasn't. And then the radiation went away."

"What do you mean?"

"It was just *gone*, completely. I walked around the engineering section afterwards myself. It seemed safe, at least until the scientists were marooned. They said that the radiation appeared again in the engineering section and that the other people who disappeared were near that part of the ship."

"Near the engineering section?"

"Yes. One of the people was in the hold outside where we had found the gold."

"It hasn't lost any energy, even after centuries," Dr. Westmoreland said to the *Portsmouth*'s captain.

"What hasn't lost energy? The blue radiation?"

"I'm sorry, Captain Hunter. I can't say. It might be best if you go back to your ship and move it to a safe distance. Have that pirate ship and the salvor do the same. This may take longer than two days."

I had known it all along.

"I can order my ship to a safe distance by using your communications station," I said. "I'd rather stay here in case you need me again."

Dr. Westmoreland paused for a moment and then nodded in agreement. I contacted Stacey and Mary Joanna from the bridge panel on the warship and had them move to positions about 200 kilometers out. The *Hyperion* was experiencing engine irregularities as a result of rigging power to its engines after Stunt's lasers cut the electrical lines. They wouldn't be able to move for some time, so I instructed them to get out of there as soon as they could manage it.

I found myself wishing that I had formulated some kind of a code with Stacey in case I needed to send a message to swoop in and pick me up if it looked as though the bogeyman was going to make us disappear like the crew of that other warship.

"Captain Hunter, you've dealt with this before. Would you object to joining our boarding party to the *Victorious*?" the *Portsmouth*'s captain asked.

I thought about it for a moment. "I'll go, but I'm not military personnel. At the first sign of trouble I want out of there."

"Agreed."

"How big will the party be? Who's in command?"

"You are," he said.

"I'm not an officer, but I'll do it if you say so."

"Excellent," he responded.

"Well, let's assemble the team."

"I'm sorry, I wasn't clear. Captain, you *are* the boarding party. I've just lost half of the personnel assigned to this mission—152 people. I'll need every man I've got left to complete it, and probably a few of yours as well."

They had tricked me into it. I thought about demanding to be returned to my ship, but I realized that it wouldn't do any good. They held too many cards, and agreeing to board the derelict again would give me some badly needed leverage to get more information. Part of me was certain that I'd see the same thing I saw in the *Cape Hatteras*'s engineering room after the first disappearance—nothing.

"Alright," I said, "but I want more answers."

"Answers about what?"

"What's really going on here? What am I dealing with? What's this about dark matter? I'll need to know what I'm up against."

The Captain of the *Portsmouth* and Dr. Westmoreland looked at each other. The Captain nodded.

Westmoreland sighed and turned to me. "Captain Hunter, you're dealing with a weapon."

"Oh, I see, a weapon gone wrong. Sounds like the UNAG of 200 years ago . . . and now. I suppose you want to get it back and threaten the other unions with it. Maybe I shouldn't go over there if it's just more government games. Contact my ship. I'm going home."

"No, Captain Hunter, you don't understand. It isn't a weapon we made. It's from somewhere else."

"Somewhere else? What the hell is that supposed to mean?"

"Not human," the Captain said, taking care to articulate very clearly.

That was the kind of statement for which there is no possible rebuttal. My response was silence and shock. I dutifully put on a moon suit and went to the airlock to fulfill my mission on the *Victorious*.

Chapter 19 Into the Fire

"December 21, 2259. 1600 hours. Log of Captain John Andrew Nelson, Commanding Officer, UNAG Mining Vessel* **Cape Hatteras.** *The cavern system is significantly deeper and more extensive than anticipated. Marquez is now repositioned at the mouth of the cave and has sent the second sled. Galon continues his exploration deeper into the asteroid alone. The thickness of the rock prevents direct communication with him. His reports are being relayed by Marquez hourly."

I pushed myself out of the open airlock of the *Portsmouth* and looked down its immense length. Its laser batteries bristled at regular intervals, all of the guns now retrained on the *Cape Hatteras*. I found relief in that. I was never comfortable with a laser cannon pointed at the *Amaranth Sun*—or at my salvor full of gold.

Ahead I could see the *Victorious* still listing and slowly pulling away from the derelict. I activated my suit's maneuvering thrusters and crossed the distance, aiming for the same area of the *Victorious* that I had just left on the *Portsmouth*. I assumed the airlock would be located in the same place, but it wasn't.

"Could someone tell me where to go?" I asked on open comms.

"You're near the correct area. It's located on the top of the ship between ribs 84 and 85," the Captain replied.

"Where are ribs 84 and 85?" I asked.

"Go up and over; then head toward the stern. You can't miss it."

"How am I going to get in?"

"We can operate the airlock remotely. We'll need your help in gaining full control of the ship when you get inside."

I followed his instructions and spotted the airlock. I peered in and could see a small part of the ship's interior bathed in red light. The door slid open without warning, startling me as it began to move. I felt a slight brush of residual air push me gently backwards into space. I thought it would not have been unreasonable to expect some kind of warning. I concluded that communication with me must have been secondary to monitoring the telemetry data from my suit. I wished that I had suggested that we use the drones from the *Neptune's Revenge*, but I doubt they'd have trusted them.

The airlock immediately began closing, again with no warning. I noticed a camera in the lock. I realized that if they could see me, they'd probably be able to watch my every move anywhere I went on the ship. My gut feeling that I was an expendable guinea pig grew stronger. I was there to figure out how to safely enter a ship in which everyone had just vanished. It might even have been to their benefit if I disappeared.

It didn't seem as though there had been enough time for the cycle to complete itself before the interior door opened. I checked my suit's display on my right forearm. It was reading a normal atmosphere, but I felt it best to keep my helmet on. I didn't want to add the extra step of putting it back on if I had to escape quickly.

Boarding that ship was different from what I had faced when I entered the *Cape Hatteras* for the first time. The

Victorious wasn't dead in space. It was lit up and operational, red and yellow alert lights flashing away as buttons that needed to be pushed went neglected.

"Where should I go now?" I asked.

"The bridge should be first. We will need you to assist us from there in gaining full control of the ship. You should see a corridor immediately on your left. Take it."

I followed it, moving toward the bow and passing through a rotating artificial gravity ring. When I stepped onto its floor, I immediately detected the ship's list. I pushed myself upward and back into the zero-G air to avoid disorientation. I felt a new uneasiness as I sensed that my escape route was getting progressively more complicated as I moved through the ship.

I was passing through a hatch into the zero-G environment of the bridge when my peripheral vision caught a slight movement. It was a sleeve moving through the air. I briefly thought that I was seeing the crew, alive and well, still working on the bridge and that the ship had merely lost contact with the *Portsmouth*.

I was fear-stricken when I realized what I was actually seeing. While the people had disappeared, their uniforms were floating around the room, still filled out as if there were living persons in them. They were moving on the last momentum of non-existent bodies, looping and turning in mid-air like slow dancers in a ballroom.

I blinked, or I think I did, and they were gone. I was seeing ghosts again.

"I'm on the bridge, and there's no one here. They've disappeared," I said chokingly. I looked out the bridge windows to see the *Cape Hatteras* and the *Hyperion* still near each other. They were still having engine problems on the salvor, I thought.

"You'll need to go to the captain's station at the center rear of the room. You will see a screen that is the commanders operations panel. You will need to access it," relayed Westmoreland.

"I'm here. It's giving a long list of warnings."

"You'll need to touch the screen and back out of there to the main interface menu. Access the global operations interface at the top of the list."

"I'm there. It's asking for the commanding officer's access code," I said after following his instructions.

"The code is 41-54672-4783-BH."

I never thought I'd ever have a captain's access code for a UNAG battlecruiser. The screen that came up wasn't anything like my display on the *Amaranth Sun*. The ship had a full complement of weapons, all of them fireable from that station.

Westmoreland and the captain of the *Portsmouth* gave me a series of technical instructions. I saw their remote presence building in the system bit by bit as I put in the data.

"You're clear to leave the bridge and move on now," said Westmoreland. "You'll need to go back the way you came."

I stepped back into the the gravity ring and felt the ship righting itself as the *Portsmouth*'s crew gained attitude control of the *Victorious*. I then jumped back into zero-G and passed into the main corridor with its red lighting and flashing yellow lights, just as they went green.

"What's next?" I asked, hoping they'd say the mission was over.

"We need you to enter engineering at the stern and give us a visual on what its condition is. The engine status indicates operational, but that doesn't mean there isn't a chair floating about ready to destroy an instrument panel if we reposition the ship."

Great, I thought. Now I had to go to the exact opposite end. I wanted out of there badly, back to whatever inhabited ship I could reach first. The *Hyperion* and even the *Cape Hatteras* were both closer and safer than that place. At any moment I might lose consciousness or hallucinate again, as I had on the *Cape Hatteras*. There was no way I could escape in that state. I didn't want to tell Westmoreland about the uniforms, not thinking it mattered. Whatever had made the crew of the *Victorious* disappear could make any of us vanish whenever it wanted, so I moved on as bravely as I could force myself to be.

I floated down the corridor past the airlock entrance, more than a little tempted to jump in and escape, but I mustered up enough courage to move onward. At the end of the corridor I found the airlock again, or one like it. I turned around, and there was another airlock. My heart raced as I turned again, and there was another. In every direction was an airlock. They opened all at the same time, and I saw stars and deep space. I sensed that there was no ship at all and that I somehow had fallen overboard and was floating freely. I closed my eyes tightly.

When I looked again, I found myself back in the corridor and staring into a common room just forward of engineering.

"I think I'm hallucinating, Doctor."

"Try to make it, Cam. You're fine. We're not seeing

anything unusual."

I was badly disoriented. Whatever had happened left me confounded and with a headache forming. I felt slowed down, my thoughts governed by something that wasn't me. Half awake and half asleep, I tried to use the comm again, speaking but not receiving an answer. Before I could check my display to see whether the radio was working, everything went dead.

The whole ship and my suit lost power. Instead of panicking and heading for the airlock, I inexplicably tried very calmly to figure out how that could happen. It wasn't a time for problem analysis, but I was doing it nonetheless. Thoughts formed and aborted as my mind wandered to places far away. In the end I found myself thinking about a trip to an accountant I had made a decade ago.

I'd lost my senses, though it wasn't apparent to me. I wasn't even awake; I was something else. I thought it was perfectly normal to think about that accountant. I didn't think it was important that ten feet away the blue glow had appeared and was rising in intensity.

"We warned you to leave," said a very calm voice.

I discovered exactly what Sanjay had meant by a voice inside his helmet. It was right next to my ear, or in my mind's dialogue with itself like thoughts in bold typeface. My senses returned with a vengeance, and fear paralyzed my body.

"You didn't listen," it said in its detached, almost mechanical tone.

"What did you do with our people?" I asked aloud, absolutely terrified.

"They came here in a way that they could not exist."

"Can you send them back?" I asked.

"They do not exist."

"Am I about not to exist?"

"Yes. Run."

Wide awake again, I turned as fast as I could and dropped to the floor, running with my hands grabbing anything I could. I had no idea whether I was making any progress. I was no longer even certain that it was all real. Either I was moving entirely on reflex, or whatever it was that had been talking to me was helping me to escape.

I saw the airlock. Again it was not where it should have been, by my reckoning, but I threw myself into it nonetheless. I hand-cranked the door shut as fast as I could, then started cranking the outer door without bothering with the manual decompress. I looked briefly at the interior window to see the blue light glowing very brightly, flickering and getting more intense, as though it were moving down the corridor. It was following me.

As soon as the seal broke, I felt myself drawn along with the blast of air. I held onto the hand crank and kept at it as the lock went to vacuum. As soon as it was wide enough for me to slip through, I pushed against the wall with my feet and shot like a torpedo from the ship. My suit regained power without warning. Just as I stabilized my attitude, the *Victorious* came back into view, and I turned toward it. It was glowing intensely before vanishing in a brief and blinding flash. I was left floating freely in space, desperate to make sense of what had just happened.

And then, for only a moment, I saw something suspended

in space a few hundred feet away. It was a blue ring of light, shrinking and growing dimmer. Inside it was a void that looked almost like normal space but with a faint gray cast and indistinct stars. It gave me the sense that wherever it led was abnormal, somehow very different. It was moving slightly at the last velocity and direction of the former *Victorious*. It continued until it eclipsed the sun relative to me. As it did so, inside the ring I could see a stark white sun, not yellow as it should have been. It was ill-defined, dimmer, and much larger. And then the ring closed. The vision seemed to melt away into normal sunlight, ending the eclipse.

Chapter 20 Confusion

"December 21, 2259. 1700 hours. Log of Captain John Andrew Nelson, Commanding Officer, UNAG Mining Vessel* Cape Hatteras. *Marquez reports that Galon has found a large chamber at the heart of the cavern system. The walls look to be made of a perfectly smooth and solid mass of the same crystalline mineral found in the samples. I have sent Marquez to accompany him, and they are both now out of contact. I have ordered them to return to the surface and reestablish communications within eight hours."

Back on the *Portsmouth* the military men were in an extraordinary state of organized disarray. It was something to see. The chain of command was desperate to maintain the illusion that everything was under control, so they had one half of the crew mired in a hopeless tangle of confusion while the other half dutifully manned their stations. Everyone was collectively trying to convince themselves that the *Victorious* hadn't just disappeared.

It was obvious from the chaos that they had no idea of what had happened, or didn't want to believe their eyes. The one thing everyone was avoiding was a cursory glance out the window to confirm that the ship was gone. I couldn't blame them. Not only had they lost an entire crew, but they also had lost an entire ship. And they had no obvious starting point for figuring out why.

At least someone had the presence of mind to let me back inside the *Portsmouth*. I was on the verge of banging on the airlock door when a young lieutenant's face appeared in the window and gestured for me to move away so that he could decompress the lock. I repositioned myself to avoid the burst of rushing air and spent a few moments checking my communications. I still was getting nothing, and it wasn't because my suit was defective. I had regained power the instant the ring disappeared. The silence was because no one on the bridge was paying the slightest bit of attention to me.

I slid myself into the lock, and the lieutenant began the compression cycle by closing the outer door. After a moment I heard the faint sound of rushing air, and I waited for him to give me the thumbs-up. When it came, the young lieutenant opened the inner door. He could see on my face that I wasn't happy about being ignored and abandoned out there.

"Did you guys forget about me?" I asked.

"I didn't. From what I hear the bridge is a complete mess. I suppose they forgot about you."

"Do you know whether Westmoreland is up there? I need to see him immediately."

"I'm sure he is. I'll take you there when you're ready."

I took my suit off fast. I wanted to give the *Portsmouth*'s captain a dressing-down that would have rivaled that of an angry UNAG admiral. The young lieutenant escorted me to the bridge. He didn't have to since I knew how to get there, but I suspected he was looking for an excuse to be near the heart of the action. I understood his desire completely.

When we entered the bridge, the Captain and Dr. Westmoreland were in heated debate at the command station. I maneuvered over as coyly as I could, hoping not to attract their attention while floating just within earshot. It was one of the juiciest conversations I'd ever heard.

"The readings indicated negative pressure coming from inside the anomaly," Dr. Westmoreland explained to the Captain.

"What does that mean? There isn't any kind of pressure in the vacuum of space."

"There was immediately outside that thing. Pressure is a terrible word for it. Space-time itself was being drawn toward the object. Think of it as like water being pulled in a tide or going down a drain. Anything sitting in the water goes along with it. We were drawn several tens of feet in the direction of the anomaly while it was active, the *Cape Hatteras* and *Hyperion* even more because they were closer. It stands to reason that the *Victorious* was drawn entirely into it."

"So it's a type of wormhole that sucked the ship in?" the Captain asked.

"No, I don't think that's a good analogy. A wormhole is a connection between two places in normal space, *our* kind of space. The medium would be static or equalized, distorted by gravity perhaps but not moving in the fashion that we saw. Whatever we were seeing inside the anomaly was not normal space. It was space with its properties altered."

"It wasn't part of our universe?"

"I'm not certain."

"It seems clear that there was energy there. It was glowing," the Captain remarked, obviously hoping to sound smarter than the scientist.

"Well, something was emitting photons, but that doesn't

mean there was a lot of energy, just some light. High energy always shows a signature. It interacts with things. We didn't detect anything other than some weakly visible light emissions."

"That's it? All those instruments in the lab, and you only detected light? I could have told you that with my own eyes!"

"Well, we saw more than that. We could see objects in our space moving toward it. We could detect emissions coming out of it, originating from the matter being drawn in, but that was separate from the anomaly itself. The light the ring itself was emitting was entirely in the visible spectrum and largely blue. There were no other frequencies. I suspect even that was simple Cherenkov radiation emitted by subatomic particles falling into the blackness and exceeding the speed of light in whatever medium surrounded that hole."

"Exceeding the speed of light is impossible!" the Captain exclaimed. He was getting increasingly frustrated by the scientific mumbo jumbo.

"In regular space that's correct. The speed of light in space is the fastest anything can go, but that doesn't mean that light can't be slowed down. If you run it through water, or air, it moves more slowly. If you've got some kind of energetic subatomic particle that has enough energy to move faster than light in a medium, say water, then it glows blue like an old nuclear reactor. That's Cherenkov radiation. It may have simply been subatomic particles falling into the edges of the ring. We don't know."

"So this thing was sucking space into it?" I asked. It was the first time they'd noticed me floating near them. Their conversation stopped for a moment before they hesitantly continued, including me in a watered-down version. Or at least that's what they tried to do.

"Yes. We registered movement on this ship *visually*, but everything else indicated that we hadn't moved at all. Yet our position, relative to the sun, had changed. The only way that could have happened was by space itself moving. We moved along with it like boats floating in a river's current. Moreover, when the warship disappeared, we saw a flash of emissions, but then they tapered off as the hole closed. We believe those residuals were dust falling into the hole. Based on the radiation readings, I think we were seeing the matter changing state as it entered the other side, wherever that might be."

"Changing state?"

"Possibly becoming dark matter, annihilating or losing its cohesiveness in some way. I'm not certain."

"How do we find out for certain?"

"I don't know yet. We don't know what kind of space they inhabit. It might be a hyper-form of our space or a lack of space-time altogether. The movement could simply have been the universe itself expanding into the hole. There's no way to tell with our current understanding."

"They?" I asked. "Those aliens you hinted at. How do you know anything about them? How did you know about what had happened on the *Cape Hatteras*? You've only given me a few pieces of the puzzle. I demand to know, especially after that thing almost killed me."

I had grown as frustrated as the Captain. He was clearly anxious at that point, and I could see in his eyes that he was ready to jump at any chance to exclude me. Dr. Westmoreland must have taken my side because he kept offering answers and seemed determined not to let the Captain intrude into the conversation.

"We know because we were contacted from the other side, Mr. Hunter," said Westmoreland.

"That's enough," the Captain said, waving his hand in front of Westmoreland.

"Oh no you don't. I'm in! I already have enough classified information to have coffee with an admiral at headquarters. You can go a bit further, Dr. Westmoreland. Please continue, contacted how?" I asked. The Captain responded by silently crossing his arms.

"It happened during the *Cape Hatteras* mission. We're not certain why they were there or whether they had always maintained a presence at the asteroid. Something allowed them to detect us. They appeared to Captain Nelson while his crew was on the surface. He established some kind of contact with them, and then they killed him. We know little else except that they must have left evidence of their presence somewhere on the *Cape Hatteras*."

"What evidence?" I asked.

"We know there is a connection to them on that ship. Something physical. It was probably originally on the asteroid, and the mining crew brought it back. At any rate the logs on the *Cape Hatteras* will make it clear. You've got them, and we can't stop you from reading them. Our intention was to find whatever it was they left on the ship in the two days we requested, Captain Hunter."

"How did you come up with two days?" I had to ask.

"Before your salvage two days was the longest anyone since Captain Nelson had been on that ship without something's happening. We have instrumentation that we hope will allow us to detect the anomaly before it becomes a problem."

I didn't mention it, but it had taken less than two days before Sanjay and I had our encounters. I have no doubt that other members of the engineering team saw things as well but kept quiet about it.

"You son of a bitch! You detected it before I saw it on the *Victorious* and didn't warn me?"

"No, no, Captain Hunter. We didn't detect it until the moment the *Victorious* disappeared. Believe me, you saw it before we did. We saw nothing in the telemetry of your suit before it went dead."

"In other words you're saying that you can't detect it until it sucks something in?"

"That appears to be the case. But remember, that only needs to be a few specks of dust."

"So how do we fight it? It obviously wants to kill us, so what do we do?"

"Study whatever physical object on that ship allows them to manipulate our space. Assuming, of course, that it can be found. Then we can figure out how to fight them."

"What do you think it is? I mean, what are we supposed to look for?"

Even though that was an obvious question to ask, I was injecting it to stake a new claim: I wanted to be on the team looking for whatever it was on the derelict. I wasn't going to let them tear it apart without me. I would have liked to have those scientists on the *Hyperion* involved as well. I planned to ask for that later.

"If it's something so simple as an artifact, let's get to it," I said.

"It might not be. It could be something so small that we can't see it, something on the level of the subatomic, or it might just as well be a pink box with an X painted on it. We won't know until we go over there and start searching and eliminating possibilities. What I can tell you is to retrieve ANY surface material you find. The logs suggest that Captain Nelson was inordinately interested in some geological samples, but he was a miner, so that may not mean much."

"Alright," I said, "that's a start, but what exactly do we know about these aliens? You mentioned before that dark matter was involved."

"Only that they aren't from here and that they're very hostile. We know that dark matter is at work somehow because of an anomaly that was seen by the *Cape Hatteras*. The asteroid's gravity increased very slightly when the aliens first appeared. It started producing more than its mass should produce. They literally saw Walton's Rock grow heavier."

"Nothing can do that except by adding more matter," I said.

"Or by adding dark matter."

It seemed like a good time to drop a bombshell. "We believe there are missing documents from the initial disaster investigation that we weren't able to access. We know they existed. There are references to another set of documents in what we've got. What are they?"

Westmoreland glanced at the Captain, deferring to his knowledge on that subject. I lost hope of getting a real answer.

"We have them, or at least something that might fit the

description of what you're talking about. But they're unrevealing, and you'd need security clearance to see them anyway," the Captain said.

"I think I have clearance enough already."

"Not that kind of clearance. I haven't even seen them entirely. I doubt that Dr. Westmoreland has read them without some parts redacted."

"He's right, Cam," said Westmoreland. "I haven't seen much of them, but I can tell you that what I have seen isn't relevant to what we're doing here."

I was intrigued even more. What was so important in those documents that I couldn't see them? I thought it must be some kind of physical description of the aliens or the content of another message from them. Or maybe it was incriminating evidence of the cover-up.

"Were the aliens hostile from the beginning?"

"Yes," the Captain said, cutting off Westmoreland before he could say anything. "They are inherently hostile."

The Captain took over the conversation from Westmoreland, but as much as he might have liked me to believe that he had more information—information is power—I don't think he did. I believed him when he said that he hadn't seen all of the classified documents, but I couldn't be sure about Westmoreland. He always seemed to be marginally on my side, at least when he was giving me information.

One thing was clear: it was surprisingly easy to get them to allow me to board the derelict with them. I'm not certain I needed to worry about trying to get myself included. I think they intended to have me along from the beginning. In hindsight

I guess it was just more evidence of my expendability. It may even have been worse than that. I am tempted to believe to this day that if I'd had an accident, or been deliberately killed, they would have had a free hand to do as they wished with the *Cape Hatteras*. I never found out if that was part of their intentions.

As we turned to leave the bridge, I noticed that the poor lieutenant had been hovering behind me during the entire conversation and must have been ready to interject some minor detail that he knew from his own clearance level and passed out. Westmoreland and the Captain seemed not to notice him floating there. A moment later two men came onto the bridge with a body bag to collect him. He wasn't unconscious; his implant had killed him.

Chapter 21 Boarding Party

"December 22, 2259. 1700 hours. Log of Captain John Andrew Nelson, Commanding Officer, UNAG Mining Vessel **Cape Hatteras.** ***It has been 24 hours since I last heard from Galon and Marquez. I have dispatched Hunter and Goreman to the surface to search for them. The ship is experiencing a strange and unexplainable acceleration toward the surface of the asteroid. I have stayed behind to mind the ship and monitor this phenomenon."***

Unlike the case with my exploration of the *Victorious*, this time I was given a boarding party. I shouldn't say "given": I was just an advisor who knew the terrain. Other than that I was at the bottom of the ladder. My companions were four very gung-ho UNAG marines loaded with every kind of weapon man had yet devised. They had guns that shot old-fashioned bullets and lasers that could zero in on whatever they thought worthy of killing and incinerate it in fraction of a second. They could fire a grenade and blow a building sky high without the blast's even slightly straying in their direction. All of it was utterly useless against the anomaly. I warned them before we left that their weapons might merely annoy whatever was on the other side, but they maintained that they were following standard procedure and that they would treat the mission like any other.

I didn't get anywhere by arguing, so that was how the initial team was set up—except that they didn't give me a gun. I can't tell you how much that worried me. I wasn't concerned about fighting the anomaly; I knew that was impossible. I was worried about those marines and their guns when all I had in my hand was a portable welding torch. After seeing that dead lieutenant, my paranoia index had risen considerably. They could choose their moment, shoot me, and call it friendly fire, and I'd have no way to fight back except with the flame from that welder. I therefore intended to watch their every move very carefully.

At the time when the *Victorious* crew disappeared, the warship had been in the process of adjusting its position relative to the derelict, so its thrusters were firing. With the crew gone, there was no one left to shut them down. That caused the ship to list away from the derelict until the pressurized and flexible docking tunnel they had strung between them ruptured and tore in half. The mishap set off the *Cape Hatteras*'s automatic air-pressure sensor, something we didn't even know had electrical power, causing the ship to shut its own airlock doors to keep its atmosphere from being sucked out. Expecting that 200-year-old network of safety features to work together flawlessly was like going into a barn and expecting a dead horse to pull a wagon. It was inconceivable that it would still work, yet it did. It also had locked us out.

The only way to get onboard was either to cut a new hole or to take the welds out from our first entry point. We chose the welds because that option seemed easier. The airtight bulkheads on either side of the corridor were closed, courtesy of those marooned scientists who had hoped that shutting doors might keep the anomaly at bay. Once we gained access, we reasoned that all we'd need to do would be to seal ourselves back inside and make certain that the joint was airtight. Then we would empty a few tanks of pressurized air to fill the corridor. There were at least ten of those stored in the corridor by the engineers. Once we did that, it would be safe to open the bulkheads and take off our helmets. The marines wanted their ears and eyes free from the restraint. If the ring showed up, we'd have to leave through the airlock anyway, so they said we'd have plenty of time to put our helmets back on during the cycle. I didn't believe a word of it, but I went along with the plan.

I was able to cut into the ship with surprisingly little trouble. I simply made a small hole in one of the weld joints and moved out of its way. The air escaped fast enough to cut most of the rest of the bead loose.

The real problem I had was in sealing it shut and closing us in. My son might be a great welder, but I am not, so it took me a lot longer to close up the ship than it should have. None of the jarheads knew what to do, and by the time I had finished they were impatient and cranky. When I finally was done, they released the air from the tanks and opened the bulkhead door. We all took off our helmets at the same time. It was at this point that I expected they'd shoot me and get down to Westmoreland's work, whatever that *really* was.

"Where do we begin?" I asked, hoping that one of them had some kind of knowledge about what exactly we were looking for.

"Odd movement," Sergeant Chen replied. He produced a handheld device that could have only come from Titan.

"One of Dr. Westmoreland's toys?"

"Bingo, genius. We're supposed to move through the ship with this thing and look for any kind of deviation in the readings. It's your junkyard. Where should we go?"

"I'd suggest engineering. That's where the thing was when we first came onboard. After that I'm told it moved around the ship. We'd have to ask the scientists on the *Hyperion* about specifics."

I knew they'd check the entire ship anyway. I still wanted to try to get some of my specialists onboard if I could, if for no other reason than to serve as a deterrent against foul play, but they ignored my suggestion. We moved through the corridors slowly, Chen waving his detector back and forth. I noticed the pitch of his voice rising about halfway down the enclosed promenade. I remembered that we'd equalized the pressure in the redundant rooms with helium. Obviously one of them had leaked when I depressurized the corridor.

We passed through the cavernous cargo hold. The last few bars of gold had been moved to the *Hyperion* during the evacuation, and now it was just an open space with nothing in it but a few pieces of leftover mining equipment. The prospectors on 974-Bernhard had reused the original drilling platform from the mission. I remember marveling at it on my earlier visit because it was a tangible piece of the legend. My feelings were so different then. Despite the fact that I was standing on the famous wreck, I couldn't wait until this adventure was over. I wanted the ship safely in lunar orbit as a museum and the gold in the bank. I also wanted to forget that the anomaly had ever existed.

We made our way to the engine room, where I paused to examine the door. I wanted to make absolutely certain that there were no flickers of glowing blue light. There wasn't a trace. The engineering section was brightly illuminated with normal lighting, and a few of the panels were giving figures for the reactor we had repaired. It didn't seem like the room of dread it had been.

We moved from room to room through the engineering compartment. Chen seemed disappointed: his needle didn't so much as move a tenth of a millimeter. We then moved through the corridors again, stopping at each sealed door on the ship and trying to find something. By the end of our tour we were joking that we wished the damned anomaly would show up and take someone so we'd know whether the detector was working. So much helium had leaked into the atmosphere that we were all talking funny by that stage, and the air seemed as thin as that on a mountain top. It was not a problem, though. The atmospheric controls of the ship had been repaired by the marooned engineers, and it would be only a few hours more before the scrubbers and pumps returned the air to normal.

The last room we checked was Captain Nelson's quarters. I'd never been in there. Sanjay had inspected it briefly but left it pristine to ensure that his colleagues could methodically record later everything that was in it. I had deferred to them, but I admit that I'd always wanted to take a look. This was where Nelson had lived and spent his nights while running the *Cape Hatteras,* much as I did on my own ship, mulling over the day's activities and wondering what to do next.

At last I'd finally get a look. It was a disappointment. There were no secret handwritten journals, no cache of information about what had happened to him. He seems to have lived simply, though I guess that's no surprise—I did too. There was just one thing of interest in the room: his desk was covered with geological samples. I assumed that they were the rocks Westmoreland wanted, so I collected them up before stopping for a moment to examine one. They were crystals, black as coal and extremely heavy for their size. They had a sheen like cut onyx but were soft and seemed as though they might crumble if I applied too much pressure. I'd never seen anything like them before. They didn't register on the meter at all, but I assumed that Westmoreland would want to see them. I shrugged and put them in a box.

After a full eight hours on that ship, five tired men returned to the *Portsmouth*. It was nearly a full day since the *Victorious* had disappeared, and the mood onboard had improved. The crew was acting calmer and less confused, and the command structure seemed to be working again.

I had a quiet dinner with the Captain and Westmoreland. There wasn't much to say. We had found nothing with the detector, and there wasn't anything we could have done about it if we had. Westmoreland then broke the silence like an exploding fuel tank.

"We should tow the *Cape Hatteras* to Titan," he said. He knew full well that I'd go ballistic.

"I'd sooner cut off my own foot!" I exclaimed. "Why don't we just tow it to Earth? That's where I was going with it anyway, and that's where all your admirals and scientists are."

"My laboratory isn't on Earth. If we're going to learn about the foothold, we'll need my full equipment and resources."

"The foothold? Now there's a loaded word. I get the feeling you've been studying this phenomenon for a while."

He sighed before glancing at me. "Yes, as had my predecessors. We've been studying the anomaly for many years, Captain Hunter, longer than you've been alive. Officially it's called Project Halcyon."

"I thought you said we barely knew anything about it."

"That's true. We don't understand much at all, considering the time that's been spent on the project."

Surprisingly, the Captain wasn't interfering in the conversation. He was simply staring blankly at a light fixture.

"Captain, how are my ships?" I asked, just to make sure he

was alright.

"I've ordered them to take a position nearby but not too close. Your *Hyperion* has full engine power restored. I have to be clear, though: distance may not offer safety from the anomaly. In the event something else happens, it would be better if they were close to my weapons but still far enough away in case the anomaly comes back. That's assuming the *Portsmouth* will be the next target."

"I'm sure you'll also want to keep your weapons locked on my derelict and my fleet," I said. "Don't think I didn't notice that."

"That too," he said, still looking at the fixture.

"Why the paranoia? We aren't going to do anything," I said, as he redirected his gaze toward me.

"You've got a lot of gold on that ship, Mr. Hunter. You've already had a mutiny and two theft attempts. I'd have thought you would appreciate the free security that a Poseidon cruiser can provide. When all is said and done, I may even escort you back to Earth. For free."

I hadn't thought of it like that. I felt a little embarrassed, so I changed the subject.

"Dr. Westmoreland, you said that the crew were found on the asteroid. What had they been doing?"

"They had taken shelter in a cave. It had collapsed by the time the UNAG fact-finding mission reached them, but they dug it out, recovered the bodies, and then sealed the cavern again."

"How did they seal it?"

"Bombardment from orbit, as I recall."

"Why seal it? Why not leave it as it was?"

"Same reason you'd seal an abandoned well. If anyone went back there, like those prospectors who were working the asteroid, they didn't want anyone hurt if they ever ventured to the stony side of Walton's Rock."

He appeared a little uncomfortable. I wondered whether I had struck a nerve.

"There was something in there, wasn't there?"

"No, Captain Hunter, there wasn't. Now if you'll excuse me, I have work to do."

"Those crystals came from that cave, didn't they? They are important."

Dr. Westmoreland didn't answer but simply left the room. He usually shared information freely, but not now. Maybe I had outlived my usefulness, and there no longer was any reason to dangle carrots.

I sat with the Captain in awkward silence. He had gone back to concentrating on his meal, and I tried to focus on finishing my own. I was relieved when another officer appeared.

"Mr. Hunter, Captain, you're both needed on the bridge."

"On my way," the Captain said as he left the room like a racer hearing a starting gun.

"Why?" I asked as the officer and I shot toward the bridge.

"The *Hyperion* has contacted us. Someone's disappeared."

Chapter 22 Home

"December 23, 2259. 0800 hours. Log of Captain John Andrew Nelson, Commanding Officer, UNAG Mining Vessel* Cape Hatteras. *I have had to expend a great deal of fuel to maintain my orbit. I have confirmed the reason why: the asteroid's gravity has increased. There is no other explanation; no other known mechanism in the laws of physics could cause it. Yet, it is physically impossible.

I have no contact with my men on the surface. I do not know how the increased gravity will affect them. I cannot help them. The crystals are important. They seem to be growing, gaining mass through an unknown process. It could be related to the gravity. I feel ill, unclear, and very tired. I sense there is someone here with me, but I know there is no one."

I was relieved to get off that warship. I couldn't take any more of Dr. Westmoreland and the Captain of the *Portsmouth*'s double talk, and frankly they both had become outright strange. I couldn't tell what parts of the picture were misinformation and what parts were the truth. I returned to the salvor first. At least there everything made sense. For all the faults of Dr. Webb and his team, they spoke openly and candidly.

I was greeted in the *Hyperion*'s airlock by my ex-wife. Seeing her was a pleasure, which was a conflicted feeling to be sure, because I was seeing the first honestly readable face in days. I could tell from her expression that things were not well on the ship.

"We lost someone, Cam," Janet said.

"Are you certain? Have you searched the ship?"

"Yes, and we know where he was. It had to be the anomaly again."

"Who was it?"

She hesitated. "It was Sanjay Maheshtra."

I experienced a sinking feeling in the pit of my stomach. This wasn't someone I barely knew. It was Sanjay Maheshtra, someone I had grown close to and liked.

"What happened?" I asked.

"He'd gone off duty after finishing an analysis of the archeological placement of some objects on the derelict. He was alone for less than an hour before another crewman stopped by his quarters to drop off his laundry and found him missing."

"You searched the entire ship stem to stern?"

She didn't answer but just darted the usual look she gives me when I say something ridiculous.

"Still, we'll need to do a second search. I want to be very thorough before I inform Dr. Westmoreland. If I don't, he'll want to send a crew of his own over here to investigate. I'd like to keep the military off our ships as much as possible. Hopefully, a solid report will satisfy him."

I was being only half truthful. I hoped we'd find Sanjay alive and well, perhaps reading in some remote part of the ship. You do that out of shock, grasping at straws and praying that the news you've been given is somehow wrong. I didn't want to alarm Janet, but the other thing left unsaid was that a boarding crew would probably be made up of soldiers, and they would not leave their arms behind. Soldiers on my ships meant that they could seize control of them, using whatever excuse the UNAG devised. We would have no way of stopping them. I trusted Westmoreland to at least be civil, but I didn't trust the Captain at all.

Janet was hard at work, hoping to get more of the *Cape Hatteras*'s systems running, and wanted to get back to it. That left me alone in one of the two main halls of the salvor. I looked out the gallery windows that ran down the corridor. From that vantage point I could see all members of the fleet. It was a minor comfort to see our ships together again with the derelict, but I longed to get back to the *Amaranth Sun*. I hadn't talked with my crew in two days, and as much as I wanted to share my wealth of new information with the academicians, I felt that the time was not yet right. If I kept my mouth shut, I might prove my trustworthiness to Westmoreland and the Captain, such that they would be more forthcoming.

I stayed on the salvor long enough to supervise the search. Sanjay was nowhere to be found. I dutifully sent my report to Westmoreland, but I went much further than simply telling him about the disappearance. I included a very detailed account of my hallucinations up to that point, especially those on the *Victorious*. He'd asked me about them before, so if anyone would understand and not think I was crazy, it was he. Westmoreland didn't personally come over to the *Hyperion,* but he did send two officers to check things out. I was pleasantly surprised: they were unarmed and left quickly. My respect for Westmoreland rose again, albeit slightly.

Another surprise came in the form of a progress update *he* sent. I suppose he felt obligated after receiving mine. He and the Captain had been busy with devising a way to tow the *Cape Hatteras* to Titan. It seemed workable, but nothing would make me enthusiastic about the idea. I had to face reality: at least until that disappearance business was solved, I needed the authorities more than they needed me. Without them we would be at the mercy of whatever it was we were dealing with.

I reluctantly endorsed the plan. Early the next day the *Portsmouth* took the derelict in tow, and our little fleet charted a course for Saturn's largest moon, Titan.

I was preparing to return to the *Amaranth Sun* when Janet returned and pulled me aside. "Cam, there's another matter," she said. "Our week on the derelict gave me plenty of time to look at the logs."

I still hadn't had a chance to see them. One of the things I did on the *Hyperion* was to transfer copies to the *Amaranth Sun* so I could finally read them.

"What did you find?"

"Cam, Nelson went crazy. He abandoned his men on the asteroid. The last ten or so communications he received were pleas for rescue, but he ignored them all. He just kept talking about some kind of crystals in the geological samples and how important they were. He kept assuming that his crew was dead, even while his communications panels were lit up with messages from them. It's all damned odd."

"I found the samples in his quarters. Westmoreland has them now. Not very interesting crystals, if you ask me, just dirty black things."

"Do they have anything to do with the disappearances?"

"He doesn't know, and I'm sworn to secrecy. I can't really say much else."

"Well, going nuts is one thing, but there was no corpse. Do you think the phenomenon might have been manipulating him and then made him disappear like our people?" she asked.

"We don't know that it did. He could simply have shot himself out an airlock. Crazy people do crazy things. Look, I promise to tell you more just as soon as I can," I said.

She wasn't happy with that, but it's not as though she'd have told me what she knew if I were in her position. When I finally got back to the *Amaranth Sun*, the ship was a hornet's nest. Not one person there was any happier with me than my ex-wife was. All they'd heard from me in days were relayed messages from the *Portsmouth*, along with orders to go here and there without any explanation, and not a word about why that huge warship disappeared into a hole with a blue ring around it.

"Where the hell have you been?" Stacey asked angrily.

"Busy!" I said. "And do I have a story for you!" I might not tell the academicians what I knew, but I could tell my own crew some of it. They were my family and best friends whom I trusted implicitly. Telling them would also divert my attention from Sanjay's death.

"It had better be good," Stacey said, "or we're going to have a mutiny."

"It is!" I replied, before recounting everything that had happened on the submarine. Then I told them about the disappearing warship and the chaos onboard the *Portsmouth*. They were spellbound, listening intently over drinks as I triumphantly aired the UNAG's dirty laundry. It felt great to get some of that off my chest.

It continued going well until I told them why we were

going to Titan.

"Titan?" they said in unison.

"This is a treasure salvage, not a tour of the outer planets," Neil reminded me.

"Don't worry. Everything is under control. We'll get our treasure home, and it's not every day that you get invited to Titan," I replied, hoping to calm them down.

"I've heard that secret things happen there. Aliens and secret projects, that kind of thing," said Kurt.

"I've never heard that. They do engine research," I answered, not wanting to betray Westmoreland's trust.

"Yeah, I know an engineer who worked there for a few months on some kind of fuel-efficiency project. He said that most of the complex was off-limits. I told him it wasn't surprising that engine research would be secretive, but he said it was more than that. He also said that strange things happened while he was there. He even heard a rumor that they had an alien spacecraft hidden there so they could reverse-engineer its engines."

"They said that about Area 51 some 400 years ago," Stacey retorted. "It was just an elaborate hoax to draw attention away from the test projects that went on there. Now it's a museum."

"I'm just saying what I heard," Kurt replied.

"I heard it from the horse's mouth. Westmoreland is doing secret research there," I said.

"Talking to horses," Neil quipped. "No wonder you didn't call home. Why don't we give them the *Cape Hatteras* and get the *Hyperion* back to Earth and be rich?"

I glanced at my son disapprovingly.

"It's an old saying. And I couldn't call you. Those people on that warship kept me busy. Besides, Ed Iron wants that ship," I said.

"I know. I'm just glad to have you back and I'm sick of your being in constant danger and not letting me help."

I was going to try to come up with something reassuring but quickly gave up. A few hours later Janet interrupted us with a transmission.

"Cam, they've released us to board the *Cape Hatteras* again. We're not supposed to remove anything, but that Westmoreland creep doesn't think the danger is any worse there than on any of the other ships. I don't like it one bit that we need the military's permission to board our own derelict."

"I don't either. Open it up to the specialists then and see whether you can get anything else out of those logs."

"Will do. Oh, I have some good news. I know it will waste a lot of time to have Ed's tow ship go all the way out to Saturn to retrieve the *Cape Hatteras*, but I think we've solved that problem," she said.

"What have you got?"

"I didn't want to raise your hopes until we were sure, but we believe that we can get the engines running and bring her back to Earth under her own power if you refuel the *Cape Hatteras* at Titan. She's not a slow ship with those 100,000 lzs helium thrust giants she's got."

I was floored. It was hard to imagine an ancient ship firing its own engines and entering Earth orbit with every camera in the Earth-Moon system watching. It would be a sensation. I knew that Ed Iron would adore the idea.

"Refueling certainly isn't a problem at Saturn," I said. "It's a giant ball of helium. Do it. You have no idea how fantastic that will be! Ed will probably give your team a huge bonus, and I'll personally give you a huge kiss."

"Bonus yes, kiss no," she said before ending the transmission abruptly.

We passed into the Jupiter system without significant problems. Time seemed to pass faster thanks to the security of those two powerful ships traveling in my convoy. I felt safe, at least from claim-jumpers and pirates. I spent most of the travel time poring over Nelson's logs from the *Cape Hatteras* mission. I wasn't disappointed. They were as fascinating as Janet had made out. They seemed to make perfect sense for a while, but then his manner changed. He began saying bizarre things, coinciding with the moment he got hold of those crystals. I contacted Westmoreland.

"I've been reading the logs as you suggested. It has got to be those crystals, Doctor."

"We agreed with that inference until I got a chance to study their structure. Don't concern yourself with the crystals any longer."

"Are you certain? What did you find out?" I asked.

"Well, they have an unusual matrix and are extremely pure. They're not physically impossible and structurally they're just normal crystals. There's no magical or unknown element missing from the periodic table, no unusual properties. They're just a new kind of silicon-based crystal that we haven't seen before."

"That's not unusual? Something completely new like that?"

"Not at all. We find all kinds of new minerals in space. Conditions vary in the solar system, and all manner of unusual molecules can form that we might never see on Earth. These are no different. Look, if they were related to the foothold, it should have formed by now and made me disappear. They certainly shouldn't have driven Captain Nelson crazy. They're just rocks. We must have missed something. Make certain that your people on that derelict let me know of anything unusual they run across."

I realized why Westmoreland had let the academicians back on the ship: he wanted them to comb for anything that I might have missed. There was always an ulterior motive with that guy.

"I'll do that, but from what I can tell that ship is just an archeological site now. Completely normal, with nothing unusual happening whatsoever."

"We'll know more when I have access to my equipment at Titan. We're still weeks out, but I have to reiterate that you should keep this business about the crystals quiet along with everything else. The less your people know, the better."

That sounded ominous. First he downplayed the crystals, and then he wanted them kept secret. It had to be more misinformation. Also, I hadn't heard him speak quite that way before. He was forceful and authoritative rather than benignly good-natured.

I had no idea what he wanted me to say to the specialists.

I'd have to tell them that everything was normal and fine but that, if something weird happened, I should know immediately. I didn't see how that would be believable, but that's what I did say. They seemed to shrug it off and go along with things for once.

Just before leaving the Jupiter system, another transmission came through for me.

"Cam, there's a message for you," Stacey said. It was Mary Joanna.

"Cammy, come give me kisses before I leave!" she said, seeming more like her alter ego of Sister Mary Joanna. I think she was slipping back into character.

"Leave? Aren't you going to Titan with us in your big powerful ship?"

"I'm taking the *Neptune's Revenge* back to Europa. They're not going to like it, but someone's got to tell them that Stunt was the pirate."

"Kisses and hugs!" I said, though I would have preferred to keep that ship and its immense weaponry with us.

"Watch your back, Cammy. You're in with a tough crowd right now. That's all I can say."

"Thanks, Agent Mary Joanna, and best of luck on Europa. Any plans?"

"I'm thinking of running for mayor," she replied with a giggle and a squeal.

Chapter 23 Day 314

"December 23, 2259. 0900 hours. Supplemental Log. I have spent as much fuel as I can afford. I have been waiting for my crew to return but can delay no longer. I have no choice but to break free and set a course. I can feel others with me, voices that speak to me as I sleep. They whisper to ask me whether I am John Nelson, Salus, or one of them."

We entered Titan orbit three months after the anomaly's last appearance. We immediately began refueling the *Cape Hatteras* at the orbital maintenance station. So few people had a reason to visit Titan that its station was unmanned. It was just a self-service facility designed as a waypoint to the Uranus system rather than a destination in itself.

It was strange to see the ship cradled in a space dock, active and alive with my engineers working feverishly to mate outdated connectors to new ones. At Westmoreland's request I reluctantly transferred back to the *Portsmouth* to work more closely with him. I ran into him on my way to the bridge.

"Odd place for a secret UNAG installation," I said, "on a planet controlled by the Eurorussian Union."

"Why would you say that? What better place could there be to hide it?"

"Since you put it that way. . . ."

"No one in the UNAG believes we'd have a facility here, and the public in Eurorussia have no idea that it's a UNAG installation. It's perfect!" he replied.

"Even so you had to have cut a deal with them."

"That's reading between the lines. Maybe you should have been a spy," Westmoreland said.

"Maybe I am one."

"I'd know about it if you were. To answer your question, yes, we did cut a deal, along with the Asian-African Union, which has a presence here as well. Cam, this is a problem that Earth itself dealt with sans union squabbling. It was deemed too critical."

"Critical enough that everyone united, eh?" I was skeptical that the unions would ever set their differences aside and consider anything in the universe pressing enough to suspend their little games. Westmoreland's tone became more somber as we delved deeper into the topic.

"That's exactly what happened two centuries ago. And we're still united on this issue."

"The anomaly is a bigger threat than I know, isn't it?" I asked.

"There's nothing to indicate that it couldn't destroy Earth."

"And that's why we came here. It's the real reason," I said. "Being in your lab won't let you do anything more than you could have done at the Trojan asteroid. You wanted to get this thing as far away from home as you could."

"Yes, that's true, or partly so. I'm just one scientist, Cam. There are more on Titan, and I have no doubt that Earth will fast-track their best out here to join us. This is still the most effective way we can study the phenomenon, and the safest."

"Who else knows on Earth?"

"Just the admiralties of the unions, all three of them."

I dropped the conversation at that. I couldn't argue with him. I didn't want Earth—my home as much as anyone else's—destroyed, and I had moved far beyond any need for public secrecy. The UNAG would take care of that for me.

Titan loomed close in the *Portsmouth*'s windows. It was a dim orange ball whose surface features were hidden by a thick smog that never dissipates. Moments later Saturn rose from behind the moon's limb as we orbited close and fast. The glory of its rings and subdued tan color made this place seem very alien. Of all the planets Saturn is the most captivating. It mesmerizes you when you're near it, always reminding you that you are very far from home. It's these kinds of places that lie in the universe beyond, if we can ever find a way to reach them.

I boarded a military transport bound for the surface with Dr. Westmoreland. He was silent throughout the entire voyage, reminding me of a penitent monk returning to his monastery from an excursion into the secular world. Westmoreland's old life, his normalcy, was resuming with all its layers of secrecy and isolation, shrouding the man I'd first met on the *Portsmouth.* His almost childlike delight in annoying the Captain by giving out just a little too much information was gone. Here he had to safeguard his secrets.

I had never been to the surface of Titan before, since there was little reason for any ordinary person to go there. It was the place of the geniuses and their engines, and if you didn't have an IQ the size of Jupiter, you didn't belong there.

We landed softly on a pad outside what appeared to be a research station. I paused at a window to marvel at the orange landscape stretching into the smog beyond. It was raining large, clear drops of liquefied hydrocarbons that undulated and fell slowly to the surface, collecting and flowing to a lake just barely discernible as a black smear at the limits of visibility.

To get to the laboratories, we had to use a different kind of suit. More like something designed for diving, I couldn't get accustomed to it. It was comprised of a paper-thin layer of highly efficient insulation along with a tight-fitting plastic mask that left no part of your skin exposed. It was very cold on Titan, but that system was all that was needed. It made me feel naked standing on an alien world without the bulk of a moon suit surrounding my body.

Through the Titan suit's thinness I could feel the rain drops slowly undulate down my arms before dripping to the ground below. They seemed almost alive, behaving like giant versions of amoebas living in the different rules of low-G. What felt like soft rocks crumbled beneath my feet, yielding to a permanent substrate as hard as concrete. They were made of a wet methane slush that thinly covered water ice that was permanently frozen. Water was a rock on Titan, a mineral that never became a liquid except deep below its surface. Miles underneath the surface was a liquid ocean, but there was no life in that sterile mix of water and ammonia.

Titan's life existed on its surface in the form of extremophile microbes adapted to live on a methanological cycle instead of a water one. Metabolizing hydrogen instead of oxygen and pulling life-giving energy from acetylene in the bitter cold of −290° F, they were no more related to our warm organic chemistry than an elephant was to a desk. We were nothing to them, and they were nothing to us. That is expected to change in six billion years when the sun expands and Earth's role in the solar system's grand production ends, making a warmer Titan into evolution's new forge. No one knows what life on that world might become.

Westmoreland led me into an entrance located at the eastern side of the research institute. I knew that I was not at the famous engine technology center. There were no domes, though they could have easily built them. The buildings were more like the airtight steel sheds at a science station in Antarctica. The door sealed behind us. It was a kind of airlock, but instead of air rushing into a vacuum, the air pushed out the denser Titanian atmosphere. I removed my helmet and smelled the strong residual lighter-fluid stench of this world.

"This lock is the most dangerous place on Titan, Captain Hunter. One spark in the presence of oxygen and this stuff becomes highly flammable, like hydrocarbons on Earth. We went to great lengths to prevent accidental ignitions. We coated everything in rubber and installed fire suppression systems, but we still have the occasional accident every few years. My predecessor died precisely where you're standing."

"I had no idea," I said, moving quickly out of the antechamber as a glass door slid open.

"Accidents generate public interest. When something happens that might attract eyes, even from just the Propulsion Institute, we have to cover it up. As far as anyone outside this station knows, Dr. Halsey died in a vehicle accident on a trip to check a weather station."

"What caused the fire?" I asked.

"Just a simple spark from a malfunctioning battery in an instrument he was carrying. We tried to get him out, but it happened so fast that there was nothing we could have done. The hydrocarbons are in the atmosphere itself, and the moment the oxygen started flooding the room, the air simply ignited. We now have an intermediate stage. Inert neon is pumped in before the breathable air. We think it's safer. At least we haven't had any further accidents . . . yet."

The door closed behind us. In a place like that, it was only natural to wonder whether Dr. Halsey's death was *really* an accident.

"Are we safe now?"

"Perfectly. It's the necessary smallness of the lock that makes it dangerous. In a larger room like this one, the gases diffuse. Even so we have to filter the air constantly to prevent explosive concentrations from accumulating. No smoking please. I understand that you were on Europa recently."

Westmoreland might have thought it safe, but I still smelled lighter fluid.

"Where is the Propulsion Institute?" I asked. "I didn't see it when we were landing."

"In another complex about 400 miles from here. They don't know much about us. They think we're a science outpost with a crew of two. In reality, we've got 18."

We bounced down the hall. It was perfectly white from floor to ceiling with closed black doors along its length, all with labels and warnings on them.

"Vaporization Threat. Do Not Use the Floor," I whispered aloud to myself as I read some of them. Another read: "Warning: Time Distortion."

"Bizarre things happen here, Captain. I wish I could tell you more, but believe me when I say you don't want to know."

I was compelled to accept that at face value, especially when I saw a warning on a door covered with locks. It said: "Existence Alert! Abnormal Space. DL-828 Access Only."

The doctor led me into a large central hall. It was circular with long corridors radiating from it in all directions. In one corridor I could see scientists in lab coats moving between doors and two more standing around talking to each other. Most of the other corridors were empty. I assumed them to be living quarters, other labs, storage areas, and the like. He led me down one of the deserted ones, turned to a door about halfway down, and unlocked it.

The lights sensed our presence and switched on. The room was a disused laboratory filled with covered equipment. At the opposite end of the room was another door. Westmoreland opened it, revealing a relatively straightforward office. He sat down behind the desk and motioned for me to have a seat.

"We can talk freely here," he said. "This lab hasn't been used in some months. I doubt anyone's bugged it."

"Easy for you to say. The anomaly could have bugged it," I said, intending to be facetious, but I think I sounded serious.

"I wouldn't discount that. We can't discount anything. Captain Hunter. Let me level with you. We face an alien species . . . no, I can't use that term. A species occupying the same physical space as we do, but living in a higher vibration of matter."

"Higher vibration?"

"Yes, that's the only way to say it. Their matter, what we call dark matter, exists in a completely non-interactive state with ours, at least on this side of the gateway. It doesn't parallel ours except in one way: gravity. Otherwise they could be all around us, and we wouldn't see them."

"Yes, I understand that much."

"We think that these aliens detected us much as we detected dark matter initially. They can see that there's more gravity in their universe than their own kind of matter can produce. We're the same to them as they are to us."

"Makes sense so far. So they can't see us. They just see the gravity that our matter creates in their universe."

"Right. And that should be the end of it. But it isn't.

Somehow they're able to open a gateway, a method for bringing our matter into their vibration of the universe. The problem is that our matter can't exist there; it would have to change state and become dark matter. We don't know whether whatever is drawn into the foothold does that or is destroyed. They may even be able to choose what happens."

"That's what they told me before the warship disappeared. In so many words, anyway. Whatever goes through the anomaly stops existing."

"Either way, that's why we refer to the foothold as a weapon. That's how they've always used it—to kill people. Except once: the initial contact on the *Cape Hatteras*. They seem to have manipulated Captain Nelson and then possibly tried to bring him through without killing him. That raised an important question at the time. If they could bring us there, could they come here with an invasion fleet? Could they use the foothold to destroy our defenses and conquer us?"

"But they haven't done that. Could that mean they are peaceful? Did we make them angry?"

"We don't have the answer to that, Captain Hunter."

"But you said that there was contact. What happened when your clean-up crew disappeared? Why did they fill the *Cape Hatteras*'s engineering room with ice?"

"We think that the density of our matter changes the equation for the foothold. Density somehow alters the properties of the anomaly on the other side. It could be that while we think there is no interaction in our universe between gravity, there may be an interaction on the other side that we aren't aware of. That's why this facility was built. We were to answer that question and find a way to use the anomaly against them. But I have to be honest. It's been decades, and we have little to show for it."

"Where do the crystals figure into this?"

"Having matter around isn't enough to form the anomaly. If it were, we'd see them everywhere as a normal part of the universe. There must be a special kind of matter, and that's where the crystals come in."

"You found out what they do?"

"Not precisely, and I'm still not certain they mean anything. But I'm confident that we can find out the answer here. I've already had them brought to one of the labs."

I wasn't comfortable in that station, and I had a mounting suspicion that I might not have the freedom to leave it. I decided to test my gut feeling.

"And why am I here? Let's be frank: you don't need me. I would be just as useful sitting on the *Amaranth Sun*."

"The reason should be clear, Captain Hunter."

"What do you mean?"

"You're the only person since Nelson to whom they've spoken to instead of outright killing."

Chapter 24 Day 316

"December 23, 2259. I am Lieutenant Philip Marquez, Staff Mining Operations Specialist on the UNAG Vessel **Cape Hatteras.** *I am recording this log in the event that we are not able to return home. We have been sending messages to Captain Nelson for hours, but he does not respond. I have been joined by two more members of the crew. They very nearly crashed. Something has changed. Gravity is different somehow. We feel heavier, and the transport pods register that they cannot take off from the asteroid. I worry that Nelson has been incapacitated or that the* **Cape Hatteras** *has been destroyed. Something is very wrong with this place."*

Westmoreland was kind enough to allow me access to a communications station to contact my fleet, so long as I agreed to oversight by his assistant. That man listened to every word I said with unnervingly close attention. His piercing and unflinching gaze made a normal conversation impossible, along with the fact that he was holding a kill switch to end my transmission the moment I let something sensitive slip.

Janet had received word from Ed Iron. The owners of the salvor had disavowed any knowledge of Keating's plan, though they did admit they were paying him poorly. Ed was furious. He had been under the impression that everyone would receive a proper cut, ensuring that no one had a motive to try anything underhanded. He took the expensive step of purchasing the *Hyperion* outright to avoid any entanglements that might have required the ship to return to Earth to pick up a new crew.

He had given day-to-day operational command of the

Hyperion to my ex-wife after she told him about her plan to resurrect the derelict's engines. He loved the idea, but he was very concerned about the time we were spending at Titan. He was on a schedule and needed to get that antique ship home to coincide with the grand opening of the hotel. Unveiling the *Cape Hatteras* was to be a publicity stunt, and along with exhibiting the gold it would be the ultimate two-for-one.

My ex-wife as a captain! I knew her head would swell to epic proportions as a skipper with a nearly equal footing with me. I figured that she'd make herself a stubborn pain in my side just for the fun of it, but I was also aware that she was eminently qualified. I could live with Ed's decision. I was still the commander of the overall operation and of my little *Amaranth Sun*. That's all I had ever wanted to be.

On my ship things were going well. Although it had been two days since I last spoke to them, much to my surprise Neil and Stacey hadn't fought at all. Kurt had come up with a new recipe for tarpotch cheese dip, and the *Amaranth Sun* was running as though she had been built yesterday.

On Titan I hadn't done much of anything in those two days except cool my heels in that room. I hadn't even seen Westmoreland, just his nameless assistant. I'd tried to call him Dr. Lyman, but he looked at me mystified before realizing that I was reading his name tag. He said that the coat belonged to another scientist and that Lyman wasn't his real name. But he would never reveal what his name actually was. When I finally did see Westmoreland in person, he seemed bothered.

"You act as though you have something serious on your mind," I observed as he walked into my quarters, rubbing his forehead.

"Well, it's just the stresses of running this station. Your

problem isn't the only thing we're working on."

"I'd love to hear about some of that."

"Need to know only," he said. "I didn't mind giving you bits and pieces that the Captain of the *Portsmouth* wouldn't, but here it's an entirely different situation. I'm more accountable and very closely watched."

"I understand how you feel. I have investors who watch me. I just hope that you can figure out how to get rid of the anomaly. Have you had any luck?"

"We're working on it," he responded. "We've got some theories and a few leads, but nothing of significance to report yet. But there's no reason to keep you cooped up in here, Cam. I apologize for not thinking of you sooner."

"It's alright. I've enjoyed my time in this room looking at the walls. Can I walk around the station?"

"Not really, sorry, but you're welcome to suit up and explore Titan if you wish. It's a fascinating moon; there's no other place like it. We've got a shed full of skimmerloons if you'd like to take one out for a ride."

"Skimmerloons?"

"Our name for the best mode of travel on Titan. It's a cross between a sort of hot-air balloon and a rocket sled. The engines were designed specifically for Titan. They won't work anywhere else in the solar system."

"Sounds interesting, a specially designed engine just for Titan. I might do that if I get cabin fever, but for now I'd rather not take the risk. Going through that lock is something I'd like to do as seldom as possible." I wondered whether the song-and-dance about the death of his predecessor was intended to scare me and keep me from wanting to go outside. If so, it had worked.

"I can't blame you," Westmoreland said. "I always wonder when I'll be on the losing end of the statistics. I pass through it at least three times a week. But the offer's there for you anyway. Just ask my assistant, and he can escort you to the lock and show you the skimmerloon shed."

"What is his name anyway?"

"Who?" Westmoreland asked.

"Your assistant?"

"Oh!" he said with a chuckle. "We're supposed to use code names here. Most of us call him Dr. Lyman."

"He seemed surprised when I called him that."

"He's odd like that."

"Is your name really Westmoreland?" I asked.

"Usually," he said as he opened the door, before pausing to say something else. "Cam, I can't say much yet, but I'll tell you one thing. The crystals are interacting with some of our experiments."

He walked out and shut the door before I had a chance to press for more information. I spent most of the rest of that day reading some of the books that filled the shelves in my room. I'd hoped they might shed light on some of the things that go on there, but they essentially fell into two categories: manuals about living on Titan, and books so technical that I had no idea what they were about. I tried for a little while to make some sense of a ten-volume set full of equations and tables, but I gave up and contented myself with the colonization manuals.

One I found particularly interesting. It was a survival manual detailing what you should do if you got lost on Titan. That wouldn't have been hard. Visibility was typically very low, and if you wandered more than a few hundred feet from a settlement, you might not be able to find it again. I had read that visibility dropped to ten feet during really bad weather, but sometimes it would inexplicably clear and you could see for some distance.

The author of the book had formulated a methodology for surviving days in that environment with only an intravenous sustenance backpack. He was so convincing, and covered so many contingencies, that I thought he must have lived on his own out there for an extended period of time and tried everything himself. The only thing that would kill you, no matter what, was the cold. If you weren't wearing a long-term exposure suit, you would freeze to death well before you starved.

He even had a plan if your pack failed and you ran out of water. It showed how to identify which rocks were the water ice. Then you were to slip one under the face mask very quickly, wait a certain amount of time for it to warm up to nearly the melting point, and then manipulate it with your tongue against the glass mask and into your mouth—though it wasn't recommended to do that for very long with all the ammonia and hydrocarbon contamination. I was just getting into a chapter about setting a broken leg by yourself, which also seemed to come from personal experience, when the door slid open again. It was Lyman.

"Someone is here to see you. A Captain Janet Allison. She

transferred down on an unauthorized transport pod, and we found her banging on the atmospheric lock door. You should warn her that we're technically supposed to shoot intruders."

"I'll tell her. Please send her in." I wasn't used to my ex-wife’s new title or reversion to her maiden name, nor had I seen anyone carrying weapons. I guessed that the latter was just more misinformation.

"Of course, but I'll have to stay here and monitor the conversation," Lyman said.

Janet came through the door looking very angry. I cringed out of habit, though I didn't intend to.

"What are you cringing for?" she asked.

"You must be in a bad mood," I said.

"You always were a bit of a coward."

"I've salvaged some of the most dangerous wrecks in the solar system. I am not a coward. You're just mean sometimes."

"I've polished that act over the years, but I'm not here to oppress you, Cam. I came to check on you. They weren't telling us much up there, and the crew got worried. Of course, I was more concerned with a malfunctioning toilet on my ship, but I didn't want any of the others to take the risk of barging in down here."

"I'm surprised they let you in," I observed.

"Are you really?"

"Well, I guess not." If anyone could bully their way into a place, it was she. "I can't say much because it’s all classified. Just studying something we found on the *Cape Hatteras*."

"I assume you're referring to Captain Nelson's crystals."

"Yes." I half expected Lyman to pull a gun. Instead, he shot a dagger glance with those damned eyes of his. They reminded me of the dark windows of the *Cape Hatteras* when we first found it.

"Your son is very worried. You told him more than you told me, didn't you?"

"Just his overactive imagination. Don't worry. We'll get past this and be on our way to make Ed Iron happy with his gold and his ship."

"Speaking of which," said Janet, "Ed asked us to check the assay of the gold as a precaution. He said that the thieves might have replaced it with coated lead and moved the haul onto a third ship without our knowing. I thought that was a little paranoid and unlikely, but he mentioned that you've fallen for that trick before."

She was referring not to a salvage but to something I'd bought. I'd run into an old shipmate on Mars once who said he had a small unrecorded treasure from an unmanned transport pod that had hit an asteroid and embedded itself in its side. It was carrying a consignment of gold coins, and he just wanted to sell them for whatever the melt price was. I bought the whole lot. I figured that they could always be taken back to Earth and sold as shipwreck salvage coins to collectors. Every single one of them was a fake.

"I deny every word of it."

"Yeah, well anyway, we drilled through one of the bars to make sure it was solid, and then we assayed the dust. Everything's fine. It's pure gold. But we also measured the weights in the gravity ring on my ship. The bars are heavier by several grams than their markings indicate. The *Cape Hatteras* mission must have taken faulty measurements."

"I wouldn't be surprised. You can't just weigh something in space when there's no gravity. You have to use other methods such as measuring volume. That introduces unreliability. Our measurements could be off just as easily if the *Hyperion*'s gravity ring were rotating just a little too fast. Either way, I won't complain if we've got more gold than we thought."

"Neither will I. The crew thought it would be nice to use the leftover gold dust to make a gift for you. Neil made the mold and cast it, and Ed Iron composed the inscription himself," she said. She handed me a gorgeous pendant in the shape of the *Cape Hatteras*. On the bottom was written: "To Captain Camden Hunter. The haul! With love from Ed and your crew."

"Thanks! It's beautiful," I said, holding the pendant up and admiring its detail.

"It's not from me. The best I'd have given you is a checklist to make that bucket you command safer for space travel. I have a son living on that thing."

"The *Amaranth Sun* is not a bucket. It was a great ship of exploration before I acquired it. Do you know who owned that ship before me? Guiscard Van der Boort."

"The guy who was eaten by a shark?"

"Well, yes, but he's more famous for his exploration of the Kuiper Belt. He mapped something like thirty percent of the rocks out there. He discovered more minor planets than any other person in history, and he was the first to see the Eye of Minerva!"

"I just remember how he died. You've got my son on a ship formerly owned by a man who wasn't smart enough to get out of a tank full of sharks to eat a roast beef sandwich."

"He was a great marine biologist too!"

"And lazy. Really, just climb out of the tank to eat lunch," Janet jibed.

"You're hopeless. No sense of adventure or greatness."

"Oh, and I'm sitting on Earth right now knitting a sweater to send to my son."

"I didn't mean that," I said.

"I know you didn't. I've got to get back. Listen, take care of yourself here and return to your bucket as soon as you can. I don't like this facility. The military won't tell us anything about it. When I looked in the databases to investigate, all I found was that the damned place doesn't exist. The only thing that's supposed to be on this moon is the Propulsion Institute and a few peripheral science stations. I'd have never have found it if I hadn't triangulated its location from your transmission."

"That took work and foresight. I'm touched that you care."

"I don't want any interruptions in my alimony payments."

After Dr. Allison and Lyman left, loneliness returned. There was only one advantage to being in that room: I slept well. I must have slumbered for twelve hours that night. The odd thing was that I don't remember a single dream during my entire time on Titan, except that is for one. I remember standing on Titan with no suit; there was no wind or anything, just orange fog. In front of me I saw a black cloud vaguely forming into the shape of a man, but I somehow could tell that he was experiencing great difficulty in forming fully. When I popped half awake, it struck me as very profound and unnatural, but that feeling quickly faded as I awoke fully and dismissed it as just a very strange dream.

The next morning, when someone finally came to my quarters, it was Westmoreland. "Cam," he said without preamble, "we've got something."

I sat up in bed. "What?" I asked, still a little groggy.

"We know what the crystals are reacting to. It's the gravity here."

"Here?"

"Yes, there was no gravity on that derelict. But when we brought them here, they began to grow. Microscopically slow at first, but it's beginning to progress faster."

"Faster doesn't sound good. How fast?"

"Exponentially, and we think we have discovered why. The orbit of Titan is slightly elliptical like a squashed circle. At one point in its orbit it's further out from Saturn, but then it gets a little closer. We're halfway to the closest point. The added gravity of Titan and Saturn itself seems to be driving the crystals to grow."

"How? What's the mechanism?"

"We don't know. But one thing is clear: there could be some kind of critical mass involved. If the crystals multiply to become a certain amount, does the equation change? Does that allow the foothold to form? Or is there more to it? We just haven't got the answers yet."

"What makes you think there would be a critical mass?"

"They reached a certain point this morning while you were sleeping. It was a ratio: twice the size that they were before we brought them here. At that exact point, they began to emit blue light," he said.

"The same blue light as in the *Cape Hatteras*'s cargo hold?"

"Yes, but it's very weak. You can barely see it; however, it's getting steadily brighter. That's all we know, Cam. I'll keep you posted, but I may be able to bring you in to see them within a day or two."

"Do you think the crystals will shrink if we get them off this moon?"

"I don't know yet, but that may be important. There's something about these crystals, Cam. They hold some kind of key, but I don't know what that is. It's maddening. I can hardly stop studying them and leave them long enough to speak with you. I'll return for you in a day or two at most."

Westmoreland abruptly left. His words chilled me to the bone.

Chapter 25 Day 318

"December 24, 2259. Lieutenant Philip Marquez, Staff Mining Operations Specialist on the UNAG Vessel* Cape Hatteras. *The heaviness is unbearable. I can move only my arms. It is impossible to stand. The cavern is beginning to collapse around us. Gravity is so much stronger. We cannot move; there is no way out. Immediate rescue required. Captain Nelson, why won't you respond?"

I received a cryptic message from Westmoreland at lunchtime the next day. I had just been sitting down to a chicken sandwich dropped off by a very untalkative Lyman. He didn't seem to know me. Shortly afterwards he came back and handed me a messenger pad. He was in a hurry to get away from me, apologizing by citing other pressing duties. I surmised that Westmoreland must have been tightly limiting contact with me.

"My assistant will bring you to Lab 24b in one hour. We think you'll be useful," the pad said in yellow electronic handwriting.

There was one recurrent pattern in my dealings with Westmoreland: being useful always meant being exposed to danger. He had mentioned having me try to talk to what I now thought of as the Dark Matter Beings, and I was prepared to do that, but I didn't like it. After all, the last thing they had said to me was that I was going to stop existing, though they had also suggested that I run. That didn't seem hostile on its face; it seemed more like a warning. But there is also such a thing as a dumb move, and trying to talk to them felt like one.

I didn't think I had any choice anyway. My quarters were effectively a prison cell. They let me have contact with my ships but not without supervision. They'd allow me go outside, but the hostile environment would eventually force me back into the fold. I could probably even have returned to my ships and left the Saturn system, except that there was a giant warship parked off the *Amaranth Sun*'s starboard bow, not to mention an anomaly that was still loose and ready to kill. I was trapped, and they knew it.

When the hour was up, no one had come for me. I waited another ten minutes before I decided to go out the door on my own. It was the first time I had tried to leave the room. I was surprised to find that it had been unlocked the whole time. In hindsight that's just the kind of thing Westmoreland would do: tell me I couldn't leave to cover himself, but then leave the door unlocked so I could meddle. I found no guards outside.

I tried the door across from mine. It was unmarked and also had no locks. As the door slid open, it revealed itself to be a storage room full of lab coats. Every one of them was marked "Dr. Lyman."

I walked down the hall and saw Westmoreland standing in the central hub. He seemed surprised and glanced at the clock on his pad, causing me to wonder whether he'd simply lost track of time. He motioned for me to sit down at the meeting table that occupied the center of the hub.

"Titan orbits just under once every fifteen days," he said. "We're nearing its closest point to Saturn. It's just a few hours away, and something else has happened. It's what I was afraid of, Cam. The crystals seem to have reached the critical mass I spoke of, and we are no longer seeing just the blue radiation. We're also seeing footholds."

"Footholds! How many?" I was thinking I might be ready to take that skimmerloon trip and get out of the laboratory for a while.

"Thousands, but they're very tiny. They can only be observed with the aid of an imaging scanner. The largest one we've seen was about a tenth of a millimeter. They don't seem to be dangerous at that size."

He showed me a series of microscope images on a pad. The anomalies all appeared identical to the full-sized model that destroyed the warship.

"For now they're confined inside the crystals. We're not certain why. There isn't any reason we can think of that would restrict them to anything specific. It seems to be that crystalline matter contains them, at least until they have enough available energy to escape. Or they may require a catalyst."

"Is that why the engineering section of the *Cape Hatteras* was flooded with water so that it would freeze into ice and hold the anomaly?"

"Very perceptive. Yes. The expedition hoped that confining the anomaly inside ice might keep it bottled up indefinitely and possibly even weaken it. We think it did, at least to some extent, but there seem be other phenomena involved. We think that whatever is on the other side can communicate through the gateway, even if it is confined. That's how it put you to sleep and affected your dreams."

That seemed to make sense. The anomaly didn't kill Roberts until we'd melted the ice, but it was affecting Sanjay and me well before then.

"So how does the anomaly gather energy and escape?" I

asked.

"We're not certain yet. With the microscopic rings appearing, we think that whatever was speaking to you might be able to do it again now. That must be how they established contact with Nelson—by somehow manipulating the gravity of 974-Bernhard to increase the power and size of the crystals he had on the *Cape Hatteras*."

"How do you increase the gravity of an asteroid without adding more rock to make it bigger?"

"That's not the only way you can do it. All you have to do is to add something else that possesses gravity. Add dark matter to the asteroid, and you will increase its gravitational pull."

"Well, when do I try to speak to them? I'll talk to the crystals all day long, but that doesn't mean they'll answer."

"We should start now, but I want you to know that the risk is very high. We don't have a good understanding of this."

"You were never worried about the risks to me before. I must be very special now. You can't find anyone else that the crystals will talk to, can you?"

"It's shown no reaction to anyone except you."

Westmoreland led me to Lab 24b. It was set up much like the one we'd visited when I first arrived, but the equipment was powered up. Dr. Lyman was in the room working with what appeared to be some kind of a fusion reactor connected to a chamber. I guessed that it was some kind of attempt to contain a ring with other kinds of energy, but I wasn't certain I'd want to bet on its working. On the far table were the crystals. They were easily ten times the size they were when I last saw them, and the blue radiation was unmistakably bright.

Westmoreland motioned for Lyman to leave the room.

"Doctor," I asked, "why is there a room full of lab coats with Lyman's name on them?"

"Let's just say that the Propulsion Institute's belief that there are only two *people* at this station isn't entirely inaccurate. But now to the matter at hand. Walk toward the crystals, and let's see how they react."

When I walked nearer to the crystals, they instantly flared. The blue radiation rose in intensity until it was so bright that it became difficult to look at. The heightened glow was followed by some kind of reaction that caused sparks to emanate from most of the machinery in the room.

"Step back!" Westmoreland yelled, and I quickly did.

The crystals dimmed somewhat, but not quite to their former level. They had gained some kind of energy from me.

"Well, Captain Hunter, it seems they still like you."

"Should I speak to them?"

"Might as well try."

"Greetings from Earth!" I yelled from across the room, waiting for a response. There was none.

"Try again," Westmoreland suggested.

"Earth sends a friendly hello to the dark-matter universe." The crystals still seemed unimpressed.

"I don't think this is working, Doctor. Those things looked as though they were going to explode when I got close to them."

"Stay here for a while in the hub. I want to take more readings before we try anything else."

I waited at the conference table for what seemed like most of the rest of the day. A strong feeling of anticipation had filled me and made the time pass slowly. In reality it was barely past four in the afternoon when Westmoreland reappeared. He was holding a sample of the crystal.

"Cam, I want you to stand at the other end of the hub."

I stood up and walked to the far wall. He approached me slowly. The closer he got, the brighter the crystal became.

"We think this sample is still well below the critical mass," he said as he drew closer.

"Be ready to throw that thing across the room if this goes badly," I said. I'll admit that I was frightened out of my wits.

As Westmoreland inched closer, the crystal grew brighter and brighter. When he got about three feet from me, the blue glow began to detach from the crystal and form a weak transparent ring around the rock. There was no black hole as with the full-power anomaly, but I could sense that it was getting close to breaking through. Westmoreland slowly handed the crystal to me. I held it in my palm, which became encircled by the blue light. My hand felt as though it were being lightly shocked with waves of electricity.

"Cam, this small crystal is growing as we speak. I believe the main group in the lab will achieve the critical mass needed to open the foothold within a few days. But there's a mystery: unless they've shrunk over the years, the mass in that room is much larger than it was on the *Cape Hatteras*. And there's something else. You are the catalyst. But now the question is why they are responsive to you and not me. You've got some kind of connection to them that I can't explain. I'd like to try the lab experiment again," he said as I set the crystal on the conference table.

"Do you have a working theory on how gravity is making them grow?"

"I do. I think the presence of gravity is allowing a molecule to form that incorporates not only normal matter but dark matter as well. Think of it as a hybrid molecule. It's a normal crystal here, but it has a counterpart in their universe that creates a molecule existing in both universes at once. The growth derives from more and more dark matter attaching itself to the crystal lattice in a organized way. We think it's robbing the table and the air of the atomic building blocks it needs to grow in our universe. It's consuming the table. But we don't know why certain people would be the catalyst for the energy release. Why they needed you or Nelson, and killed all the others, is very unclear."

We stepped into the lab again, and I started walking closer to the mass of crystals. They hadn't lost their accumulated glow; they were still blindingly bright.

"The energy hasn't dropped, has it, Doctor?"

"No. It appears to be cumulative. The more they are around you, the more energy they build, and then they seem to retain it, at least for a while."

I moved closer in baby steps. I was within five feet of them when I began to feel the same strange sense of intoxication that I had felt on the warship and the *Cape Hatteras*. My vision seemed to have multiple blind spots; my sense of direction went awry; and I felt very sleepy. I fell forward as I lapsed into semiconsciousness, inadvertently getting closer to the crystals very quickly. They blazed momentarily, and I could see the the weak version of the ring flare out, the center darkening and expanding fast like molasses poured on a table. It was opening, I thought, prompting me to stagger to the other side of the room.

"Cam, get out! You need to leave the station!" Westmoreland screamed. I struggled to focus on opening the door. I looked back to see whether he was following me, but he wasn't. Instead, he was walking toward the crystal mass.

"Westmoreland! We've got to get out of here,"I shouted.

"I've got to save them, Cam. They're important!"

"Don't do it! Come on," I yelled.

I watched Westmoreland approach the anomaly. His body contorted and then slowly disintegrated as he was drawn into the vortex. Soon all that was left was the anomaly floating in the center of the room and sucking everything into it. Even the mass of crystals was being dragged slowly toward it.

I ran from the lab and screamed for everyone to evacuate as I made my way to the hub and past the conference table. I am uncertain why, but I felt compelled to grab the crystal lying on it, pocketed it, and made my way to the airlock. When I had finished with suiting up, I hit the recompress button. I turned and saw Dr. Lyman—five identical copies of him—trying to put on suits on the other side of the glass door.

The exterior door opened with a slight pop. I stepped out not knowing what I should do next. I then remembered the skimmerloon shed Westmoreland had mentioned, and I walked into the Titanian wilderness until I spotted it barely visible a few hundred feet away. I made my way toward it, feeling a stiff wind trying to drag me backwards. Finally making it to the shed, I opened the door and glanced back long enough to see blue light emanating from every window in the station, all of them broken and sucking Titan's poisonous air into the building. Almost immediately the oxygen inside mixed with it, and flames erupted before the building crumpled and began to implode. I was the only one who had escaped.

I slammed the door and saw the skimmerloons parked in a row. They were a sort of pod, pressurized with an atmosphere, on skids and tracks but with a large compartment attached to the rear. After I climbed into one that looked the newest, the cockpit closed around me and pressurized. A green button marked "Deploy" flashed on the panel in front of me. I took my helmet off and pressed the button, assuming that it was the first step in starting the craft. I was wrong. Opening the shed door should have come first. The craft shot forward through it and dashed into the landscape beyond. I heard the compartment behind me blast open and release the balloon, filling it with hot gas in an instant.

The high speed was nerve-wracking. The balloon was enormous, rising rapidly into the air and being pushed by the wind and its engines. It dragged the cockpit on its skids, violently bumping over large chunks of ice. It was obvious that it wasn't supposed to operate that way, so I frantically searched the area around me for any kind of control that I hadn't previously noticed. Near my left thigh I saw a lever that had a vertical arrow sign on it. I hoped it wasn't an eject mechanism, but I took a chance. When I pulled it, the pod rose rapidly into the air, gaining even more speed.

I tried to make sense of the instrument panel and managed to find a map function. Accessing it, I saw a layout of the Titanian surface along with the course I was following. There was only one other feature on the map: a yellow dot marked with a series of numbers. I hoped that it designated the main colony. I placed my finger on the dot, praying that it would steer the skimmerloon.

The craft seemed to right itself, settle down, and head in a straight line for that yellow dot. But it was covering kilometers in seconds, so fast that I feared I might pass it. I had no idea how to stop the skimmerloon, so I frantically tried hitting the deploy button again. The balloon began to descend and retreat into its bay. I realized that I was still in the air and had not bothered to land the damned thing. My judgement must have been badly affected by the crystal in my pocket.

The skimmerloon fell, but in the low gravity its descent was more an uncontrolled float to the ground than a real crash. When I hit, it was hard, but not enough to injure me. I at least had the presence of mind to put my helmet back on as the craft skidded to a dry lake bed and onto a plain of house-sized pieces of ice before rolling end over end until coming to rest against a boulder. The canopy was broken and the orange atmosphere was seeping in like smoke. If there were a damaged wire or some other source of ignition, the whole compartment could explode. I put my helmet on and opened the canopy as fast as I could, dumping myself headfirst onto the ground below.

I had to get rid of the crystal, I thought, but it was sealed inside my suit. I remembered advice from the survival manual. I opened my helmet just enough to reach in and grab the crystal. Frostbite burned my neck as I zipped the suit closed. I dropped the crystal and fell to my knees, then onto my face, and there I slept for hours bathed in the crystal's bright blue glow holding back the ruddy orange hues of Titan.

Chapter 26 Dreamscape

"December 23, 1700 hours. Log of Captain John Andrew Nelson, Commanding Officer, UNAG Mining Vessel* Cape Hatteras.** ***Gravity's power has been revealed to me in an epiphany given from the perspective of a god. It is a gift to our universe that allows it to exist. It is a crutch to give me strength and understanding. It feeds the crystals and grows them."

I saw a man standing deep in black fog. Shrouded, faintly outlined, and wispy, he shimmered against a field of nothing else that my human eyes could see. He had no sharp lines, no reference points to lend clarity to my vision. His indistinctness made him feel like the presence sensed when there is someone in the room that you cannot otherwise see.

I stepped closer, hoping to see him better. It was like looking through a prism at a man. I saw his back, sides, and front but never all of him at once. He was like a twisting kaleidoscope, parts of his image lingering as others evolved into something new. He seemed like a shattered representation of the human form, looking at me, I believed, with comparable feelings of mystery and incomprehensibility. I saw a face flash across his visage. It was me. Then again it was Captain Nelson and all the others it had encountered in the past. Hundreds of faces flashed in a series, some old, some young, some bearded, some male, some female, and then finally me again.

But the faces weren't quite right. They were something like clay statues looking at the people who were their subjects. They were approximations or facsimiles made without a clear knowledge of how a human being actually appears to another person.

I felt that the figure could not comprehend me entirely but was linked to me in some other way. Intimate and cerebral, I could feel his presence much more precisely than I could see him. He held out his hand, upward and palm forward in greeting, projecting to my mind a sense that I was seeing a version of myself. It was me, in a way, but it was a different from me, a dark-matter equivalent that occupied the same place in his universe that I did in mine. He was trying to speak but couldn't. He neither understood language, or even the concept of it, but even more he did not understand air and sound itself.

I didn't know where I was. It could have been the other side of the anomaly, where they might have taken me. Or could I have been dreaming, lucid but only semi-conscious? Even a dream seems rational when one is immersed in it, but you always wake to a different truth and find that it was only a dream.

The place grew darker, the only light coming from the kaleidoscope man. It faded as he seemed to give up. The next instant I was on the bridge of the *Cape Hatteras*, staring through its windows at a gray and unnatural space with a white sun burning dim and indistinct.

"Captain Hunter," I heard behind me.

"Who's there?" I said, turning around but seeing nothing.

"Captain Hunter," again the voice said, this time with frustration telescoping through to my subconscious but still providing me with no direction in which to look for the voice's source. On that bridge he could not be seen. It was he that could not exist in my universe.

When the image changed again, I found myself in the laboratory on Titan staring into a ring blazing with furious blue fire. I was barely inches from it, bending forward to see inside without the fear that would have stricken me when fully awake.

"Are you trying to speak to me?" I asked it.

"The difference is too great," the voice said. I thought it was in my head, as before, but I realized it wasn't. It was my own mouth speaking the words.

"The time of the bridge is coming," it said through me.

"The bridge? You mean the anomaly?" I responded to myself.

"It must go into the well," it said.

"What is the well? You must be clearer."

And with that my mind's eye flashed Saturn. But it was different too, unrecognizable were it not for the planet's rings. Very much like the white sun, it was nearly formless and encircled with rings of mist instead of ice and rock.

"Gravity," the voice said through me.

"Gravity well. You want me to throw the anomaly into Saturn," I responded with the elation that comes with sudden and unexpected understanding.

"The bridge will close," it said.

"You want me to close the gateway? You are the ones that opened it. You have control."

"No," the voice said.

"Why do you make the crystals grow? Why don't you stop them?"

"There are others, the enemies of us all."

I awoke startled and gasping for air, the ruddy orange of Titan pouring into my eyes once more. My oxygen was low, and my suit read carbon dioxide levels near to the point of forcing unconsciousness. But that is not sleep; it is the black void of an oxygen-starved brain. If I had passed out, I would not have been dreaming.

My body felt as though it was made of lead, even in the weak gravity of that world. I reached back to the oxygen flow valve on the rear of my suit and opened it fully, hoping to give myself enough of a blast of residual air to give me strength enough to make it to the emergency bottle stored in the skimmerloon.

I asked myself whether the episode had been real as I fumbled through the broken cockpit and found the bottle, securing it to my suit and breaking its seal. I watched my oxygen levels return to normal. It had to have been an authentic message.

Dreams are not a credible basis on which to form an operational plan, certainly not one that I could sell to Janet. But if the voice was a communication, a kind of tuning of my consciousness to them, then it *was* legitimate. It was something I could trust, which I desperately needed given that Westmoreland was dead. My task seemed unambiguous: I was to drop the crystal I had taken from the table into Saturn. But treading the line of knowing what to do without admitting the questionable basis for it was a challenge. To my crew I would say that it was a direct communication while I was fully conscious. I would never tell anyone that it was really something far less certain.

I stood up and brushed off the ice dust and hydrocarbon sludge. I was very cold, even with the superinsulation and heating provided by the suit. It was not a long-exposure suit, and I had exceeded the temperature threshold for which it had been designed. In short, I was beginning to freeze to death. The frostbite burned my face and chest, and my head ached awfully. Any sudden movement made the pain unbearable. I could see the crystal on the ground, or more accurately where it had been. It had melted itself several inches into the ice, its presence suggested only by the streaks of blue light radiating from the hole.

I didn't want direct contact with the crystal. It was affecting me, I thought, and the closer it was, the worse the effects would be. I pulled out one of the balloon's lines from the compartment and cut it, then tied the crystal securely, pulling it along twenty feet behind me as I staggered across the desolate Plain of Dilmun, paradoxically named after the Sumerian garden of paradise. It was no such thing, however. It was a muddy and flat marshland awash with gasoline's chemical cousins that led to a mostly dry ocean bed occasionally filled by downpours every few centuries.

I had no way of knowing precisely where I was. I knew that I was somewhere near the yellow dot I had seen on the navigation map in the skimmerloon, but as I looked around I couldn't see a settlement. The plain seemed to stretch endlessly in every direction, but I could see only a few hundred feet ahead before the orange smog swallowed the horizon. I explored for hours, mindful of the sinking needle on my suit's oxygen meter. I was terrified and expected that I would die out there. But a stiff and welcome wind cleared the smog just enough for me to discern the domes of a settlement just over half a mile away.

I reached the colony just after midnight by my calculations. I hadn't even seen it when it materialized, lost as I was in contemplating imminent death. Encountering a plastic wall, I couldn't tell whether it was a boulder or a structure. I just knew that I was annoyed that it was in my way. I looked up and saw the hulking mass of an atmospheric dome. Realizing what it was, I slammed my fists against it until I couldn't anymore. I fell to my knees, staring face-up at a hazy and barely visible Saturn. Soon men with lights shone them in my face, blinding me. The brightness persisted in my eyes as they dragged me inside along with my crystal. I awoke two days later in their medical facility, feeling substantially better.

"God damn it, Cam!" my ex-wife said, looking down at me as I struggled to open my eyes. "I've been planning your funeral for hours, and here you are improving."

"Hello, honey," I said.

"You wouldn't believe how surprised the researchers were when a strange man wandered up and started banging on the Propulsion Institute's dome."

"What happened?" I asked. "I remember seeing men, but that's all. I'm drawing a blank after that."

"The first thing they did," said Janet, "was to post a guard here and do an orbital search to see whether there were any mafia ships marooning you for pissing off a Triton boss. They found something alright: our fleet. I got down here as soon as they contacted us and told us that they had Camden Hunter in their hospital."

"How did they know it was me?"

"That gold pendant around your neck has your name on it."

I sat up in bed, hurting awfully, but overall I felt alright, in fact better than I had while lying by the crashed skimmerloon. Thinking of it reminded me of the crystal.

"Where is the crystal I was dragging? It's important."

"It's on the transport. I'm surprised you were able to drag that thing that far."

"It's not that big," I said.

"Yes, it is. It must weigh over fifty pounds," Janet responded.

It was growing, I thought. I figured it was best not to tell her about that aspect of things until later. "I'm ready to go," I said, as I started to climb out of bed.

"Not until you're well enough for the trip. You've got frostbite, and the physician says your brainwave profile is abnormal. You need more rest."

"I can rest on the *Amaranth Sun* better than I can here."

"Always the idiot," she said.

The doctor on duty wasn't pleased that I was leaving. He claimed that my brainwaves were like nothing he'd ever seen before and that I should stay for observation. He looked as though he wanted to sedate me, but I told him that I was going to leave no matter what he said. Eventually he acquiesced and gave me some medicinal salves and a stimulant injection to get me back to the ship. It helped. I felt wonderful for about half an hour. But the moment I sat down in the transport, I fell into another long, deep sleep.

I awoke alone, zipped up tightly in my bunk bag on the

Amaranth Sun. I felt pretty good, I thought, as I pulled myself out. Zero gravity is very therapeutic during illness, like floating on a cloud, though it can make nausea and dizziness that much worse. I opened the door and floated into the hall, looking both ways toward the bridge and then the engineering section. I didn't see anyone.

"Hello?" I said, not getting an answer. I repeated myself a bit louder. "Hello!". . . Still nothing. I pulled myself sluggishly along a wall to the bridge. There was no one there. There should always be someone on the bridge, I thought, though in truth we often left it unattended when nothing was going on. I panicked. If the crew wasn't there, they might have been taken by the anomaly.

"Hello!" I yelled again at the top of my lungs.

"Yeah, what? Jesus, Dad, what are you screaming about?" Neal said as he popped his head out of engineering. I was quite relieved.

"Where the hell is everyone?" I asked.

"Kurt and Cranky are onboard the *Cape Hatteras*. That crystal thing you brought back is getting bigger, so they dumped it over there," he said.

"I know. We've got to drop it into Saturn and get rid of it."

"I think they wanted to get rid of it anyway. It's filling up the hold over there already. How the hell can a rock grow like that?"

"I need to warn them," I said, as I pulled myself to the communications station. "*Cape Hatteras*, this is Cam. Get that crystal off the ship!"

"Cam!" Stacey responded. "It's wonderful to hear your voice! We were worried about you."

"No time for chat, Stacey. That thing could hit critical mass at any moment and open the anomaly!"

"There's no way to get it out of here now. It's too big."

"Evacuate! You are in terrible danger!" I yelled.

The minutes counted down. I sat on the bridge of the *Amaranth Sun* in frantic and helpless suspense until finally I saw Stacey and Kurt emerge from the airlock and fire the jets on their suits to cross the gap. As soon as they were in the *Sun*'s lock, I plotted a course to bring us to a position several hundred kilometers ahead of the *Cape Hatteras*. I hoped that it would be close enough to monitor the derelict but far enough away to avoid the anomaly. The *Hyperion* had been following a higher, slower orbit and had drifted to the other side of Titan relative to us. I tried to contact those still there, but the effort was futile. It would be hours before they were in range.

I thought about the irony of it all. A few months ago I wanted to be as close to my salvage prize as I could get, and now I wanted to be far away. I didn't think Westmoreland had been right: the crystals reacted to me for some reason, but they didn't need me around to form the ring. It formed on its own and had taken two people on the *Cape Hatteras* while I was 20 million miles away on Europa. There was something else in play, another aspect of the mechanism. I desperately needed to figure out what it was. I made my way to the airlock to let my crewmen in.

"Why are we moving? What the hell is going on?" Stacey asked the moment the airlock door opened.

"Those crystals could form the anomaly at any time. They destroyed the research station and killed Westmoreland and his scientists," I said.

"The crystals are growing, but I didn't see any sign of immediate danger. Why the urgency?"

"I'm not at my best," I said. "At any rate, we should be alright when we get a good distance away."

I felt relieved that everyone was safe. When my thoughts returned to the message from the Dark Matter Beings, a terrible realization hit me. To destroy the crystals now would destroy the *Cape Hatteras*. Ed Iron wouldn't get his museum piece. We would have to try get them off the ship somehow, and every moment that passed meant that the task would be harder.

Chapter 27 Day 327

"December 25, 2259. 1900 hours. Log of Captain John Andrew Nelson, Commanding Officer, UNAG Mining Ship **Cape Hatteras.** ***I am passing a dead trojan comet. The voices call it the signpost. I am nearly out of fuel, but they assure me that we will reach our destination. Even when they do not speak through me, I know they are always here. They guide my actions with a reassuring hand. They are me, and I am them. It has always been this way, but it is only now that I am made aware of it. The signpost leads to the well, and I am to take my ship into it so that the forces of our enemies can be silenced forever."***

I didn't understand it. Not that I expected anything in that mission to add up to something sensible, but at least the powers that be—whatever those were—could have given me the satisfaction of some tiny measure of predictability. I would have been grateful for anything consistent with what I'd already been through that would have helped me get by without second-guessing myself every damned day. But that's not what I was given.

We had watched the *Cape Hatteras* for nearly a week through the telescopes on the *Amaranth Sun.* We spent hours in shifts gawking at that derelict trying to detect the slightest change in its appearance—blue light in the windows, any unusual movement—that might have signaled the crystals' reaching their critical mass and conjuring up the anomaly. Unfortunately, I didn't know what we would have done if we *had* seen something. I was putting enormous trust in the only thing I had: the Dark Matter Beings. If my understanding of them was correct, they didn't open the anomaly, but once it was there they had some kind of limited control over what it could do. I hoped they had enough influence to make certain that it didn't eat us if we flew nearby to attach a tow line.

After a week of round-the-clock surveillance, everyone's patience had badly eroded. We engaged in seemingly endless debates over whether or not one of us had seen something. At first they were simple discussions. If someone had noticed a flash, we'd all look through the telescope and study the instrument readings. Then we would disagree and invariably blame it on an errant cosmic ray skittering across the spotter's retina. But things got worse. My crew was annoyed with the false alarms. Tempers flared, and one by one each of us acknowledged the emerging truth: nothing was happening on that ship. Only I held out.

They therefore started directing their anger toward me. At first they tried to hide it, and then came occasional small outbursts. But by the end of that week they were openly furious for my keeping us idle and stationary, on edge but doing nothing. Stacey was the first to succumb. She was also the loudest in trying to persuade me to do something. Impatience was in her nature, and the more frustrated she got the harder it was to live with her.

Safe as the *Cape Hatteras* may have appeared, there was still no way I could bring myself to put any trust in those crystals. I took every precaution I could think of. I instructed the *Hyperion* to remain in a diametric orbit opposite the derelict while warning my ex-wife of imminent catastrophe. I had been telling the *Portsmouth* to stay even further away in a high orbit of Saturn on the orders of Westmoreland before he died, which I'd made up hoping they'd buy into the ruse and comply.

I was still convinced that the *Cape Hatteras* was eventually going to blow just as soon as those crystals reached critical mass. The captain of the *Portsmouth* was the only one who seemed remotely persuaded that I was right. He was a cautious sort, so he kept his distance, dutifully following the false orders of a dead man.

I was worried about that lie. Westmoreland had said no such thing. I had to be vague yet scientific in sounding like a man with far more education than I really possessed. I knew that if I said anything that the *Portsmouth*'s captain found questionable, his crew would have taken over the entire affair and thrown me into his ship's brig. But the risk was worth it. I needed them far enough away but not too far. It would take them a few hours to get where the *Amaranth Sun* was if we needed them, but not so close as to be able to meddle.

I certainly couldn't tell the military that the *Cape Hatteras* had to be destroyed. They wanted to study the anomaly, not destroy it, but I worried that I was weaving a web with the UNAG that would get increasingly difficult to maintain. All I knew was that I needed to be in control of the operation at all costs.

At the same time I knew that it was only a matter of time before the military would see through my deception and the admiralty would override Westmoreland's orders. I convinced myself that I could no longer afford to be inactive. I needed to move the plan forward, and do it quickly before the military took the initiative. On the eighth day I conceded that the crystals had to be past critical mass and the danger averted. That wasn't an easy decision to reach.

My first step was to move the *Amaranth Sun* closer to the *Cape Hatteras*. I didn't want to risk the lives of my crew, so I intended to go over myself and see what was happening aboard the derelict.

"It's about time," Stacey said.

"I haven't changed my beliefs, Stacey. Those crystals are extremely dangerous. But we can't sit here forever, so I'm going over to see what's happening."

"You'll need help. I'll suit up and go with you."

"No, Stacey. I need you to stay here. There's no sense in risking anyone else. I can simply take a look around and return. If you see any blue light coming out of that ship's windows, I want you to punch the *Amaranth Sun*'s engines and get the hell out of here."

"We aren't going to leave you, Cam," she said.

"You have to. You don't understand what we're dealing with. If you see that light, it means I'm already dead."

I could see her temper rising. She was preparing to waylay me with an angry speech about duty and sticking together, but I cut her off before she could launch into it.

"You've got to. I've seen what this thing can do, Stacey. You've heard my order. Now tell me you'll follow it!"

I was never that forceful with her in all the time that we had worked together. It disarmed her. My eyes flaring and my mind in two worlds at once, I was no longer myself, and she sensed it. Stacey broke down in tears.

"Aye, Captain. I will follow my orders," she said quietly.

I believed her but felt badly. It is not in my nature to be authoritarian, especially to someone who was like a daughter to me.

She also had done me a very great favor. She had had the presence of mind when evacuating the *Cape Hatteras* to override the outer airlock door and leave it open to space. Spending those few moments doing that could have gotten her killed, but there would be no one onboard to let us back in if she hadn't. I then would have had to cut into the hull a third time.

I silently turned and moved down the hall, leaving the bridge to her.

"Hey," I said to Neil while getting ready to climb into the airlock. He knew by my tone that I was going to say something personal.

"Yeah? Don't get mushy. You've been in so much danger lately that I'm numb to it. You'll be fine." he said.

"Now you know how I feel every time you do one of your insane space walks."

"Yeah, but I know what I'm doing. You just wing it and play around with UNAG spies."

"You're right that I'll be fine, but I want you to hold onto something for me just in case," I said, giving him the gold charm. "Your mother gave me that when she visited me on Titan. It's the *Cape Hatteras*."

"I know. I cast it. You should keep it."

"Oh, I want it back alright. Your mother said it was from the *Hyperion*'s crew, but I think it was really her idea. Of course, she'll never admit it. If I don't come back, it's the last link between you, me, and your mother."

"And the *Cape Hatteras*," Neil said.

"You should hold onto it just in case."

He took the charm and worked hard to suppress his tears until one rolled down his cheek. It was only the second time I'd ever seen that since he was out of diapers. The other occasion was that when Janet and I told him we were divorcing. He was still in his early teens when things finally self-destructed, and he hadn't taken it well. Janet and I could both tell that he wanted us to be a happy, functional family, exploring space together instead of being separated and angry.

"That pendant represents my greatest moment," I continued, "and your first big one, but I'll bet money that it won't be your greatest. You're going to go on and do bigger things than I ever did. I know it. The adventure is just starting for you."

"Of course I'll be great," Neil said, "but watch yourself. Remember, if you die, I get to be the captain. Kurt and I then can ditch Cranky and pick up a group of Mars babes. *Party Ship* is a better name than *Amaranth Sun*."

"It'll be a few more years before that happens. Keep those engines hot, son. I'll be back," I said as I ruffled his hair.

"I will, Dad. I'm holding you to that," he said, closing the airlock door as I snapped on my helmet. It's easy to prepare other people for your impending death, but it’s another matter entirely to prepare yourself. I tried not to think about it.

When the outer airlock door opened, I pushed myself off lightly into space. I remembered a time when that was frightening, something you did very carefully and cautiously, but for me it had become almost routine. A year earlier I considered space-walking the most dangerous part of salvage work. People at home always asked how we dealt with the stress of the constant danger. I'd never known quite how to answer, but now I would have told them that you deal with it like all of life's dangers: you just do what you have to do.

It took nearly twenty minutes to close the distance. I occupied myself by staring at the derelict. You never get to see something quite the same as the first time you set eyes on it. After then it becomes a known and familiar thing. But the *Cape Hatteras* was once again different. The known had morphed into the unknown, terra incognita once more.

I gently checked my momentum against the starboard side of the *Cape Hatteras* and hoisted myself into the open airlock. Its automated system sensed that I was inside and closed the door gently, the silence of space giving way to the sound of flowing air until a sign indicated safety.

After the interior door opened, I took off my helmet. In hindsight I probably should have done the usual tests to verify the atmosphere, but I somehow knew it would be fine. Perhaps I was growing careless or numb to what I regarded as minor dangers. Once on that ship I didn't fear anything. My emotions were strangely and unnaturally disengaged. I wondered idly whether that was the effect of the crystals or of too much reliance on the familiarity I now had with that ship. I couldn't tell.

I made my way to the hold. The entire room was coated in black crystal. They'd grown from floor to ceiling, giving the room the look of a cave. The bulkheads were a perfectly smooth wall of solid gemstone shimmering in the ship's lights, themselves shining dark violet through the crystal that covered them. It had inched itself past the hold doors and was just beginning to spread along the walls of the corridors, first in lightning-like streaks and then filling in as they grew.

I could perceive the growth indirectly. Over a few minutes I could discern a change. They were encasing the *Cape Hatteras*, entombing it in dark-matter minerals, but something had changed. I could now touch the crystals and experience no reaction. I ran my fingers along their smooth surfaces without the slightest hint of blue radiation.

I wondered whether the Dark Matter Beings had control of them now and whether the former threat had passed. I took a few photographs and left within the hour, satisfied that the *Cape Hatteras* was safe for the time being. I returned to the *Amaranth Sun*, taking care to the leave the outer airlock door open to space as Stacey had done.

"Open a channel to the *Hyperion*," I said to Stacey the moment I shot into the bridge.

"Captain Janet." I figured she'd hate me calling her that. "The derelict appears to be safe, or something close to it. Even so I think it would be best if you transferred any non-essential personnel and the prisoners to the Titan colony until we get a grip on what's going on here. No need to endanger everyone if we don't have to, and the historians and engineers won't be needed for a while."

I took a certain pleasure in the idea of abandoning Keating and his mutineers in a jail on Titan. It was a just research station, not a full colony. It didn't have a large jail with private cells but just one locked room. It might easily be a year before extradition to Earth could be arranged.

"You have such a way of instilling confidence in the safety of a mission," Janet replied sarcastically. "I can run this ship myself, at least for a while. I'll rendezvous with you in two days."

Chapter 28 Day 328

"December 25, 2259. 2300 hours. Log of Captain John Andrew Nelson, Commanding Officer, UNAG Mining Ship* Cape Hatteras. *Salus is dead. They have killed him from within me. I am an echo of John Nelson, now a marionette whose strings are being pulled from across the threshold of the two universes. Death gives me the gift of clarity. I see the signpost for what it truly is. It reveals the well, and it is Jupiter. I am to destroy the ship in the planet's atmosphere."

It must have been an effect of visiting the Crystal Palace—a nice new name for the derelict, I thought. I had developed a throbbing four-alarm headache that began the moment I left the *Cape Hatteras*, and it would not go away no matter what I tried. I went through the *Amaranth Sun*'s medicine cabinet and tried every pill and stimulator we had. Nothing worked. I finally resorted to the EES, the strongest piece of medical equipment a ship like mine carried. It was for shutting down the pain centers of the brain in those who were *very* seriously injured. It could block the agony of the severest of burns but leave you nearly catatonic until it was shut off. Even it could not block that damned headache.

The two days before Janet arrived left me with plenty of time to focus on the pain. I spent most of it in my zip-bunk, keeping the room as dark as I could make it. That helped a little, enough to let me clear my head and record a quantum-pad report for her. I wanted to tell her everything I knew about the crystals.

Recording seemed to lessen the pain, or at least distract me from it, so I made the report long and detailed. I told her almost everything, from the submarine episode at Europa to every word Westmoreland had said to me. Considering what might be in store for us, I felt that she deserved to have every piece of hard information I could give her. The only thing I left out was my uncertainty about communications from the dark-matter universe. I had laid the faltering and uncertainty aside. It was a message, not a dream. I was convinced that I was doing the right thing, but there was no way I could sell it to her without hard evidence, and I couldn't afford to have her questioning me about it, so I continued to insist that it was an unambiguous message.

There was just one thing left that had be reckoned with: saving the *Cape Hatteras*. The easy way to accomplish the mission would be to destroy the ship, but then I'd need a way to justify that to Ed Iron. I probably was making too much of what Ed's reaction would be. He might not get the *Cape Hatteras*, but the gold on the *Hyperion* would still yield an enormous profit. I think he would have taken it as a disappointment rather than a catastrophe. The real problem was me. Destroying the *Cape Hatteras* was as unthinkable as burning the *Mona Lisa* would be to an art historian. I had to save it, or at least try. I wasn't certain that I could pull the trigger if it had to be destroyed.

I was still in the zip-bunk when a way to save the ship came to me amid the throbbing pain. I considered it a stroke of genius. While the crystals were growing in the presence of gravity, getting them away from any gravity source should stop the growth. Westmoreland had been right about that, I thought. But what would happen if they were kept away from gravity for a long period of time? They might shrink, I theorized. Nelson's crystals were relatively small when I found them in his cabin. It seemed logical that they must have been larger when he was being affected by them, but that shrinkage might also have taken centuries.

Even if they didn't shrink in a timely manner, it didn't seem too difficult a thing to do: just head into deep space and steer clear of the planets. The crystals were soft. That meant they could be removed. We could chip them off the derelict, load them into suitable unmanned pods, and shoot them at Saturn one by one until the ship was clean. The only harm done would be the delay in getting the ship home to Earth for display and the pitted surfaces where the crystals had been growing.

But there was an unfortunate wild card in that idea: the unpredictability of it all. There was no guarantee that those crystals wouldn't flash to life without warning and conjure up the anomaly. I'd already been wrong about that once, and I could have easily been wrong again. I didn't want to lose any more lives over the *Cape Hatteras*—it had taken far too many already—so the first step of my plan would be to suggest to Janet that we reposition the derelict away from Saturn in open space. We would then have the *Amaranth Sun* cool its heels at a safe distance, but still within sight, until Ed Iron could get a specialized crew out there to deal with the crystals. In the meantime we would return the *Hyperion* to Earth with the gold and all non-essential personnel.

As it turned out, Janet wasn't very receptive to the plan after reading my report. I thought I'd done a good job of downplaying the danger of the crystals, but she had the annoying habit of assuming that anything I said was five times more hazardous than I made it out to be, especially if her son was involved and would be watching the derelict from the *Amaranth Sun*.

"Cam, that ship is dangerous. You've been dealing with

those crystals for some time, and based on that insulting report you sent the only thing you can count on is their being highly unpredictable. You should have told me all of this crap when it was happening, instead of acting like a spy and keeping secrets with the goddamned UNAG."

"I'm sorry, but I had to if everything was going to. . . . "

"We've got to get rid of it. You said yourself in your report that a small block of crystal in the corner of a laboratory on Titan was enough to create the anomaly. Well, now you've got several metric *tons* of crystal sitting on the *Cape Hatteras*."

Janet was still several hundred thousand kilometers out, so I had a few hours to try to convince her. I needed every minute of it.

"I'm surprised. I thought you'd want to preserve this thing for Ed Iron."

"Ed will understand! Cam, that ship kills people! You can't let the public tour it when you don't understand what you're dealing with. It will have to be investigated for years, maybe decades, and it will probably cost him too much to make the thing safe anyway. He'll see it as a lost cause and hand it over to the UNAG. He'll be happy with the gold."

"I don't think. . . ."

"I think you do. I think you know it quite well. You just don't want to give up Cam Hunter's ten minutes of fame. You want to show it off to everyone so that they can see how magnificent you are."

I knew she was right. Still, I wasn't ready to give up. Something would not allow me to. God, how my head pounded with every word she said.

"Janet, I don't think I can do it. You're right, the ship is important to me. I looked for it for so long. I dreamed about it since I was a kid. I don't want to destroy it."

"Cam, how do you feel?" she asked.

"I have a terrific headache, but that's irrelevant. I'd be saying this if I felt like a million tons of gold."

"Are you sure? You were in close proximity to those crystals again. They affected you on Titan, as you admitted in your report. They allowed the aliens to speak to you. How do you know they're not doing something to you now?"

"I don't. I really don't know what's happening. But remember, the Dark Matter Beings want me to destroy the crystals and close the bridge permanently. They don't want me to keep them around and make jewelry out of them. But they have nothing to do with the ship itself. We are doing the right thing. We can destroy them and save the ship. I know it."

I hoped that I'd convinced her that I wasn't crystal-crazy. She was reluctant, and it took two more hours of debate before she finally agreed to try my plan. I had the *Amaranth Sun* catch up to her, leaving the derelict alone. Protecting my crew was more important than protecting the *Cape Hatteras*, and there was still the warship watching everything that went on below from its God's-eye view high above Saturn.

I transferred to the *Hyperion* and ordered the *Amaranth Sun* into a similar orbit to that of the *Portsmouth*. I hoped that maneuver would keep everyone but Janet and me out of harm's way. The two of us were all that were essential, or so I hoped, and I still thought I could save the day and satisfy everyone, including the Dark Matter Beings. My mind changed when we attempted to approach the *Cape Hatteras*.

"Ten kilometers out, Cam, and closing," Janet said.

"Preparing to enter a trajectory that will bring us alongside the derelict," I said from the navigation station.

Our plan was to stop and leave a space of about two hundred feet between the ships. That would allow Janet to cross over to the *Cape Hatteras* and cold-start the engines so that we could set a course for deep space. It was going well until the distance closed to five kilometers.

"Cam!" Janet exclaimed. I had been gazing at my instrument panel blankly. I looked up and felt my heart skip a beat. The *Cape Hatteras* had lost power. The lights were out. The ship was dark again, just as I had found it near that burned-out comet over a year ago.

"I just left this thing. It hasn't been two hours. What could have happened?" I asked.

"Don't worry. It could be nothing. Those are 200-year-old reactors on that ship. We may have got them running again, but that doesn't mean they can't break down, especially if they're left unattended for days. I'll have a look at them when I go over."

"I'm going with you. It could be something else."

"I doubt the anomaly wanted to save electricity and went around turning the lights off," replied Janet.

"It shut my suit down when I was on the *Victorious*."

"It doesn't matter. You're not an engineer, and someone has to stay and man the *Hyperion*. It's supposed to run on a crew of five at all times. It won't run long on zero manpower," she said.

"I'll go over. You can talk me through it," I replied as I began to move toward the door. She gave a look that made me realize how ridiculous I was being. A cold start was a very complicated procedure that was usually performed only at space stations. Most ships spend their lives at least at idle, their engines are turned on when they are launched and only shut off again when they are scrapped.

"Then I won't get to see that crystal cave of yours," she said.

She was right, as usual, and my head hurt so badly at that point that I was starting to wonder whether I could operate the *Hyperion*'s navigation station, much less cold-start the *Cape Hatteras*'s engines. And the pain was getting worse. It had to be my proximity to the crystals. The closer we got to the *Cape Hatteras*, the more I wanted to lie down and sleep.

Somewhere around the time we reached the 300-meter mark, I lost all memory. I have no recollection of Janet's suiting up and heading for the lock, and I remember nothing about her crossing over. I should remember, but I don't. She never mentioned that I was acting strangely, or any worse than I already was, so I assume that I was conscious the whole time and doing my job. I don't remember a thing until I heard her voice on the comm telling me that she was onboard the derelict.

"In the airlock and compressing," she said.

"Be careful over there."

"Stop worrying. You were here alone just a few days ago playing around and coming up with new pet names for the *Cape Hatteras*. Interior door opening. Stepping through. My God!"

"What?"

"Cam, they're active! There's blue light everywhere in the corridor!"

I tried to tell her to get out of there, but she couldn't hear me. My mouth moved, but I had no breath to force the words out.

Chapter 29 Day 330

"December 25, 2259. 23:30 hours. Final log entry of Captain John Andrew Nelson, Commanding Officer, UNAG Mining Ship **Cape Hatteras.** *The ship no longer responds to my command. Against my will it has entered into a distant orbit of the signpost and vented its remaining fuel. I cannot get to Jupiter.*

"The voices have fallen silent. I have been abandoned. The man I was is already gone, and I can feel what I have become slipping away with each passing moment. I see it blazing in my mind's eye, depriving me of a peaceful passing. Blue light announces the bridge between the worlds, made to exist by the most terrible of enemies, but they did not have a command of normal matter to accomplish it alone. They used the uniqueness of the golden asteroid to set a trap. All that was needed was human greed to spring it. Once taken to Earth and in the prolonged presence of its gravity, they would unite matter and dark matter as one to enslave us not in body but in mind, time, and matter. I am powerless to stop them. They are coming for me. They intend to exact their vengeance."

"Cam, I've got power back, but if we're going to get this ship to Saturn and destroy it, I'll need to get those engines running and then plot a course," Janet said.

I couldn't say a word.

"I don't think we'll have any problems. The UNAG team cleaned the exhaust bells and did most of the cold-start prep. But I won't be able to leave the engine room. I will have to keep the crystals from overtaking the main reactor. I'll use a hammer if I have to."

I was still forced to remain silent.

"If we lose the engines, the ship won't be able to rotate and perform a deorbit burn. It could end up skipping into a semi-stable Saturn orbit. It might take years for it to decay and finally fall. The UNAG will have retrieved it before then."

I desperately tried to say something to her. I wanted her off that ship, and I wanted it left where it was until we could figure out a way to save it. I was physically prevented from expressing my mind and rendered mute from the intense pain. I tried with all my strength to form a word. Any utterance would have been a triumph. I tried to get up from my station and in the process flailed in zero-G, smacking into a pile of quantum pads that scattered around the bridge. The effort exhausted me; I could muster nothing else. I was left floating motionless. I heard her switch off her communications link.

My struggles probably wouldn't have mattered. If I had been able to say something, Janet in all likelihood would have ignored me. She knew that I had become unreliable and badly compromised. "God damn her," I remember thinking. I thought about leaving the *Hyperion* on automatic navigation, jamming the ship's airlock open, and dragging her back if necessary. The truth was that I couldn't have moved ten feet, much less hundreds.

But those sentiments were a play on my emotions at the direction of someone else. It wasn't about her; it was really about the ship, or what was in it. I understood then that my compulsion wasn't a simple desire to save the salvage of my dreams. A feeling had been growing for some time deep within me. I don't know when it started or where it came from, but it introduced a terrible contradiction. Something was telling me that I had to *rescue* the crystals.

It now seemed that the crystals themselves were important, more so than anything else in the universe. I felt directed to use whatever excuse I could to save them, like an addict hiding his problem. It was madness, and I was ashamed of having thought it. In those few seconds Janet herself seemed secondary to the derelict. Everything else bordered on the meaningless. I could feel my natural human priorities giving way to indifference. In my mind there were now only the crystals.

I was held in check by the Dark Matter Beings. I couldn't have moved from that bridge on my own. They would not let me be influenced by their enemy. I paid for those horrible thoughts with a loss of consciousness. While asleep, I was under their control. It seemed like only a few minutes when Janet turned her communications back on and said something that I couldn't immediately understand. In fact, she had been working for hours.

"The crystals have destroyed one of the peripheral reactors," she said, "and they're spreading through the engineering compartment. I lost power to the navigation control, but I've bypassed the damaged reactor, and it's working again. The main reactor should give us enough power to start and operate the engines."

I tried once more to spit out words telling her to escape. I felt a little stronger at that point, and I might have been able eventually to get it out, but she cut me off before I could.

"I'm going to have to stay on this ship if it's going to make it to Saturn. I'm sending you the course solutions. You need to input them into the navigation menus. The *Hyperion* will follow the *Cape Hatteras* and eventually overtake it. When you reach a distance of 100 meters ahead, it will be at the exact time when we can be certain that this thing is going to burn up cleanly. I will come over then. You'll need to drop a tow line to me. Remember that, Cam. Be ready for me when you overtake the *Cape Hatteras*. We will have very little time to spare."

I managed some sort of response, but she didn't understand it. I knew what I wanted to say: I still wanted to save the derelict. My words were incomprehensible, however. I was nearly screaming them in frustration, but it seemed that the harder I tried, the less sense they made. The power the Dark Matter Beings had over me was absolute. They could not allow me to be influenced by another power; they could not permit me to give in to them and save the *Cape Hatteras*. They were causing the pain to occupy me while they controlled my body to do their bidding. I was like a mouse being shocked in a maze: I either did as they wished, or I was punished while they forced me do it anyway. I began to react by wanting to fight them, only to be pushed back by waves of intense pain and brief periods of unconsciousness.

Other alien thoughts flashed through my mind. It wasn't a voice or anything so obvious. I felt that my ex-wife *and* the Dark Matter Beings were against me but that the darkness was not. Like a puppet with too many people pulling the strings, I could not function to resist any of them. I simply had to endure them.

In my altered state of consciousness, I could no longer tell which side was right. I tried to refocus. I looked at the orbital solutions Janet had sent. They were unambiguous: the *Cape Hatteras* would be destroyed if I typed them into the computer. It wasn't what I wanted, and given any chance I would have stopped it. That horrible schizophrenia had gone on long enough. The confusion and pain had driven things to be about more than just the derelict and the crystals. It was also a battle for control of my own self-determination given the two powers at war in my body.

I must have lapsed into unconsciousness again, though it was now hard to recognize the line between being awake and being asleep. It couldn't have been for long. I found myself standing in front of the kaleidoscope man again. He gestured that I should grasp his hand. I did but sensed no physical presence. He was not solid. I felt his sorrow for putting me through such pain, and it comforted me. He knew that I couldn't take anymore. He knew that I wanted to feel normal and that I would have done anything to make it all stop. At that moment I awoke again to barely tolerable pain, but it was far less intense than before. I knew that any second thoughts would bring back the agony, so I ordered the ship to execute Janet's calculations. I had given in to the Dark Matter Beings.

"Cam, have you entered the orbital solution into the *Hyperion*'s navigation computer?" Janet asked. I heard her but didn't respond.

"Cam!" she yelled.

"Yes," I said. It was the first clear word that I had been able to form in hours, but it was different now. It was *my* word.

The solution was straightforward. If Janet could maintain the reactors, the *Cape Hatteras* would maneuver itself into a high angle of descent toward Saturn, and at the proper moment it would rotate 180 degrees and fire its engines at full thrust in a backwards attitude. That would slow the ship until it no longer had enough momentum to maintain an orbit. It would plummet and incinerate cleanly in the planet's atmosphere.

"The *Hyperion* is flying the course you wanted," I said

haltingly, not unlike how the aliens had spoken to me. In my mind I implored the Dark Matter Beings to let me talk to my ex-wife without interference. I admitted to them as loudly as I could think that I had lost the war and that I would pay no attention to any impulse contradictory to my mission. Suddenly I felt the remaining restrictions on my speech lift like a physical fog that had been enveloping my body.

"I will overtake you at 600 nautical miles above the upper cloud deck of the planet," I said to Janet. "That will give you a three-minute window to cross over before we pass the 100-meter mark. You must be back aboard in that time. The *Hyperion* will have to fire its engines hard at the limits to create an orbit. Otherwise it will burn up too."

I had been given back free will and normal speech. I had accepted that I no longer had a chance of saving the *Cape Hatteras*, and I was being rewarded for the decision.

"The engines are ready to be started, but the crystals are reaching the main reactor. I'm going to have to hammer them away from it. I'll have to trust the computer to start the engines on its own and fly the ship. It's the only way I can keep the reactor running. You'll have to monitor the *Cape Hatteras*. If you see any deviation in course, you need to let me know. Can you do that, Cam?"

"Yes. I'm feeling stronger now." I was starting to understand more. New thoughts flowed into my brain as if from nowhere—alien images, voices, and concepts—but they were not malicious. I understood what the future would hold if I weren't successful, and a very different universe it would be. I also was made to understand that the dark-matter vibration of the universe offered a vantage point unlike my own. They saw time from an outside perspective. They saw all possible outcomes and knew that there was only one choice, only one way.

If anything survived of the crystals, we would fail. They showed me why we were at Saturn. There, in the gravity well of a giant planet, the weight of the crystals would ensure that they would make their way through the atmosphere deep into the planet's interior and entomb themselves forever in its dense core, an environment too gravitationally hostile to allow them to combine with dark matter and grow again.

"Cam," Janet said, "the engine start sequence is beginning." I could hear that she was already hammering away at the crystals.

I was struck speechless once more, but it wasn't by the Dark Matter Beings. It was by the sight of the *Cape Hatteras*, ahead of me and just to my port side, spraying a cloud of pure supercooled helium from its engine bells, followed immediately by the muted flashing of superheated compressed gas deep inside the ship. White flames burst out, stretching a third of the ship's length. The nozzles shook and rotated to direct the raw power before settling into an intense white glow.

Tears streamed down my face. I was watching the full glory of that legendary ship burst alive for the first time since John Andrew Nelson had commanded it. It was also the last time anyone would see it. It was the past and the present merging in the same moment, and I was proud that the ancient vessel could still muster its full strength. It would not die as a salvage wreck; it would find its end as the UNAG Mining Ship *Cape Hatteras*.

"I have full power. The ship is gaining speed. We're going to make it, Cam."

"It's beautiful. I wish you could see it," I said. In just a few hours Janet would be back with me, and we'd be watching the *Cape Hatteras* burn up from the safety of high orbit.

Accompanying that comfortable thought was the departure of the last vestiges of pain. I laid my head down on the navigation screen. I was suffering extreme exhaustion in every part of my body. Just before I closed my eyes, I saw one of the quantum pads I had scattered floating past my head. As tired as I was, I laughed. I must have hit a button because it was flashing red for recording and had captured every vision I had been given by the Dark Matter Beings in those hours on the *Hyperion*'s bridge.

Chapter 30 Gravity Well

"Office of Rear Admiral Jonah T. Carlin. Admiralty Administration Complex, Union of North American Governments, Montreal, Province of Verbec. December 25, 2259. Eyes only, HALCYON clearance required. To the Director of UNAG Intelligence, Dr. Augustin Sato, Los Angeles, Province of Calorwa. Agent Salus's log transmissions have grown erratic and nonsensical. He is being affected by the foothold phenomenon. We have no choice but to consider him a liability to the mission.

"The ship does not have sufficient fuel to return to Earth remotely; therefore, you are herewith requested and required to terminate Agent Salus by implant activation. Then you will override his command of the ship and order the computer to decompress the UNAG Mining Ship **Cape Hatteras** ***at its current location near the Trojan asteroid 831240 Zarathustra located at the L1 Lagrange point of the planet Jupiter. Long-term stability at that position is critical. Under no circumstance can the ship be allowed to approach a major gravity source. You are to execute this order immediately and without delay."***

"Cam, we've got a problem," Janet yelled between blows of her hammer. "I'm not going to make it."

That statement was the first thing I remember after laying my head down. I had fallen asleep, but it was a natural one, uninterrupted by the Dark Matter Beings. I think it was the first real rest I'd had since I had left Titan. I wasn't certain how much time had passed, but I noticed that Saturn now completely filled the windows of the *Hyperion*'s bridge. I must have been asleep for hours.

"We're so close to Saturn," she said, "that the gravity is making the crystals grow faster. I can't keep up. The engineering compartment is mostly filled. They're going to overtake the main reactor and destroy it. It doesn't matter what I do now."

I could hear her hammer crushing the crystals, followed by the snapping sounds as they hit the walls. She was speeding up and slowing back down as she alternately rallied and tired. She had been at it for hours, and I could tell from her voice that she was exhausted. The time had come for me to finish the job.

I felt better, nearly normal again. I had given in to the Dark Matter Beings wholly, and it was too late for me to save the ship. It would now fall into Saturn sooner or later, no matter what I did. I was resigned to be the Dark Matter Beings' instrument, compliant and ready to see their wishes through. The dark impulses had fallen silent.

"How long do we have?" I asked Janet.

"I'd say two hours tops. It's difficult to tell because the crystals' growth is increasing so fast."

I looked at the navigational instrument panels on the *Hyperion*. They revealed that, while I couldn't save the ship, it was still possible to do so with the right resources and enough time. The UNAG could still tow it with one of their powerful ships. We needed just under five hours to guarantee a fast and clean burn up.

"We're going to have to tow it with the *Hyperion*," I said. "Once we get it close enough, we'll fire our engines. We'll need to get as much from them as we can and hope to hell we escape Saturn's gravity."

"There's no guarantee we can do that, Cam. There's no safety margin. If we have an engine failure, we'll burn up just as surely as the *Cape Hatteras* will."

"We've got to take that chance. Westmoreland said that this thing was a direct threat to Earth. That's the real reason we came out to Titan. We've saving our home planet."

Janet fell silent for a moment. I hadn't told her that before. It wasn't in my report, but not out of any intent to deceive. I had simply stuck to the immediate threats and never thought to put the big picture into perspective. At that moment Janet knew that it had to be done as much as much as I did, no matter what happened to us.

"Let out the tow line," she said quietly. "I'm leaving the reactors and throttling the ship up 110%. You'll need to compensate, but at least we'll get as much distance out of the engines as we can. Then I'll suit up and abandon ship, connect the tow lines to the *Cape Hatteras*'s bow, and cross over to the *Hyperion*. I can't make it with my suit thrusters given all that engine wash out there."

She was right. Suit thrusters are very imprecise things. An accidental drift in the wrong direction meant incineration. Climbing the tow line was safer but still very dangerous. If the *Cape Hatteras*'s engines shut down while she was clinging to that line, it would go taut and kill her instantly. It wasn't a thick steel cable like what we had on the *Amaranth Sun*, those were dangerous enough. Instead, it was a thread-thin line of carbon nanotubes that could slice like a cheese cutter.

I assumed manual control of the *Hyperion* and throttled to

full power. I passed the *Cape Hatteras* and took up my position. I had only just reached it when I heard from Janet again.

"Cam, I'm outside the ship. I'm making my way to the bow. I can see inside the portholes. There's blue light everywhere. It's gotten much brighter."

I didn't want to hear that. If the anomaly formed and took Janet, I wouldn't be able to complete the mission. I'd have to call the military ship for help, and I didn't think they'd give any. They had been sending queries for hours trying to figure out what I was doing. In my condition I had been ignoring them.

I watched Janet climb her way around the exterior and onto the flat nose of the *Cape Hatteras*. She connected the line quickly, but I could see the blue light intensifying through the ship's bridge windows. The crystals had reached critical mass, I concluded. I was terrified that at any moment the anomaly would take her.

I watched as Janet hauled herself onto the cable and kicked off, covering 50 feet very quickly but then slowing from the friction of her gloves on the line. The *Hyperion* was accelerating fast to keep up with the *Cape Hatteras*. With both ships speeding up that rapidly, if she lost her grip there was a very real chance that she would be killed outright if she hit the derelict, which lay in a straight line behind her. It was a choice of that or burning up in the *Hyperion*'s engine wash.

I desperately tried to think of ways I could speed up the process and bring her to safety. I thought of trying to reel in the tow line, but there was no way its small motor could pull the entire mass of the *Cape Hatteras* closer. There was nothing I could think of to do. I could lose Janet, and it was then that I realized something that would change my life forever.

I guess I had been feeling it ever since I first saw her again all those months ago, but it hadn't been obvious to me. Maybe I should have realized it sooner, or better yet when we were still married. Because of my own stupid failings, it wasn't clear until I watched her trying to make her way to safety. I was still in love with that woman.

After an hour she was getting close, not more than twenty feet away. I had placed the ship on automatic navigation, hoping that the computer was better at calculating relative speeds than a human brain was. I suited up and sat in the rear airlock of the *Hyperion*. It must have been terrifying for her. The exhaust formed a ring of white fire that encircled her body, with her only option being to climb further into it.

As I watched her inch closer, my heart sank when I saw the *Cape Hatteras*'s lights go out and then flash once before going dead forever. We were out of time. Without someone hammering at them, the crystals had destroyed the reactor. The line would soon go taut when the engines failed. She wasn't going to make it.

I looked around, desperate to find some way of rescuing her, and then I saw it. There was a rope in the airlock. I think it was the same rope that I'd used to drag the crystals across the surface of Titan, though I couldn't tell you how it got there. I quickly lashed the rope to my suit and the other end to the lock's opening mechanism. Then I jumped.

I fell twenty feet in less than three seconds, I could feel my spine strain to the limit as I ran out of rope. I was lucky it didn't tear a hole in my suit and vent my oxygen into space, but my luck held out. I pulled myself as fast as I could toward her. We were close enough to the airlock to be clear of the engine exhaust. Janet reached out and grabbed my hand, letting go of the tow line, as I pushed us away toward an engine bell.

It wasn't a half a second later that the *Cape Hatteras*'s engines died and the line tightened. I have no doubt, watching it vibrate, that it would have killed her and propelled her corpse back into the engine streams. We hung for a moment from the skimmerloon rope, safe enough, and took our time climbing back into the ship before shutting the airlock door.

"I'm so glad to see you. I thought I was going to lose you," I said as I pulled off my helmet.

"Honey, that was a hell of a move. You saved my. . . ."

"Honey?"

She paused for a moment. "Yes, I mean it this time," she said quietly.

"You know why I did that, don't you?"

"I hope I know."

"It's because I've never stopped being in love with you. I didn't want a divorce."

"I didn't either, Cam. I was just angry. You wouldn't put your adventures on hold to be at home and help me raise our son."

"I made a mistake, a selfish mistake. I knew it at the time. I tried to make up for it by taking Neil into space when he became a man, and every day I think about how I should have been there when he was younger. It's my greatest regret. You have to believe me."

"I do. I think he'd still like to see us together."

"I'm sure he would. I think I would too."

"Then let's do it."

I kissed her in front of the utility airlock window at the rear of the *Hyperion*. We looked out at the *Cape Hatteras*, which seemed to be watching us approvingly. Or maybe it was the Dark Matter Beings.

The anomaly must have been active on the derelict. Intuitively I knew that whatever malevolent power was at work was trying to seize the *Hyperion*, but it was somehow held in check by the Dark Matter Beings. They couldn't hold it at bay forever, though, so after I kissed Janet again we made our way down the corridor together and headed to the bridge.

What we found on the monitors reinforced my belief that the universe loves a good joke. After all the previous dangers and everything that could possibly go wrong doing it, there was yet another problem. The *Portsmouth* was rocketing toward us at full speed. I tried to contact the crew, but now they were the ones who weren't answering.

Chapter 31 The *Portsmouth*

"United States Deep Space Geological Survey. Noctis Labyrinthus, Valles Marineris, Tharsis Region, Mars. January 25, 2078. Report of Dr. Leland Strunk, Ph.D., Chief Investigator of the Mars Geological Exploration and Sample Return (MGESR) Mission. We have completed the fifteenth manned exploration of the Red Planet and are preparing to depart in order to rendezvous with our return capsule. After exploring the Valleys of Mariner for the past six months, we are confident that we have gained a solid understanding of the deepest canyon system in the solar system and its extensive network of caverns.

"The caves have proven themselves to be the best candidates yet for the location of a permanent human settlement on Mars. The mouths of the caverns show evidence of fluid erosion, making their exploration a priority. We determined that this activity was recent, and it has led to the most important discovery of the mission. We found water in liquid form, salty and seeping from an aquifer deep within one of the caverns.

"I am confident that humankind will some day live here. We return home with many thousands of samples of water and rock, but most surprising are the crystalline minerals we found in the deepest levels of the caverns. They are completely new to science, and we believe them to be the most ancient rocks ever found on Mars. They are beautiful and black as night, but terribly cracked and shattered. We are uncertain what damaged them, but one thing is certain: they are important."

The timing of the reactor failure slowed us down just enough for the *Portsmouth* to overtake us on the cusp of Saturn. If you haven't been through it, it's difficult to imagine what it's like to have a Poseidon-class cruiser bearing down on your ship and preparing for an attack. The power of their weapons and the efficiency of their practiced maneuvers make even the most seasoned captain of a merchant vessel look like an amateur. Finley Pace would never have stood a chance against the *Portsmouth*.

Despite its bulk the *Portsmouth* pivoted and changed direction so rapidly that it looked more like a high-tech fighter pod outmaneuvering a hostile bogey than it did something that would weigh a hundred thousand tons if it were sitting on Earth's surface. The battleship's crew finally broke their silence when they had taken up a strategically favorable position above us, their guns trained squarely on the *Hyperion*.

"Captain Camden Hunter! You will drop your tow line immediately and send a confirmation of surrender. You will then move the *Hyperion* well clear and maintain a static position of ten kilometers off the starboard bow of the UNAG Mining Ship *Cape Hatteras* and await further instructions. If you do not comply within 60 seconds, we will fire on your vessel with lethal force."

They weren't mincing words, but I couldn't see any point in responding. I had no intention of complying, and my time was better spent trying to come up with some way of getting out that situation. I assumed that my apprehensions had been realized: the captain hadn't been satisfied with the orders of a dead man, and my long silence had only made matters worse. He contacted the admiralty for instructions, and they told him to secure the derelict at all costs. It seemed like such an obvious eventuality, but apparently the Dark Matter Beings didn't think it mattered.

Otherwise they would have allowed me to maintain contact and keep up appearances.

Only a week earlier I might have let the military have the ship if things had gone a little differently. If they had confiscated it, the loss might have been easier to explain to Ed Iron than would the decision to destroy the ship. They were more qualified to deal with the anomaly than I was, at least technically. Neither the Dark Matter Beings or their foe would have allowed it, however. If I had tried to hand over the ship, they would have overridden me and forced me to complete the mission anyway, no matter what I wanted.

The next voice I heard on the radio was that of the *Portsmouth*'s captain speaking very deliberately. "Hunter, give it up. You haven't got a chance tactically, and none of your ships are armed. I don't want to have to take that antique by force and send you home in my brig. You can still stand down."

Yeah, I thought, stand down and go to prison. With all the secret information to which I had been privy, jailing me would be a priority for the UNAG. Even If I had done everything the captain asked, the admirals would still find a way to squirrel me away on some trumped-up charge of destroying a national treasure like the NASA probe. I knew they would use anything they could against me.

"I can't do that, Captain," I replied. "This ship needs to be destroyed. I think you know that yourself."

"I've been ordered to ensure that doesn't happen, Cam. Westmoreland may have wanted it away from Earth, but I know that he didn't want it destroyed. The admirals want it safely in Earth orbit, and they want it delivered fast and secretly."

"They're not scientists. They don't understand the danger it poses to Earth."

"Maybe not, but Westmoreland wasn't the only scientist in the solar system. Look, Cam. Think about it. We need to see what kind of weapon this is and make sure that it can't ever be used against us. Earth is the only place we can do that now. The research station on Titan is gone."

"It's not a weapon. It's a mistake, one that the Dark Matter Beings want corrected as much as anyone else. They didn't create the anomaly; it was some other power that we don't know anything about. But they were enabled by something we did. If we keep messing with this thing, we may well cause our own destruction."

"That may be true, Cam, but it's bigger than you and I. Isn't it best to let the finest minds in the UNAG figure this out?"

"The UNAG was playing around with things it didn't understand," I said. "And it allowed someone else to open a damned portal to a higher vibration of the universe."

"Cam. . . ," he began to remonstrate.

"And then they lost control of it, didn't they? That's the only thing that could ever unite the unions, a common threat so great that there was no other choice left. Well, that threat isn't what you said it was, is it? It's not the Dark Matter Beings; it's the anomaly itself and whoever created it. But you'd attack the Dark Matter Beings to keep it open so you can study it and turn it into a weapon in violation of your agreement with the other unions."

"It's not my choice, Hunter. I understand what you're saying, but I haven't got any alternatives."

He closed the channel. In less than the duration of a lightning bolt, the *Portsmouth* fired a deadly accurate laser cannon at the tow line and cut it cleanly. A shudder moved through the *Hyperion*'s frame that signaled the severance. I watched the *Cape Hatteras* reel on the bridge's monitor. The derelict lurched sideways as it was pushed away by the wash of our engines. The *Hyperion*'s full thrust was freed from its load and glued us firmly in our seats before the computer sensed the problem and cut the fuel feed, sending the engines to idle.

Janet and I found ourselves drifting in midair toward the bridge windows. I looked out. We were very close to Saturn now, well inside the orbit of its rings. Even with my nose pressed to the glass, I couldn't see all of its yellow globe. But I still didn't know whether we were close enough. The tow line's severance had introduced new physics, and I didn't have a few hours for the computer to go through the calculations needed to determine whether the *Cape Hatteras* would burn up or enter an orbit. If I didn't do something decisive fast, the *Portsmouth* would get a tow line of its own on that drifting ship, and I could only watch them alter its trajectory and haul it off.

"Cam, look," Janet said. "The blue light is dimmer."

I looked at the display again. The light coming from the *Cape Hatteras*'s bridge windows was almost non-existent. It should have been much brighter that close to Saturn's gravity. The anomaly should have been running rampant, but it wasn't.

"We've got to get closer to the derelict," I said. "Set a collision course."

I wasn't thinking those words when I said them. I was trying to come up with a way to break any towline the *Portsmouth* might try to get on the derelict. Those words just tumbled out on their own, courtesy of the Dark Matter universe.

"You aren't serious!" Janet exclaimed.

"We've got to do it. If we ram the *Cape Hatteras* and break it into a million pieces, then they can't tow it. They'll never get a salvage ship out here in time to pick up the pieces before everything falls into Saturn."

Janet looked at me for a moment. She wasn't certain how I knew that the mission would be completed without the computer calculations, but I think for once she took me at face value. She glanced at the instrument panel hoping for some kind of verification but didn't see it. Still she set a new course. The *Hyperion* began a 180-degree roll and fired its engines at full thrust, sending us at high velocity directly toward the *Cape Hatteras*.

"It's going to collide, Cam. We've got to get off this ship," Janet said.

"Suit up and get out of here. I'll be right behind you."

"No, you won't," she said. "You're in some other world again. I can tell. You want the anomaly to form, don't you? You think that, if you get close enough to it, the anomaly will destroy that warship."

"I want to destroy the anomaly, not form it."

My mind wanted one thing, but my mouth said another. I wanted off that ship and knew that Janet was absolutely right, but something else was involved. I thought that the Dark Matter Beings wanted me to catalyze the reaction with whatever unique attribute I possessed, but I was wrong.

"Leave," I heard some entity say. It wasn't Janet saying it, and for once it wasn't coming from my mouth. It was a quiet and disembodied voice. Janet heard it too.

"Take the God-damn hint!" she said. "They want us both

off the ship. You aren't the catalyst. It's something else!"

I couldn't explain it. Janet and the Dark Matter Beings both wanted me to leave, but something wanted me to stay. The war in my soul was rekindled. It was countered like return cannon fire by an overwhelming thought that if I had stayed a few more moments, I would have stayed forever and would die for nothing. I needed to leave before the wrong side won.

I followed Janet to the airlock. We suited up as fast as we could, and I hit the button to start the decompression cycle. Janct realized that there wasn't enough time before the ships would collide, so she broke the glass on the emergency release and pulled the lever. The lock decompressed violently and flung us several thousand feet into space in a matter of seconds. We stopped our momentum with our thrusters and spun to watch the collision. The *Hyperion* was just a few hundred meters from the *Cape Hatteras* when the *Portsmouth* began firing its guns.

It was an impressive sight. The *Portsmouth*'s guns were blazing in salvos of green and red beams, burning holes through the hull of the *Hyperion* as though it were made of paper. Then, in a flash of blue light, the *Portsmouth* vanished completely.

The anomaly then seemed to turn its attention to the *Hyperion*. The ship distorted slightly as though the ring were trying to encompass it too, but the anomaly seemed to run out of time and collapsed abruptly when the ships collided. The shattering and dispersing of the crystals aboard the *Cape Hatteras* must have disrupted its ability to exist.

The *Cape Hatteras* buckled as it impacted deep into the hull of the *Hyperion*, but its thick steel held out better than the salvor, which rotated in the collision and tore in half against the hulk of the derelict, disgorging gold bricks into a wide debris field.

We were close enough. The debris would fall into Saturn's atmosphere within a few short hours. There would not be enough time for the crystals to grow again to critical mass, nor for the UNAG to get a ship to Saturn to retrieve the pieces. We would be successful, but we too were part of that debris field. We had no way of preventing ourselves from falling to our deaths along with my gold.

Chapter 32 Free Fall

"Office of Rear Admiral Jonah T. Carlin. Admiralty Administration Complex, Union of North American Governments, Montreal, Province of Verbec. January 19, 2258. Eyes only, HALCYON clearance required. To the Director of UNAG Intelligence, Dr. Augustin Sato, Los Angeles, Province of Calorwa. The top-secret probe sent by the Halcyon project to 974-Bernhard has returned readings that strongly suggest the presence of M-DM crystalline mineral of a much higher purity than those from the 2078 Valles Marineris samples. Recovery of the material will allow a more thorough study of the Matter-Dark Matter molecular bond.

"As you are aware, we first suspected the presence of the mineral through the delusional statements of Dr. Walton. In the years following the completion of his top-secret study of the Mars crystals, he grew inordinately fascinated with the asteroid belt. His compulsion led him to the discovery of 974-Bernhard and ultimately the loss of his sanity. We believe this was due to long-term exposure to the mineral. It was much the same effect seen in Dr. Leland Strunk, leader of the 2078 Mars mission, after his handling of the material over a nine-month period as his expedition returned home.

"They both refered to something they called 'the source,' both men using identical terminology, which is believed to be a reference to 974-Bernhard. Dr. Walton was not aware of the highly classified ramblings of Dr. Strunk after his isolation and confinement to the Ramsey Institute for Mental Health, where he remained under the previous government's supervision until his death. Due in large part to the extremely

unlikely nature of those correlating statements, we suspect some form of intelligent alien life may have been communicating information to those men. The mechanism and extent of the alien's ability to do this remains unclear.

"Within the coming month we will present you with a plan to recover material from the asteroid and the specifics of what we will need from your organization."

It had been scarcely an hour, and the show had already begun. The speed and awesome power of the collision had thrown small fragments like bullets into the upper atmosphere of the planet, well ahead of the main debris field. They looked like supersonic fireflies as they burned up. I wondered whether some of them might have been bricks of gold, but I realized their intensity was too low.

It didn't seem as though we were falling. Velocity is a difficult thing to gauge in space. You can't visually determine it due to the incomprehensibly huge size of the planet below you. Even though we were gaining speed at a mindboggling rate, it seemed more as though we were timeless, suspended forever above mighty Saturn. I held my wife as tightly as our moon suits would allow. We were in such proximity that I no longer could discern Saturn's curvature. It had become a horizontal straight line, the planet stretching infinitely as a yellow plain below us. I wondered whether we had broken a record for the closest human approach to Saturn. We would one way or another as we fell further, but I figured that we had already accomplished it. I didn't tell Janet. We weren't saying anything at all but just trying to enjoy each other's presence in our last hours before we plunged to our deaths.

There were worse ways to go, I thought. It would be

instantaneous when the friction burned our suits open and vaporized us. The loss of air would be so fast that death would be painless.

I also didn't try to contact the *Amaranth Sun*. They were in high orbit, as I had ordered, far out of the communications range of our space suits. Those were designed to talk to people hundreds of feet away, not hundreds of miles, and the interference from Saturn's natural radio emissions shortened our range even more. I did look for my ship, thinking it might appear as a dim moving star across the backdrop of the heavens and Saturn's rings, but I couldn't see it. For all I knew it was following its orbit on other side of the planet.

Even if the *Amaranth Sun* could have reached us in time, we were so close to Saturn that escaping the giant planet's gravity was no longer possible with the engines my ship had. It was best, I reasoned, to spare my crew the hours of agony knowing we were going to die no matter what they tried. I hoped they would simply conclude that we had died instantly in the collision.

I intended to use my remaining time to reflect on all that had happened to me since finding the treasure ship. I believed, in some way, that I had saved Earth's future from something so malevolent that it took two civilizations to defeat. Or was it two? If I had seen dark-matter twins of the sun and Saturn, was there perhaps a dark-matter equivalent of me? Had I really seen a copy or counterpart of myself in that vision, or was I misled? What was the anomaly? Who was the dark power that controlled it? I'll never know the answers to those questions, but I could see the anomaly, even then, trying to form in the wreckage.

Flashes of blue flickered across the entire debris field, but the crystalline matter was no longer concentrated enough to allow the anomaly to manifest itself fully. I'm sure Janet would have said they were just loose electrical wires and batteries discharging, but I knew they were something else. The distinct color and the rise and fall of their intensity was all too familiar. It was trying tenaciously to form itself and find some way to avert its own destruction.

"We're getting closer," Janet said, breaking the silence.

"And moving faster, I think. The planet is pulling us in."

"I never thought I'd die while falling into Saturn and holding onto you, Cam."

"I'm glad you're not alone."

"You, me and the Dark Matter Beings," she said. Her words triggered a thought.

"I guess you were right. I wasn't the catalyst. I might not have even been special," I said, holding her thickly gloved hand. "I was just a pawn at the right place at the right time to interact with them." The angle of the sun was making the debris field glint gold, the bricks reflecting the light as we were swept along with them.

"Why do you say that?" she asked. "That anomaly, whoever or whatever it was, could have taken you at any time. The aliens must have prevented it."

"I suppose. Perhaps they knew what I would do later. Maybe they see time from a different perspective. I didn't tell you, but they contacted me the second time I stepped onto the *Cape Hatteras*. Sanjay as well."

"What did they say?"

"They wanted us to leave. I guess that, if the ship had sat out there frozen with the anomaly contained in the ice, nothing ever would have happened. In the end my greed for the gold unleashed it."

"You might be greedy, but you aren't those military men. You never would have tried to use the anomaly as a weapon. You'd have destroyed it, one way or another. Nelson would have too, but he never made it to Jupiter. Maybe they protected and used only those people who they knew had good intentions and would overcome their greed."

"And those who didn't died in the anomaly. It killed to ensure that it would be successful in eventually getting to Earth."

"But if you weren't the catalyst that allowed it to open, what was?"

"I think I know. It was the gold."

"The gold?"

"The concentrated and dense mass of all that gold. When I was in the laboratory on Titan, I was wearing the pendant you gave me. That's what set the crystals off, not me. Moving the *Hyperion* closer brought the gold to the crystals, intensifying the anomaly's power and allowing it to appear. The gold was on the ship with the crystals when Nelson was manipulated. It was on the *Hyperion*, stalled next to the *Cape Hatteras*, when the *Victorious* was destroyed. There was gold still on the derelict when the scientists were marooned. When those ships collided, the anomaly closed, the crystals shattered below the critical mass, and the gold was dispersed, changing its collective mass."

"Still, there were plenty of things with mass that the

crystals didn't react to."

"But the crystals were native to Walton's Rock, and so was the gold. The gold must have been joined in a hybrid molecule with dark matter as well, and when they refined the gold they made it purer and denser, and it became enough to create the anomaly. You yourself saw irregularities in the weight of the gold. It wasn't an error. It really did have properties different from those of normal gold. Maybe Walton's Rock was the only place in the solar system where those two things were present in abundance. The Dark Matter Beings suggested that the asteroid wasn't natural. Maybe it was manipulated from somewhere else. Maybe whoever controlled the anomaly knew that one day man's hunger for that gold would bring us to Walton's Rock and that we would refine it to a pure state."

Meteors of debris were plunging more often into the planet's atmosphere. I almost thought I could see the haze of the tenuous outer atmosphere of the planet starting to collect around us. I closed my eyes and squeezed Janet's gloved hand. It wouldn't be long now.

"I love you, Captain Janet," I said.

"That's Doctor Hunter, and I love you too, Cam." She buried her helmet into my chest as our comm link was finally overwhelmed by proximity to Saturn and its natural radio emissions.

The flashing grew more intense. I closed my eyes. Larger meteors were falling now, signaling that the front edge of the main debris field was contacting Saturn's upper atmosphere. I tried to contain my trembling as best I could, not wanting Janet to feel it. The flashing grew brighter but not as fast as it should have.

I realized that a rhythm had formed, an unnatural one. It was a Morse rhythm.

When I opened my eyes to see what it was, I spotted something more beautiful than the wreck of the *Cape Hatteras* on the day I discovered it . . . and maddening at the same time because of its crew's flagrant disregard of danger. The *Amaranth Sun* was charging our way at hundreds of feet per second.

It looked determined and somehow brave and powerful, in the way a mouse charging a lion would seem. Her engines and attitude-adjustment thrusters fired in thousands of white blasts in all directions at the mathematical instruction of a computer struggling to counter the gravitational pull of Saturn. As the *Amaranth Sun* drew toward us, I could see its momentum slowing from the effects of drag in the upper reaches of the planet's atmosphere.

As the ship came closer, all I could focus on was Stacey's and Kurt's faces peering with looks of intense worry through the bridge windows. The rhythmic flashes were coming from the floodlights on the ship's bow, the same ones that had first illuminated the *Cape Hatteras*. They were sending a simple sentence over and over: "Get in!"

I shook Janet, who hadn't yet opened her eyes to see them. There is no sound in space, so even the explosion of a star is utterly silent, much less the frantic approach of a ship. I felt her tense up even through the moon suit. It was the excitement of someone getting the best news of her life. I waved as the *Amaranth Sun* braked and slid its port side toward us. The airlock yawned open and approached at alarming speed.

There wasn't time to climb into it. The airlock simply captured us. The ship rotated around again in the direction of its momentum and did something for which I knew it was not designed. It jolted forward in an acceleration so impossibly powerful that I worried we'd be crushed by inertia against the side of the now closed and filling airlock. And there we stayed glued for twenty minutes before the pressure finally let up abruptly.

"What the hell did you do?" I asked, climbing through the inner airlock door.

"Remember that rocket engine from the NASA probe we had strapped to the back? I welded it on, and we fired it!" Neil said.

"What? Do you have any idea how dangerous that engine is? If it had exploded, it would have killed you or left you drifting into Saturn too!"

"It's not dangerous anymore. It's out of fuel."

"Well, do we have the velocity we need to escape Saturn?"

"Yeah, and then some," Stacey said, as she shot down the hall.

"You could have been killed! I said to stay in high orbit!"

"We mutinied. All three of us agreed. We overrode your orders."

I smiled and gave Stacey a huge hug while noticing out the rear window of engineering that the bulk of the wreckage was now falling into Saturn, along with the crushed hulk of the *Cape Hatteras*. We moved closer to watch.

"Those are the gold bars," I said. "The haul is burning up."

It was strangely beautiful to watch my fortune burn away.

I'd have nothing when it was all over. When the spectacle started to subside, I turned to my son.

"Mutinied," I said.

"Yeah, I finally agreed with Stacey on something."

"My own son mutinied."

"Don't I get a hug for mutiny too?"

"Yeah," I said, and hugged him, "but I have news."

"What?"

"We've got a new permanent crew member."

"Huh?"

"Your mother! We're back together."

He looked surprised and confused but not unhappy. "Well, that's great. How long will she be with us? Surely she has obligations back on Earth, teaching at the university and all."

"Well, I don't see us returning to Earth any time soon, at least until Ed Iron cools down."

"But. . . ," he said. It had begun to dawn on him what the implications of having his mother as a crew member might be.

"And, you know, she does have an advanced degree in engineering, and you don't. But there are plenty of things to do around here. The ship could certainly use a good cleaning."

"But. . . ."

"Don't worry, son," said Janet. "It'll only be a year or two, five at most."

Chapter 33 Day 332

"Office of Rear Admiral Jonah T. Carlin. Admiralty Administration Complex, Union of North American Governments, Montreal, Province of Verbec. February 26, 2258. Eyes only, HALCYON clearance required. To the Director of UNAG Intelligence, Dr. Augustin Sato, Los Angeles, Province of Calorwa. The sensitive nature of the findings of Halcyon necessitates the creation of a cover story. A gold-mining mission to the asteroid 974-Bernhard is to be promoted to the public as a methodology for reducing the Union's debt, taking advantage of the erstwhile public promotion of the asteroid by the late Dr. Walton. At the preplanned early completion of the mining mission, your operative, Salus, is to collect the crystalline material by whatever means he has at hand. We believe that a matter-dark matter weapon would give the UNAG a significant advantage in the marginalization of the Asian-African and Eurorussian unions."

I would have to explain it all to Ed Iron in the morning. There wasn't any scenario I could think of in which things would turn out alright. Losing the derelict was one thing, but losing the gold was a different matter altogether. It was overwhelmingly unlikely that we'd be free to return to Earth any time soon—possibly for the rest of our lives. I expected that we'd have to make a run for it and hide out at Neptune and fend for ourselves. Maybe we could haul freight pods for the Triton mafia.

We all were looking for some diversion, anything to get our minds off the coming day. I had one idea that I knew would work. It was the one connection with our home planet that I could tie up neatly: the marriage of Kurt and Stacey.

I was hesitant at first because our immediate setting seemed somehow inappropriate. Kurt and Stacey assured me that getting married on the *Amaranth Sun* was a better idea than Florida anyway, but I thought they deserved something nicer.

I therefore suggested a wedding on one of the small deserted moons that circled Uranus. We'd be passing by that system anyway, and hardly anyone ever visits them. I also had heard they were uniquely beautiful—low-gravity spheres bathed in the planet's blue-green light. It would certainly be more romantic than the bridge. Eventually I was overruled, however, when Neil and Janet joined Kurt and Stacey in favor of the *Amaranth Sun*, so I gave in and dutifully donned a uniform.

Now, I hate uniforms. I'm the kind of person who's comfortable dressing in utilitarian jump suits and t-shirts. I have little interest in what amounts to silly costumes, especially after my dealings with the captain of the *Portsmouth*. I only own one set of formal attire, and I couldn't remember using it since I first tried it on when I bought it twenty years earlier. It was sickeningly classical—a white jacket complete with epaulets, a peaked cap with the merchant spacefarer's insignia in gold, and a navy blue shirt and tie. It even had my name embroidered on the jacket. It was just something to take a few pictures in and then toss in a closet after I made the rank of merchant captain.

Kurt and Stacey hadn't expected me to put it on; in fact, they didn't know I owned a uniform. After my Uranus idea was shot down, however, I figured that I had to surprise them. They undoubtedly were expecting me to show up in a jumpsuit and get the ceremony over with as fast as I could. I went to the bridge looking like the skipper of a lunar tourist cruiser. The get-up couldn't have been cheesier. I could just as well have been dressed to inform the passengers that the comedian's performance in the lounge had been canceled and that the dinner buffet would be open for an extra hour in compensation.

My attire wasn't lost on Neil and Janet. They saw me coming before the lovebirds did and snapped to attention in zero-G before flanking me as I passed through the door. I didn't know either of them could do that, its being something that takes a little practice, but they pulled it off brilliantly. Our grand entrance caused Stacey to have a rare meltdown. Tears flowing and holding Kurt's hand tightly, she seemed overwhelmed.

"Dearly beloved," I said, "we are gathered here today in the presence of these witnesses. . . ." I had memorized the whole thing beforehand to keep my mind off Ed Iron. Everything was going perfectly, if you don't count Neil's snort when Stacey came in wearing a chef's bib from the galley complete with a blood stain—it was the only thing we had that could serve as a wedding dress other than our usual blue jump suits. The wedding rings were simple plastic seals taken out during the *Amaranth Sun*'s refit. They would be proxies until Kurt and Stacey could buy real ones at a colony.

I'd never performed a wedding before, but I muddled through just fine. After I pronounced them man and wife, they kissed. We then celebrated before they retired to the honeymoon suite, which was their normal cabin decorated with some cans Neil had hung on the door and where he had written "Just Married" in engine grease.

I didn't sleep a wink that night, and not because of the newlyweds active in the cabin next to mine. I was used to those sorts of sounds already, though Janet tossed and turned so much that I had to tire her out by acting like a new husband myself. I didn't sleep because of the prospect of communicating with Ed Iron the next day. If discovering the *Cape Hatteras* had been my greatest moment, the aftermath was going to be my worst.

I tried to reduce the expected fallout with my usual written report to Ed as a prelude to speaking directly. However, my experience had been so extraordinary that I knew my usual method of downplaying the bad and focusing on the good wasn't going to work. I just had to be honest and matter of fact. Looking the report over, I recognized that it was all bad news for him: the gold was gone, the relic was gone, the ship he had bought was gone, and he now had a bunch of scientists stranded on Titan for whom he'd need to arrange transport home.

I expected nothing less than a tirade followed by endless messages from a team of lawyers ensuring that I would never make a living again. My house in Arizona would be sold, and I would be worse off than ever before. I spent much of the rest of the night planning the particulars of our escape to the outer solar system.

At 7:00 a.m. sharp came the incoming message ping. "We've got two ways to get past this, Cam," he said. "I'm satisfied with your story. It meshes with what everyone else has said. And I won't lie: I'm absolutely amazed at the quantum-pad recordings you sent. Our first communication with an alien species or something of the sort! Who'd have thought they'd do it through dreams? My people think your brain was manipulated on the subatomic level, imagine the power they must possess to control energy at such small scales and change how neurons behave."

"Yours is a story worth money," he continued, "but not enough. Let's not avoid the basics. It won't cover the money I've lost. I'm sure you understand that," Ed said with artificial calmness.

I was so nervous that I said "I do" in violation of the rule in long-distance space communication that one person talks all at once before the other person replies. That kind of thing was usually second nature to me, but I'd forgotten it entirely. Thankfully he couldn't hear me because the microphone was turned off.

"The first thing you're going to do is to write a book that will complement these recordings—a memoir telling the story of the discovery—and loss—of the *Cape Hatteras*." Ed's statement was followed by an abrupt click. His comment didn't offer a choice; it amounted to an order. I could do that much, I thought.

"I will," I said, ending that simple response with my own click. I hoped that he'd at least hire a ghostwriter for me, even if it was just a fourth-rate author of science fiction. I can't say I was too excited about having my dark-matter dreams published though. It seemed . . . voyeuristic. I ticked off the minutes until demand number two while staring at Janet.

"And while you're getting that done, the second thing you're going to do is to resupply at Mars. You'll need to stock a large amount of food and fuel in modular pods attached to your ship. You should even consider having some extra fuel tanks mounted just in case. I've got something big, and I need someone I can trust. I think that person is you, Cam. You might drop the largest concentrated quantity of gold in the solar system right into the goddamn atmosphere of Saturn, but at least you told me the truth. You're going to work my new salvage project, though at a smaller share than last time. It's the secret I mentioned to you a year ago, Cam. It's huge, and I'm confident it can be done. Will you do it?"

The end-of-message click came through. He had asked me whether I would do it, but it was just a courtesy. Deep down I knew it was really just another order.

"I'm in," I said after looking around at Kurt, Stacey, and the others and seeing nods of agreement. Waiting a few minutes for his response seemed a longer period of time than the last year had been.

"It's in the far outer solar system and comes from one of the earliest accounts of the Oort cloud when Captain Langley skirted the inner regions. He thought he saw a station or a ship out there. It was enormous, though, more the size of an asteroid than a ship. It wasn't like anything he'd ever seen, but he couldn't get close to it for lack of fuel. He just knew that it looked artificial and wondered whether one of the other unions had sent a high-tech secret mission out there before the UNAG. As far as I can tell, none of them had.

"Guiscard Van der Shark . . . er . . . Boort, also saw it, but he dismissed it as just a strangely shaped planetoid and never went close enough to investigate. Nevertheless, it gnawed at him when he got back to Earth. Eventually he came to believe that something wasn't quite right with it. He could never get the mystery out of his head and mentioned it in his memoirs. They were never published because he hadn't finished them before the shark ate him, but I obtained a copy. It cost me a small fortune, but who wouldn't want to be the first person to read about his adventures? Anyway, I pored over the instrument readings I requested from you. They were taken during that expedition. What I found convinced me to commission a long-range space telescope specifically designed to search for what he saw and photograph it in high resolution. But it's not what they thought, Cam. It's much bigger than that."

It must have been big. I can only imagine what a telescope like that cost him.

"Your mission will be to go to the Oort cloud. You will be travelling into an area of space where no one has ever been before. It's so far out that it will take over two months for a communications signal to reach Earth. For all intents and purposes you'll be out of contact and totally on your own. You'll also travel faster than any person in human history. I've got the specifics of the mission and an engine retrofit for your ship waiting for you at Mars. I can't say much more under these circumstances. Can you guarantee on your end that you trust everyone implicitly and that they'll all be going on the mission? If you can, please have Janet input her MR-2.21 encoding protocols from the *Hyperion*'s secured communication frequencies to your ship's computer and have her enter her command code."

I looked at Janet. She smiled and nodded her approval.

"I can, and she's doing it now," I replied, before ending the transmission. She entered the protocol in the computer. Minutes later a response came.

"I think it's an alien ship, but much bigger than anything you can imagine," said Ed, "a kind of artificial planet that had been coursing through space below the speed of light for millions of years. We don't know where it came from, or where it was going, but it looks as though something went wrong. It seems to be dead in space, and we think it's been there for a very long time. We want you to explore it."

Perhaps the *Cape Hatteras* hadn't been my greatest moment after all. I looked at Stacey, but I didn't have to say a word. She had already set a course for Mars.

Printed in Great Britain
by Amazon

25644152R00155